PENGUIN MODERN CLASSICS

Life Is a Dream

Gyula Krúdy (1878–1933) was bo[illegible] small town of Nyíregyháza. Krúdy moved to Budapest at the age of eighteen and lived there 'by his pen' for the rest of his life. Starting out as a precocious journalist, he soon turned to writing short stories and novels. After 1919, despite publishing many of his greatest works, he lived in reduced circumstances with his second wife and young daughter, and died in poverty and obscurity. Sándor Márai's novel *Szindbad Goes Home* (1943), a fictional account of the last day of Krúdy's life, jump-started the revival of interest in his oeuvre, which is now recognized as one of the outstanding monuments of Hungarian literature.

John Batki was born in Miskolc, Hungary, and has lived in the United States since the age of fourteen. He has published several volumes of translations from twentieth-century Hungarian literature, including the poems of Attila József, and prose by Gyula Krúdy, Ernö Szép, Géza Ottlik, Iván Mándy and others.

The translator wishes to thank the editors of *Southwest Review and Subtropics*, where two of these stories, 'The Waiter's Nightmare' and 'The Landlady, or the Bewitched Guests' first appeared. 'Last Cigar at the Grey Arabian' and 'The Journalist and Death' first appeared in *Hungarian Quarterly* (Budapest), and special thanks go to the editor, Zsofia Zachar.

GYULA KRÚDY

Life Is a Dream

Translated from the Hungarian by John Batki

PENGUIN BOOKS

PENGUIN CLASSICS

Published by the Penguin Group
Penguin Books Ltd, 80 Strand, London WC2R ORL, England
Penguin Group (USA), Inc., 375 Hudson Street, New York, New York 10014, USA
Penguin Group (Canada), 90 Eglinton Avenue East, Suite 700, Toronto, Ontario, Canada M4P 2Y3
(a division of Pearson Penguin Canada Inc.)
Penguin Ireland, 25 St Stephen's Green, Dublin 2, Ireland (a division of Penguin Books Ltd)
Penguin Group (Australia), 250 Camberwell Road, Camberwell, Victoria 3124, Australia
(a division of Pearson Australia Group Pty Ltd)
Penguin Books India Pvt Ltd, 11 Community Centre, Panchsheel Park, New Delhi – 110 017, India
Penguin Group (NZ), 67 Apollo Drive, Mairangi Bay, Auckland 1310, New Zealand
(a division of Pearson New Zealand Ltd)
Penguin Books (South Africa) (Pty) Ltd, 24 Sturdee Avenue, Rosebank, Johannesburg 2196, South Africa

Penguin Books Ltd, Registered Offices: 80 Strand, London WC2R ORL, England

www.penguin.com

First published as *Az élet álom* 1931
This translation first published in Penguin Classics 2010
1

Set in 11.25/14 pt Dante MT
Typeset by Ellipsis Books Limited, Glasgow
Printed in England by Clays Ltd, St Ives plc

978–0–141–19303–8

www.greenpenguin.co.uk

Contents

Translator's Note

Az élet álom (*Life Is a Dream*), Gyula Krúdy's last volume to appear in his lifetime, was self-published by the author in December 1931.

In October 1931 the English press tycoon Lord Rothermere donated the sum of £1,000 to the Hungarian PEN Club, to be awarded to the author of the year's most outstanding literary work. The poet Dezsö Kosztolányi, president of the Hungarian PEN, originally intended the prize for the fifty-three-year-old Gyula Krúdy, author of more than fifty volumes. Formerly a celebrated writer of bestsellers, Krúdy at the time lived in obscure poverty with wife and daughter in a crumbling hovel in Obuda on the outskirts of Budapest. Since he had no book published that year, and no publisher, Krúdy selected nine of his finest stories from recent years and had them published at his own expense, to qualify for the prize. On 23 December the printer contracted to produce 1,000 copies of the 254-page book, fifty copies to be delivered by noon on 31 December.

The stories Krúdy chose for this 'most beloved book' of his draw upon his 'dearest and finest imaginings . . . about eating, digestion, wine, illness, life's real dreams', written in 1925–8, including one story from the Szindbad cycle ('The Undead', 1925), plus 'The Green Ace', a novella from 1930.

Received with great critical acclaim, *Life Is a Dream* assured the author's eligibility for the prize. Literary politics and dissension among the directors of the Hungarian PEN Club resulted in the division of the prize money into two halves, to be disbursed over two years, and to be shared by two authors each year. To further diminish his pittance, Krúdy was requested to 'voluntarily' relinquish 10 per cent of the award to be disbursed to needy writers. Nearly half of the £225 he ultimately received was swallowed up by the printer's bill. The municipal utility authority also claimed its share for unpaid electric bills . . .

In 1957 the book was reissued by Szepirodalmi Konyvkiado in Budapest, with the addition of a tenth piece, 'Last Cigar at the Grey Arabian'. This memorable story, a complementary 'twin' to 'The Journalist and Death', was most likely left out of the first edition because of lack of space. These two stories are probably Krúdy's best known and most anthologized works, and are followed by a succession of tales that delight and astonish by opening the hidden dimensions of dream behind the seemingly ordinary events of everyday life.

John Batki,
Syracuse, New York
December 2008

Last Cigar at the Grey Arabian

On this day the Colonel had to shoot someone, on behalf of the Casino's directors; the decision had been made in the English Room (so named after a visit by the Prince of Wales).

The duel was to take place in the barracks that afternoon, and the man who had insulted the Casino was not to leave the premises alive.

'Very well, I'll shoot the journalist,' the Colonel said with a shrug.

But he was becoming devilishly hungry. This was the sum total of his nervousness on the day of the deadly duel. An abominable, unprecedented hunger now overpowered him. His stomach hungered, and so did his mouth; still half asleep, his lolling tongue explored his mouth, savouring comestibles he had never tried, never tasted before. He had been told that the journalist condemned to death in the Casino's English Room – the sentence to be executed by the Colonel, the deadliest shot in the land – this journalist was reputed to be such a pauper that he ate his evening meal of crackling with his fingers, from a paper bag, the salt kept in a vest pocket, the radishes and onions waiting in a desk drawer until the crackling was gone. Naturally the man could not afford decent wine, and so he would have to walk a long distance to find a cheap dive where he could slosh down some cold wine to quench the flames in his stomach.

The Colonel, who normally gave questions of life and death about as much thought as a bishop does in a game of chess, was dreadfully hungry now and overcome by cravings usually attributed to pregnant women. 'I'll be eating quicklime before long!' he brooded.

Today he wore civilian clothes under a roomy rain-cape and his canary yellow shoes creaked; for this pre-duel stroll in the rainy city he carried an umbrella-cane, and kept glancing into closed hackney cabs, convinced that no one would recognize him wearing mufti. Since he would never speak of these hours to anyone, after a certain amount of hesitation and cautious reconnaissance he decided at last to enter a butcher's shop in an outlying district of the city. His greying moustache drew an unenthusiastic greeting from the butcher's wife – the typical butcher's wife in her greasy white apron, sleeves rolled up to the elbows, revealing sour-smelling forearms. The wedding band on her finger had long ago cut deeply into the flesh, attesting that here was a housewife of some experience, just as the rings of former seasons recede into the trunk of a tree. Freshly fried crackling steamed, fragrant and tempting, in front of her small nose. The Colonel pointed at the platter.

'I'll take a pound of that.'

'That will be too much, sir,' said the woman. The intelligence of her intonation startled the Colonel. 'A few ounces of this crackling will be plenty for a snack. Otherwise I can't take responsibility for your stomach. This isn't light food.'

'Well, in that case give me twenty kreuzers' worth,' growled the Colonel, who did not go in for too much chit-chat. The butcher's wife reached for a volume of poems and tore out a few pages to form a paper cone. This reminded the Colonel of his journalist, who was rumoured to write poems.

'Whose poems are these?' he inquired, as if his civilian disguise demanded that he disguise his profession too, in front of the butcher's wife.

'We used to have a bearded old man come around here and he brought me poetry books. Perhaps you know him. His name was Vajda . . . Janos Vajda.'

'I know him,' said the Colonel, blushing to have to tell a lie. But no one could expect him to engage in a lengthy discussion with a butcher's wife on outer Ulloi Road.

The butcher's wife picked a few choice green peppers from a basket and cut off a hefty hunk of rye bread. 'Here, take these along,' she said generously, as she handed over the packages wrapped in paper for the Colonel to tuck under his cape.

The Colonel did not know why he was obeying this woman he had never seen before. 'Is there some tavern around here where I could eat this?' he inquired with a touch of condescension.

'There's a tavern nearby called the Grey Arabian. The sign has a Gypsy on it with a peaked cap. They'll have salt and wine for you there,' said the butcher's wife, and she was already gazing out through the open door as if expecting another customer.

The Colonel touched two fingers to his Tyrolean hunting hat and, swinging his umbrella-cane, left the butcher shop, and before he knew it he was already seated inside the small tavern known as the Grey Arabian. Once you take the first step on the road to depravity, the rest will soon follow. Our Colonel, a member of the Casino, had never dreamed that one day he would be a patron at the Grey Arabian. Back in the members' lounge at the Casino, that grand salon where not only the ornaments on the mantelpiece but even the leather armchairs appeared to be cast in bronze, he had heard rumours about the wild carousals of certain younger Counts, who partied with cab-drivers at taverns in the outer districts where, to the music of a hurdy-gurdy, they gave the scullery maids a whirl; but as for himself, it was inconceivable that he would be a guest at one of those out-of-the way dives. And here he was now, seated at a table with a red tablecloth, black-handled knife and fork, and a plain white china plate set in front of him by a young man with rolled-up shirtsleeves whose ambition in life was to lift a barrel of beer with one hand when the tavern was full of customers.

'What is your name, son?' asked the Colonel in a paternal voice.

'They call me Janos,' the young man replied, non-committal.

'Well then, Janos my son, I'll have you know that today I am going to shoot a man I don't even know and have never seen before, a man who'll be put in front of me like some target at the rifle range.'

The young man called Janos may not even have heard the Colonel's words, because he had for some time now been expecting the assistants from the nearby clinic to arrive so that he could tap a fresh keg of beer. The arrival of these uniformed men signalled the beginning of the customary ceremonies surrounding a fresh tap. The horse-traders, who were playing cards at a corner table presided over by the stout tavern-keeper, usually ordered glasses of wine spritzer, and set them down by their side, to fish the cigar and pipe ashes out at their leisure. The few patrons who dropped in on the run – coachmen and drivers of freight carts, cabs and hearses, official messengers, mailmen, tramdrivers whose business brought them this way – they would always order wine, for it packed more of a wallop than beer. Only the assistants from the clinic counted as serious beer drinkers, with time enough to savour their brews and hear out the conversations that customarily accompany beers – because across the street the day's autopsies will have been concluded, the world-weary professor washed his hands with a sense of finality, and tagged the cadavers that could at last be buried now, while others might need to be pulled out again tomorrow, the devil take their ways. As I was saying, the clinic assistants proved long-staying customers once their duties were done. And so Janos said nothing in response to the Colonel's comment.

But perhaps the Colonel did not expect a response, for without another word he spread out in front of himself the paper wrappers containing the cracklings and the cool green peppers; with great relish he cut a slice of brown bread and was at the point of digging into his snack when Janos stepped forth from behind the bar.

'What will you have: wine or beer?' he asked brazenly.

'A nice mug of beer,' replied the Colonel, even though an army doctor had forbidden him to drink beer on account of his heart murmur. Janos nodded, secure in the knowledge that he had a pitcher's worth of beer left in the keg that was tapped yesterday. He was on his way when he suddenly stopped. No, he could not give the Colonel yesterday's beer, because he had intended it for the janitor of a neighbouring building who had stolen away a girl from him, but still sent his small son over every evening for beer.

'Why don't you drink wine instead?' he called out, turning back towards the Colonel.

The Colonel flared up. 'Have you served in the army? Is this how they teach you in the army these days? I asked for beer, because I feel like drinking beer. Why, you . . .'

The hearse drivers and other transient guests all looked up towards the Colonel's table, for in taprooms, just as in drawing rooms, people love to pay attention to a raised voice. A man who dares speak in a loud voice cannot be an ordinary mortal.

'Let 'im have it, Janos,' said the owner, deeply immersed in his card game. 'Let 'im have it!' he shouted and slammed a card from his hand on top of another one that happened to lie on the blue tablecloth. After this stroke he sent an inquisitive look in the direction of the man who dared to raise his voice in this tavern. The owner had once been a cab-driver and as such had a good knowledge of all types, but even his knowing eye could not peg the gentleman wearing yellow shoes as a member of the Casino.

So Janos, by repeatedly tilting the keg, managed to squeeze out a last pitcher of beer from yesterday's tap, then with a show of strength ripped the spigot out of the barrel and decanted the leftover liquid into a dish to be saved for his rival, the janitor. Next he kicked the keg away as if it had no further use in this life. After all, the new barrel was already under the bar counter, to make the clinic assistants happy, so that they would keep the promise they made to Janos, and find a remedy for the long-standing rash his sister-in-law suffered from, back home in the village.

Meanwhile the Colonel was using all of his fingers to dispose of the cracklings. Some were crisp, some melted in his mouth. Just like life, thought the Colonel, and he recalled his youth when he had served in provincial garrisons where, towards the end of the month, he always had his orderly secretly bring him cracklings from the butcher's while he kept to his quarters, as if he, a young lieutenant, were already studying for his examinations to become a staff officer, instead of doing like his fellow officers who supped on credit at fancy restaurants and, ashamed of small debts, made sure to guzzle enough champagne to run up a tab that was respectably large. No one could raise objections to a bill garnished with plenty of champagne. He had learned to shave himself, and claimed it was only because he could not allow a stranger's hand near his face. He even drove the boot-trees into his boots himself, because his orderly was so clumsy. And he locked away the expensive moustache wax because he once caught the orderly casting a covetous glance at the container. Ah, those old-time orderlies were willing to swallow the castor oil prescribed for their officers, but could not resist the temptation of a box of moustache wax.

As he ate, the Colonel raised the mug of beer towards the light and peered at it mistrustfully. 'Surely that good-for-nothing I'm about to dispatch to the other world is drinking stuff like this today, because he can't afford any better!' he reflected, closing his eyes while he drank from the mug as if in silent toast to the salvation of that good-for-nothing's soul.

The Colonel found the beer tasty. God only knows what makes flat beer taste so good. It was as if in it the hops flowered once more, to soothe, relieve and fill you up with flavour. Flat beer has its aficionados just the same as the freshly tapped. Why do people in certain regions drink beer out of a 'boot', when nobody can empty one in a single gulp? And who can tell why real beer-drinkers, the common run of folk, do not down the freshly drawn beer straight away but wait instead until it settles, all the while eyeing the mug meditatively? There is a mystery about beer that will never be fathomed by the mind of mere mortals. – Such were the Colonel's thoughts as he drank his bitter beer, finished up the last morsels of his cracklings, discovered a few fleshy bits near the stem of the green pepper, and cut them out one by one, what a pleasure. And that brown bread was almost as phenomenal as the army bread he had once enjoyed during some field exercise, bread that gave off the scent of the saddle and other horse accoutrements. In a friendlier mood now, he surveyed the scene in the little tavern on Ulloi Road. He still had plenty of time left until the execution of that scribbler.

Life can be strange, reflected the Colonel of the Casino, catching a glimpse of the tavern-keeper's wife who must have just risen from her afternoon nap, and waddled across the taproom to check on her husband before doing anything else. Would she catch him in some heinous act that she could seriously reproach him about tonight in the privacy of the bedroom?

'My little chickadee!' shouted the hefty tavern-keeper, noting his wife's stealthy approach in those silent and indestructible felt slippers. He snatched the red-tasselled skullcap off his head (a thing he never did for anyone else), and waved it in the air. 'My little chickadee!' he shouted again, and slammed a card thunderously on to the table, as winners like to do. This slam was no doubt intended to set things right concerning his wife's afternoon dream, for these afternoon dreams of housewives may portend perils untold. At times they can dream the truth and once that happens no amount of kisses will restore their former good spirits. Usually it is jealousy that rouses these publicans' wives who nap in the afternoon, so that they leap out of bed with their sensible shoes half pulled on, hoping to catch the husband making love to the serving girl. No matter how respectable a tavern-keeper's past, he may boast of a father and mother who had instilled the best of family morals in him – all the same, the world has never known a tavern-keeper whose wife's jealousy was not justified. Although it is not easy for a publican to absent himself from his premises in order to pursue some shameful passion! It is most difficult for him to wander off to some other pub to carouse on credit, as a member of the trade, after the wife sequesters his wallet at night! And it's next to impossible, isn't it, for a well-known tavern-keeper to get entangled in amorous adventures in his own neighbourhood, for this is bound to have a bad effect on his business! And so tavern-keepers' wives the world over lay their heads to rest in the afternoon amidst great unease. And that is why the proprietor of the Grey Arabian, sitting among his pals, slammed his card down so hard, upon seeing the approach of his wife.

The Colonel, too, sized up the tavern-keeper's wife. She was a phenomenon indeed, whom every guest had the right to look over, entertaining notions mild or wild. The Colonel entertained the following thoughts regarding her:

– This woman no doubt has her points, although it would be folly to compare her to Countess Denise or any of my other acquaintances. None the less, one would like to see more specimens of her type among the women of common folk and the middle class . . .

As we can see, the Colonel was subject to the occasional onrush of arrogance, whenever he recalled his own destined role. After all, this very afternoon he had to execute a man who in a newspaper article had insulted the Casino . . . But now a nerve stirred in the region of his vest pocket, a nerve he had hitherto known precious little about, and once again he was seized by an abominable hunger. Had the Colonel been superstitious, he might have suspected some special warning at work. But he was not a superstitious man and therefore his eyes reverently followed each move made by the tavern-keeper's wife, movements that were becoming quite sprightly, once she had ascertained her husband was surrounded by his card cronies and not by a bevy of kitchen maids. No greater shame can befall a housewife than her husband deceiving her with her own serving girl. In this relieved mood of tolerance the tavern-keeper's wife deigned to take notice of the unfamiliar customer's nodding salutations.

'What can I do for you?' she asked, after the Colonel had nodded at her about ten times.

The Colonel, as if speaking in a dream under the vaulted ceiling of the Grey Arabian, replied: 'Do not believe for a moment, my dear woman, that I am what my strange outfit indicates. I have quite a decent standing in society, but circumstances at the moment compel me to show myself in the apparel of an ordinary citizen. I repeat, my good woman, that's all there is to it: I simply do not want to be recognized prematurely, before I settle an affair with a certain gentleman at a certain location in this neighbourhood.' And the Colonel pointed in a direction that the tavern-keeper's wife could hardly be expected to guess was the military barracks on Ulloi Road.

She reached into an apron pocket and rattled her keys impatiently. 'If there's something you want maybe you should speak to my husband,' she replied in a matter-of-fact tone, and she was already on her way in her felt slippers.

But the Colonel pressed on: 'This matter, my personal business, concerns solely you, madam,' he announced, suddenly decisive. 'I would like to eat something that in my opinion can only be found here at the Grey Arabian.'

'And what would that be?'

'I beg you not to laugh at my strange request. I feel like having a bit of stew left over from lunch, you know, from the bottom of the pot, with thick gravy. I don't mind if it is slightly burned. I happen to hold that each dish is best at the bottom of the pot, where it's cooked the longest. Don't worry, I've got the money.'

'Our guests prefer to have their stew early in the day,' said the tavern-keeper's wife, pronouncing the word as 'stoo'.

'You mean their stee-ew.'

'Their stoo,' countered the tavern-keeper's wife. 'I'll see in the kitchen if we have any left over. We had beef stoo at noon.'

The Colonel's eyes lit up, even though his bushy eyebrows had not experienced such a manifestation in years. After a short while the tavern-keeper's wife called from the kitchen: 'Janos, give this to the gentleman,' and she slammed the window shut.

The plate served up by Janos's stubby fingers indeed contained some leftover stew. It came in gravy as thick as stewed tomatoes. The meat was burned and consisted mostly of bony pieces that the proprietress would not have served to one of her regulars.

After all, most likely she would never see this peculiar gentleman again. The Colonel inspected these bits of meat with special delectation. He used his fork to turn over some, especially the pieces that were most charred, as if he took greatest delight in these. The barman, with some condescension, lingered by the guest's side for a while. This kind of food would not have pleased even the cab-drivers who happened to drop in here; they liked their food freshly prepared. The Colonel, after selecting a bony piece to his liking, shifted the meat about in his mouth, and just to be stylish, used his fingers to remove the bone sliver stuck between his teeth. Apparently he had made up his mind to degrade himself at all costs . . .

'You know, Janos,' he said, sucking on another bone, 'I happen to love oysters, but today I had a strange craving to eat the kind of food consumed by a certain someone, somewhere, so that I could imagine myself in that fellow's place. That's right, I want to be just like that miserable nonentity who ought to be writing his last will and testament just about now, if he had any brains. Yes, I am eating this "stoo" as an act of penance. I'm asking for pardon in advance, I announce my intentions in advance, because I do not wish to be the cause of anything unexpected. A gentleman, before he slaps your face, gives warning that sooner or later you will receive a slap. Only a bandit strikes you treacherously from behind. I give the gentleman fair warning that this affair will end poorly for him. But now that his death is imminent, I lower myself to his level to make peace with him and do joint penance together with him, even though I am quite innocent . . .'

The barman was using a matchstick to delve into his ear; it seemed he had understood not a word of what the Colonel was saying. 'I wouldn't advise you to fight here. The boss can be very tough.'

The Colonel smiled under his moustache, as if to acknowledge that his disguise was working – no one had spotted him as a member of the Casino. He dropped the remaining piece of bread into the gravy and speared it with his fork: 'I can see you know how to prepare the foundations of a stew here. I suspect you put tomatoes in the gravy, even though not everyone does that. The burned green peppers and potatoes are a nice touch. But the most intriguing part is that the dish tastes as if it had been waiting for quite some time for some cab-driver or other customer who for some reason or another could not come back for it. He's probably standing around waiting on the street somewhere, under the eaves, staring at the faces of passers-by, amusing himself by trying to guess who among those pedestrians will be the next fare, in case the cab is not reserved. But fortunately the cab already has a customer, some chap who is courting a fair lady in an apartment upstairs, the number of which is none of the driver's business. Don't cab-drivers come in here anymore?' inquired the Colonel.

The barman had no idea why he kept listening to this stranger, who under no circumstances would fit in among the regular customers. Nor could you say that he was here from the police to investigate something in the neighbourhood, for one can easily tell a police officer, if not by his behaviour then by his tone of voice.

The barman therefore had to condescend even more to answer the guest (who had finished the beer intended for the janitor). 'Would you be wanting to sell a horse? The carriage owners generally show up here after six, on their way back from Franciscans Place, Gizella Place, or wherever their business takes them.'

The Colonel almost burst out laughing. It was indeed worthwhile to don disguise every once in a while, just to get to know the 'common folk'. Crown Prince Rudolf had often been criticized at the Casino for not acting in a manner worthy of his title, but lo and behold, the Crown Prince was right after all to wear a disguise in order to mix among common folk. All he needed now was to be seen here at the Grey Arabian by Luczianovics, Wampetics, Muller, or any of the Casino's other cab-drivers! There would be no end to the ribbing at the Club the next day! He laughed, but went on to wipe his plate clean of all traces of red gravy, using the last remnants of bread crust for this operation.

'They say magnates eat a lot,' he said, winking at the barman. 'I do not know if I am permitted to go into the kitchen for a visit with Madame, for I am not familiar with her moods. But in any case I would like to know, is there by any chance a bit of leftover pork out there? Of course I mean cold roast pork, just an end piece, the stump, or "butt" as we like to put it. Just a bite or two, some small piece that cannot be sold as a full portion, but most welcome for an afternoon guest such as myself. I am sure that the rascal who's condemned to die is used to eating something like that when he wakes up after a night of debauchery in his tenement room or dosshouse where people of his sort are likely to hang out. I am convinced that his stomach must be on fire, his head splitting, his eyes seeing double; perhaps even now he's heading for the pawnshop to retrieve the overcoat borrowed from a friend.'

The guest of the Grey Arabian had undeniable good luck with everything that his untameable appetite conjured up on this day. The Colonel's stomach, which had the same identical gourd shape as most other stomachs, somehow did not feel right today, manifesting nervous symptoms that affected even the Colonel's disciplined mind. Why on earth did that stomach crave all sorts of victuals the Colonel usually never noticed, save on this day, when the Colonel's good heart, pitying his impoverished opponent, made him lower himself, out of sheer chivalry, to imitate the other man's humble way of life? No one should say the poor fellow had been snuffed out by some lord from on high in a plush box – but by someone who empathized with the trials of those less fortunate. The barman now returned bringing a piece of roast pork, an end part that was roasted to a turn, even singed a bit, featuring bones that tasked the teeth. Some like the nice and tender and even parts of the pork chop, but the Colonel, eager to identify in every way with his miserable opponent, was convinced that the other man could not afford a better piece of meat. He even asked for radishes and onions on the side, although he usually refrained from these pungent items.

'I could have had elevenses at the Casino, perhaps some crayfish, they're best during these months,' the Colonel explained to the barman, who was gradually falling under the spell of this odd guest. 'I happen to know Miss Finkelstein, who provides the crayfish for the Casino's kitchen, and during my morning stroll at the market hall always tells me about the shellfish she delivered that day. Last week she informed me that in addition to the small crayfish caught in the river, that are best as stuffing or in soups, she had sent up to the Casino one unusually large specimen that had only one claw, sort of like a sword. And its tail was a veritable battle-axe. She advised me to keep tabs on this crayfish. I immediately proceeded to the Casino and laid claim to the single-clawed crayfish. Indeed, it proved a nice mouthful, accompanied by three of his smaller cohorts. The three smaller crayfish must have been members of the same family for they were all outstanding specimens. But none of them could compete with their elder. Well, you just have to keep your eyes peeled if you want to eat well. Am I right, Janos?'

The Colonel's torrent of words would have confused even a far more significant individual than the barman of the Grey Arabian. As it was, the Colonel kept sawing away at the cold pork, then gnawed at the bone, in order to resemble as closely as possible that miserable person who was perhaps presently feeding in the same manner at some low dive, if indeed he was able to afford a meal. The Colonel was a benevolent man and would have gladly invited to lunch the poor wretch whom, in consequence of the Casino's decision, he was scheduled to dispatch to the other world at six this afternoon; of course the man would have to sit at another table, for not even the kindest heart may transgress the rules in the code of chivalry. How often, for instance, must a gentleman in high society sit under the same roof with his deadly enemies . . . After all, one cannot create a scandal at every chance encounter. This leftover roast pork was truly well done, and the Colonel, while still eating, promised Janos that the next time he had business around here (and pointed over his shoulder) he would make sure to drop in at the Grey Arabian.

'Alas, I am unable to tell you exactly when that would be,' said the Colonel, cutting open a radish and attentively examining its texture. One could tell by the radishes that the Grey Arabian's customers were connoisseurs, for every single radish he tried proved top grade. A light perspiration bedewed their ivory bellies that had not a trace of the brown worm that insidiously eats its way to a radish's heart, nor were there any spongy, decaying parts, the sight of which is so discouraging for the lover of radishes, leading him to imagine there were no decent folks, or radishes, left in the world, because looks are deceptive, and even the most honest-looking fruit is rotten to the core. But the Colonel's radishes did not deceive. Their insides delivered what their outsides promised: good health.

The Colonel munched on these radishes, food of the poor, the consumption of which had given occasion for many an amusing remark at the Grey Arabian as well as other, higher-class hostelries.

'I like to eat oysters, too,' remarked the Colonel during the ceremony of radish-eating, whereupon Janos began to eye this customer somewhat distrustfully: was the man trying to make a fool of him? 'But today I feel compelled to abstain, and eat this penitential fare, because you must obey the voice of your conscience. Were I to shoot down that poor devil after a feast, high on French champagne, I might later reproach myself for having had an unfair advantage. In a carefree and reckless mood my victory would have to be a foregone conclusion, since luck is yours if you have pluck. As I was saying, I am quite in favour of oysters but I never eat more than a couple of dozen at a time. As a matter of fact, a friend of mine died after putting away twenty-eight oysters. Yes, twenty-eight, although they were the smaller kind. Now, your octopus is quite something else. The fishermen have to use axes to kill the bigger ones! The tentacles of an octopus, pickled in a sour sauce with plenty of onions, pepper and spices makes as wholesome a dish as any eel. Say, would you happen to have a small piece of salami around?' the Colonel demanded rather anxiously, as if he had caught the scent of salami in the air. 'I just want some end piece that's been put aside because it's too small to slice. A little end piece that's tied with a string. Not everyone can chew that, but thank God my teeth are still pretty good, I believe I could bite a copper penny in half.'

By now the barman was completely in the Colonel's power, swayed by some kind of magic spell cast by the stranger's voice that he could have listened to all night. He only needed to check in the icebox. Yes, the icebox of a small tavern often contains these small sticks of salami, remnants that sometimes wait around for weeks until they find their connoisseur, while at other times they are taken right away by some cab-driver in a hurry who will pull them out of his coat pocket while waiting for a fare somewhere.

Thus the Colonel's uncanny appetite led him all the way to a helping of sharp Liptauer cheese with a penetrating aroma, spread in thin slices on a salt roll; most cheeses are usually harder. He was about to conclude his meal when a hansom cab came to a spinning stop in front of the Grey Arabian and a pale-faced, lanky young man leaped out.

Had the Colonel possessed the least receptivity towards the way civilians dressed he would have surely noticed the recherché quality of the young man's outfit. He wore a black cloak with a high lapel befitting the hero of a nineteenth-century novel. He also sported a Byronic shirt collar and lacework cuffs. His blue necktie had white polka dots and was loosely knotted about his neck, and his vest was an honest-to-goodness embroidered white vest. He seemed to have taken every item from the wardrobe of some theatre. Possibly on permanent loan. His legs were as spindly as some comedian's. The tight black pants emphasized the thinness of these legs. His boots had effeminately high heels.

This ashen-faced young man burst into the premises as if looking for help. His frenzied features betrayed an insurmountable fear, as if he were trying to run away from something. His long hair tumbled over his forehead and ears. The face was smooth-shaven, passionate, yearning . . .

– Well, he might as well be a musician, thought the Colonel, whose attention had been instantly drawn to the young man the moment he leaped from the hired carriage, even though as a rule he was not in the habit of paying attention to fellow mortals. He felt a certain attraction to the strange young man; he would not have minded if, for lack of a better place, the young man had joined him at his table. But the newcomer, without looking left or right, headed straight for the bar, as in an emergency at a pharmacy. His writhing fingers fumbled at a coin and with the urgency of an alcoholic he tapped on the galvanized iron counter. The barman half turned from the Colonel to size up the young man.

'A glass of your strongest slivovitz, please,' said the young man in an otherworldly voice. 'That's right, plum brandy,' he added, his acrid laughter seeming to mock himself for landing in a situation that demanded plum brandy.

The Colonel, although he had just ordered his second wine spritzer (perhaps intending to resemble in this respect, too, the dissolute journalist), quietly shook his head, wondering about the fate of a man so young wasting away in taverns.

But the young man had all this time ignored the challenging glances the Colonel cast his way. He stared goggle-eyed straight at the bartender's face as if that was where he expected to find reprieve from life's tribulations. However the bartender handed him the shot of brandy without the least sign of sympathy. The young man snatched up the glass, raised it to his lips and was about to toss it back when his glance unexpectedly fell on the Colonel's sardonic, arrogant face. Although the Colonel had probably not meant it, his expression was most insulting, as indeed it was most of the time. Alas, a life in the *haut monde* demands such expressions – they are nothing but masks. Some people show their true faces only when death removes the mask.

As soon as the young man glimpsed the Colonel his face was seized by such terror that one would have thought he had seen the devil, or death itself. The shot glass slipped from his hand and broke with a crash on the slanting floor, even though it was a thick and sturdy one. The young man's hands flew up to cover his eyes as if he could no longer stand to see what was in front of him. Blindly tottering, he turned and crashed ghost-like through the door. 'Head for the barracks!' he yelled in a hoarse voice to the driver, who cracked his whip at the horses, as sudden as death itself. (Indeed, subsequent discussions revealed that no one in the neighbourhood knew this driver, even though every cab-driver of any standing had been to the Arabian, even if it took him out of his way.)

'Hey! What about paying!' screamed Janos, and even the owner sprang up from his tranquil game of cards, for this sort of thing rarely happened in his tavern and must not be tolerated even if it was only a matter of a few kreuzers. The owner was about to tell Janos to run after that cab, even if he had to go all the way to the barracks, when the other stranger, the Colonel, now quiet and grave, motioned to him: 'I'll pay for that drink.'

The Colonel's words, although he spoke very quietly, created a stir in the tavern. What secret connection linked these two strangers? What mystery were they hiding? At last a sagacious old cab-driver (retired) resolved the problem with native common sense. 'Most likely he's the boy's uncle!' he opined, thumbing in the Colonel's direction. And the game resumed, since the assistants from the clinic still had not arrived. Some days there is no end of autopsies.

The Colonel by now sat in his place in silence as if a depressing presentiment had seized hold of him with the young man's entrance in the tavern. Although never accused of having an adventurous mind, the peculiar notion now flashed through the Colonel that the young man might have been the journalist he had to fight on this day in a duel to the death. After all, the Colonel had never seen the journalist; it was at the Casino's behest that he was to do his utmost to gain redress, even if it ended in death.

Janos, still worked up over the previous scene, stood behind the bar and addressed his complaint to the Colonel, seeing the owner was again absorbed in his card game. 'We'd be in a fine pickle if all our guests slammed their glasses to the floor and ran off without paying!'

The Colonel merely nodded at these words while pulling out his pocket watch again. He still had more than a quarter of an hour before the duel; he planned to arrive exactly on time. (It was two minutes' walk from here to the barracks.) Truth to tell, the Colonel had no interest whatsoever in mingling with civilians, duelling seconds, and doctors any longer than was necessary, and anyway the duel was unavoidable, a done deal. His seconds (two other Colonels) and his doctor Emil Kosztka were sure to be in their places. No one has the right to suppose that he, a retired Colonel of the Hussars, could possibly arrive late because of pusillanimity. He merely wished to avoid unnecessary chit-chat. He would fire on command, then wait, hands in pocket, to see if his opponent was able to return fire. Most likely he would not be. Although he heard it said that once a dying man mustered his last remaining strength to fire a shot, and hit the mark. Stuff and nonsense; that sort of thing happens once in a hundred years.

If he were to find himself, in the riding ring inside the barracks, indeed facing that barmy-looking young man, with the white Byronic collar and long white shirt-cuffs providing an ideal target, standing in front of his pistol – if indeed that paltry, irresponsible young man were to be his opponent, that would be most unpleasant, but would not change the situation at all. After all, the Colonel had nothing to do with the fellow personally, or with his kith and kin, his lover if he had one, or his father or mother. The Casino had decided in this matter, and against the Casino's decision there was no appeal . . .

'Let me have some of that brandy,' the Colonel now spoke, as if against his own will, for by now he had come to feel somewhat ashamed of identifying himself to such an extent with his opponent, who could only be that journalist, wearing an embroidered white vest for a duel with pistols.

Janos at first did not understand these words, for he was not a writer of short stories who anticipates the thoughts inside a Colonel's head, but slowly recovered his wits and poured brandy into a shot glass that could have been the one dropped by the young man a little earlier. After a quick sniff or two the Colonel tossed back the drink with a firm hand. Indeed, it was unusually strong brandy – obviously a favourite with cab-drivers who arrive here at the outskirts of town in a winter blizzard after spending the whole day driving around all sorts of worthless gadabouts. Or this brandy was the favourite of coachmen who transported cadavers to the post-mortem room of the neighbouring clinic. But in fact the Grey Arabian's plum brandy was famous throughout the whole neighbourhood – so why shouldn't a Colonel like it.

'Well, we might as well get going,' announced the Colonel, after surreptitiously clearing his throat once or twice, for he wouldn't have let on for the whole world that the coachmen's brandy had slightly befuddled him. But he downed it in lieu of that wretched scribbler.

When he asked for the bill, it was the tavern-keeper's wife who came out of the kitchen bringing a slate writing board and chalk, to the Colonel's keen amusement. He imagined what a capital prank it would be if Stettner, the head waiter at the Casino, pulled out a writing slate to add up the bill, and gave change out of a skirt pocket instead of on a silver salver. To show his gratitude to the woman, the Colonel fished in his wallet for the crispest banknote that was ironed as starchy smooth as if it were a leftover from last month's pension. Her head bowed, as always, respectful of money, the woman did her addition, earnestly, naively, as if she were performing the most important act entrusted to her in her life.

'I do hope everything was to your liking?' she asked after handing over the change and snapping the crisp banknote one last time before filing it away in her manly wallet. – 'But perhaps that stoo . . .'

'The stee-ew . . . was most delicious,' replied the Colonel testily, for he was starting to suspect the woman invented that pronunciation expressly to annoy him.

Next, he rummaged through his cigar case, inspecting one by one his treasures, the various cigars that he sometimes saved for weeks for the suitable and proper occasion to light them up. He quickly found a short cigar for the barman, and bestowed it as if it were some badge of honour, but he had considerable difficulty finding a cigar for himself. Finally his choice fell on a Havana shaped like a bludgeon, a cigar the like of which had never been lit here in the entire history of the Grey Arabian.

Under no circumstances did the Colonel wish to resemble that worthless buffoon, now that he believed he had seen the man. He felt sure that the young man dropped the shot glass because he had recognized the Colonel. For the Colonel supposed that the whole city knew him – especially his opponents. No, that look of preternatural terror could not have appeared on anyone but his opponent's face.

Gravely and ceremoniously the Colonel lit up his miniature bludgeon, after scornfully ripping off the red and gold paper band. How foolish of him to try to forget, even if only for the duration of one afternoon, his rank, his social position, the circles he moved in and his customary way of life, just to 'lower himself' to the level of an unknown person and his supposed habits, as if in atonement for shooting that man before the day was over, and thereby liberating him from the torments of earthly existence. 'He who asks forgiveness is the biggest fool, for we cannot speak of true forgiveness,' said the Colonel, as he lit his little club of a cigar. 'Back off, if you fear for your life,' ballooned the Colonel's first billow of smoke, which he proceeded to blow away and disperse about him, as if he had meant to obliterate everything that had happened that afternoon.

The Havana indeed proved to be savoury, proper and fitting for a last cigar.

Given this tableau of the lit cigar, we are just about done at the Grey Arabian, and the diverse gentlemen who were about to arrive there from all over the city, impelled by various inner motivations. We may be sure that the assistants from the clinic showed up at long last, because not even pathology labs conduct autopsies day and night. Hearse-drivers from all over the city will have arrived, for even the transport of cadavers must pause at times. And as evening fell the gentlemen who owned hansom cabs pulled up in front of the building, for their stables were nearby. The bar became busy, and every time the kitchen door opened a scent of fresh 'stoo' wafted out. Janos and the tavern-keeper's wife, as well as the others, had by then plenty of time to forget the Colonel who had rolled his goggle eyes so formidably around the premises that afternoon, but who turned out to be quite a sociable fellow, after all, and did not mind chatting with the barman. At some point in the evening a belated hearse-driver showed up at the bar, and stood gruffly in front of the counter, as one who is disgruntled with his profession. Standing, he rubbed one foot against the other leg, and said not a word before he downed two shots of strong brandy.

'I had to haul some Colonel wearing civilian clothes,' he announced, wiping his moustache with a filthy kerchief, and even Janos looked up to listen. 'These gentlemen wear shiny uniforms all their lives and we never have any business with them because the military handles all that. That is, if they die in uniform. But my load went and dressed in civilian clothes before he died, just to give us some business. They said he was shot in a duel at the barracks, and no one knew what to do with him until now. But that's what we are here for, to take anyone. So he's at the morgue at last.'

The bartender did not respond to the hearse-driver because an Inner City cabbie had just entered and the man had a lot of friends here, so you had to listen closely to his order, for this customer liked to make trouble at the drop of a hat.

Around midnight, when the patrons were beginning to thin out, Janos the bartender at last had a chance to catch his breath and with his back against the cupboard reflected on the odd customer he had served that afternoon. And no, it never occurred to him that the cadaver so recently transported had been that same customer. The one who left that fancy cigar band lying in the corner.

(1927)

The Journalist and Death

The journalist Titusz Finedwell was sentenced to death by the Casino's board of directors in the chamber where members held their confidential meetings, sessions of the court of honour and tribunals of the duelling code – the chamber where, once upon a time, at the festivities held in honour of Albert, Prince of Wales, gentlemen ended up going at each other with champagne bottles, and grabbed the Gypsy musicians' violins and wind instruments to beat each other. After that dark event the chamber saw no further carousing, and became dedicated to the service of honour. The destinies of rooms can change just like those of their human occupants. Only women can be as shamelessly fickle as rooms.

In his newspaper Finedwell had published an article offensive to the Casino, and for this he had to die. To execute the sentence the Casino delegated from among its members a retired colonel of Hussars, P. E. G., known as the best shot in all of Hungary. With that, the fate of the journalist was sealed. He might as well start giving away his worldly goods (if he possessed any), for soon he would no longer need anything.

This time Finedwell did not have to invent the usual family disaster to request an advance from his employer. An advance has a way of reconciling a journalist with both life and death.

Having received the advance, the journalist lost no time leaving Elderberry Street, where for years he had struggled at a recalcitrant desk with cheap pens and watery ink, in ever more refractory attempts at producing copy that always refused to materialize just when Finedwell intended to write his finest articles. With the advance in his pocket, he decided he would die like a gentleman. Let's see how Finedwell, facing imminent death, went about transforming himself into a gentleman.

First of all the journalist had to obtain a proper hat, for the one he wore throughout his nocturnal way of life (when no one sees your hat anyway) was getting to look like the hats left behind at coffee houses in lieu of payment. Long after the patron has fled, the hat is still waiting there, and grows a beard. Very few patrons actually return for a hat left behind when they stepped out pretending to 'go next door'. All of Finedwell's hats, umbrellas and walking sticks had been acquired at a café – by no means fraudulently! – thanks to Olga, the lady at the cash register of the café where Finedwell was a nightly regular. We must not presuppose anything improper about Olga and Finedwell's friendship. The journalist would simply stop and chat at the cash till – as so many other nighthawks did who pass their lives in cafés. He stood and talked to Olga about all sorts of things heard at the editorial offices. From these disquisitions Olga could have learned all there was to know about the world of politics and literature. But Olga never showed any sign of special interest in anyone featured in Finedwell's lengthy narratives. Nor was she ever surprised when, in certain inevitable situations, she was asked to extend credit to one or another journalist (including Finedwell) for orders to be served by the head waiter, who had an imperial-style beard; orders such as scrambled eggs, ham on the bone, bologna sausage with oil and vinegar, sardines, frankfurters with horseradish, sliced salami, bread and butter, pickled herring with onion, lean bacon, or smoked sausages – the sorts of food that impecunious journalists generally like to consume.

And so Olga was not the least bit surprised when Finedwell, pale, spindly and solemn as a martyr, announced, with hat clutched under his arm, that he could no longer evade his doom: he had to die young and full of promise, without being able to complete the great work that he, in the manner of old-style journalists, had always dreamed of in the midst of his tribulations and counted on for the betterment of his lot – a *magnum opus* he had not even begun, although he had spread rumours about working on it each day at dawn. There stood Finedwell by Olga's throne, his face unshaven, lips blue as plums, a glazed look in his eyes, expecting some miracle from her, a drowning man clutching at a straw. Olga, however, remained quite indifferent, safe in the knowledge that her Paisley shawl, cape and hat were as always within reach, in case she had to run from a drunken patron. Yet on other occasions, whenever some trivial sum was needed to get home or to buy cigarettes, she had been extraordinarily friendly! Still, after giving some thought to the situation – Titusz Finedwell's fatal situation – she was unable to suppress a wry little smile, which was at the same time a bitter comment on her own fate as well.

'We all have to die some day,' she said.

'But not in a crummy hat like this!' remonstrated the man sentenced to death.

Olga possessed a southern temperament, capable of quick changes of mood. After inspecting Finedwell's hat her natural benevolence soon gained the upper hand. 'You're right, this hat has seen better days! It's beyond redemption!' she said, handling the hat delicately with a woman's touch. Then, descending from her throne she went to a small closet where the café staff stored a variety of objects.

Olga emerged from the closet with a green Tyrolean hunter's hat and a so-called 'umbrella-cane'. First she dusted off the hat.

It was decorated with an eagle claw and a tuft of chamois-beard.

'This was left behind by a customer who swore he was going to jump in the Danube. Try it on!'

Finedwell put on the hat and spent some time contemplating his image in the mirror. He checked himself out from all angles. He liked the hat but hated to admit it in front of Olga, so he spoke as follows: 'Strange how this hat reminds me of the small town where I lived for a while in my childhood. This kind of hat was worn by men in green trousers, with all sorts of loops and wires and knives dangling from their belts. They usually worked in pairs. The sight and scent of these men made all the dogs bark like mad – they sensed the blood of animals on these men.'

'Ah, the swine-gelders!' – exclaimed Olga, taking a more mirthful look at the hat, for as a country gal she was familiar with those itinerant men who professionally altered the sex of domestic animals. 'Titusz, I guarantee that none of your colleagues has a hat like that. They'll be green with envy when they see you wearing it. The editor of *The Concord* had asked for it but I wouldn't give it to him. I have been saving it for some gifted new poet, but there are no gifted new poets nowadays.'

Finedwell kept the hat on because he thought it made him look like one of the landed gentry. He stood there somewhat cheered, as if suddenly the pressure over his heart had vanished, a choking pressure he had been feeling for several hours.

Next, Olga thrust the umbrella-cane at him. 'Tell me, Titusz, is there a scribbler in Budapest who has an umbrella like this, an umbrella that's a cane at the same time?'

Finedwell was indeed amazed by the strange walking stick that turned into an umbrella with a turn in the weather. He immediately opened the umbrella and held it over his hat. 'Veteran accountants used to receive things like this as souvenirs for their twenty-fifth jubilee . . .'

'I wouldn't be surprised,' said Olga.

'Or else those middle-class husbands who in the course of their long married lives have received just about every type of gift from their wives on their birthdays and name days and anniversaries until they have everything they could ever want, including tobacco pouches. My vest pockets are of course full of tobacco shreds.'

Titusz could not quite hide his excitement as he turned the rare object in his hands. Although his face was still overcast, a new hope glimmered in his eyes, for it occurred to him that he might accidentally survive the duel and live to rise in the world, as the owner of the umbrella-cane and the big green hat.

Olga is a fine woman, after all, thought Titusz as he exited from the Ferenci Café, without the least intention whatever of heading for the editorial offices in Elderberry Street, even though his new accessories would have created quite a sensation there. But that would have exposed him to the likelihood of a cantankerous editor assigning him, on the very eve of his death, the task of collating the latest news dispatches. He would rather die than see another news bulletin tonight! Lose his job, rather than work like a dog on the night he came into possession of a new hat and umbrella-cane! How degrading it would be to sit even on this night in that ill-smelling editorial office, milling about in a swarm of reporters begging for work, for something to make himself useful at any cost! Leave that to ninnies and novices without the least experience of life, not to mention a duel fought with pistols – which in their case would most likely take place somewhere around here on the Danube embankment, where the bullet would end up in the river, 'if the pistols were loaded' – as old-time duelling seconds like to say.

The clock struck ten at Franciscans Place when an irresistible impulse made Finedwell direct his steps toward the National Casino, whose court of honour had sentenced him to die.

At first he only dared to sneak a peek from the opposite side of Hatvani Street at the baronial castle-like two-storey building, through the wide open gates of which carriages drove in to pull up thunderously in front of the red velvet carpeted stairs leading to the entrance. After the gentlemen got out, and the doorman in cherry-red uniform slammed the carriage door to set the large lantern overhead in the archway swaying, the carriages drove through the courtyard, around the fountain, and exited through the side gate to Szep Street. The Casino's windows were dim and shut tight, as if no one needed any air inside – although it was a balmy night in early autumn with the sky full of stardust.

Lurking in a doorway, Titusz surveyed with rapt attention the solemn structure where life and death were of no importance, as if the gentlemen frequenting this exclusive building had notions of living and dying that were different from those of ordinary mortals! For instance, what would happen if Finedwell were to cross the street and inquire from the cherry-red uniformed doorman after P. E. G., retired colonel of the Hussars, so that he might at least have a word with the gentleman who was going to shoot him dead the next day? Most likely the doorman would refuse to have anything to do with him, or chase him away in case he recognized the journalist, for an old employee of the Casino would be familiar with the duelling code. The rules stipulated that opponents may not be in contact with each other prior to a duel, and Finedwell would only expose himself to a nasty humiliation. Before, when he still wore the decrepit old hat, he probably would have done it; but now his 'swine-gelder's hat', as he started to call it, imbued him with a certain amount of pride. Therefore he abandoned his hiding place, walked up to

Kerepesi Road and crossed over to the Casino side of Hatvani Street.

Presently he returned as a nonchalant stroller, without casting a glance at the baronial castle as he passed its open gate, swinging his umbrella-cane, for its crooked handle allowed it to dangle from his wrist. Yes, that umbrella-cane swung and tapped Finedwell's knee from time to time, as if to goad him on. In the possession of such an umbrella-cane who could conceive sinking so low as to beg for mercy for one's wretched little life. And so Titusz turned into Szep Street as if he really had some business there, other than maintaining his dignity in front of the Casino's cherry-red doorman who, he suspected, was casting scornful, mocking glances from the entrance after the journalist, as if the insolent servant had guessed the reason for this promenade in the neighbourhood of the Casino . . . On Szep Street Titusz walked past those windows behind whose dim glow the gentlemen were probably seated at their dinner table, admiring the colonel as if he were some rare exotic lobster.

Meandering through the dark little byways of the Inner City, Finedwell once more found himself on Franciscans Place, led there by years of habit. He had mulled it over, and concluded he would be an utter fool if, his upcoming deadly duel being the 'talk of the town', he did not now proceed to some fancy restaurant to parade in front of the world, as long as 'everyone' was discussing his case. If only to exhibit his dash, verve and sangfroid, which would be all the easier now that he had the proper hat and umbrella-cane for the occasion. Simply to enjoy to the very last drop the delights of being in the limelight, which must be considerable since multitudes struggled ceaselessly to attain such delights. When would the obscure journalist T. F. ever again attain the position of being pointed out in public as the reporter who, in the line of professional duty, dared to face death? . . . When would he ever again command the attention of those circles that believed duels were impressive? When would those mocking, scornful, quarrelsome, nasty glances turn respectful around him if not tonight, his last night, when that advance in his pocket allowed him to have a carefree, hilarious time?

In his mind's eye Finedwell saw himself in the middle of a very exclusive restaurant where the Gypsy violinist was playing only for him, and the women, dressed for the theatre, all kept turning their heads in his direction, their hearts a-flutter, for he was the most fascinating man about town, getting ready to face the lion – and certain death. And all for what? For the sake of honour.

Treat yourself to a decent supper, advised the spendthrift Tyrolean hat. Why not have a beefsteak at a first-rate restaurant where they not only print the correct English spelling on the menu, but also know the proper way to grill a steak.

Served with a fried egg, sunny side up, added the umbrella-cane, tapping along by Finedwell's side.

You've got the money and you still don't know how to be a gentleman, the hat accused, as Finedwell persisted in directing his steps towards a small tavern located in the building of the Athenaeum Press. You'll never be a gentleman if you pass up this opportunity. You must go to the Bristol or the Hotel Hungaria if you want people to notice that you are still in this world, and preparing to die on the field of honour. If you don't like beefsteak, there are plenty of other comestibles on the menu the waiter hands you, with a bow. Maybe a bird of some sort . . . or perhaps a hare, it's been in season since the middle of August. A saddle of hare, with a piquant sauce full of bay leaves, and if you find buckshot in the meat that means you'll be lucky in your duel. You should avoid crayfish, which is cheap in the market this time of the year; and anyway your fingers lack the skills to eat crayfish in a stylish manner. But you could have a fresh roast, and enjoy the humble, apologetic glances the waiter sends towards you while it is being prepared. Just think, what if your editor faced a duel that's been spread all over the newspapers for days! Why, he'd be cashing in on it for sure! And you don't even have the wits to get acquainted with some nosey society lady.

Finedwell was about to yield to the incessant goading sounded by the tap-tap of the umbrella-cane and the rustle of the goat hair in his hat: be a social lion, at least for a day, before you die!

His way led him past the stand of a nocturnal vendor selling all sorts of fruit from a small cart. Since it was still early in the season, grapes and walnuts were too expensive for the daytime folk but the spendthrift nightbirds were only too happy to buy them. Finedwell, just to indulge in some extravagance on this extraordinary day, bought a paper bag full of grapes and walnuts, and paid without even trying to bargain.

I wasn't born a gentleman, but tomorrow I'll have to die like one, reflected Finedwell glumly, as he entered the small all-night tavern, with the paper bag tucked under his arm. The place stayed open mostly for typesetters working the night shift and other characters of nocturnal but presumably sober habits, who came here to eat, not to carouse. Kerschantz was the name of the tavern-keeper, and he rarely saw journalists who lived the café life, for passing the night away eating and drinking at Kerschantz's was a more expensive proposition than surviving on mocha and cappuccinos at a coffee house. At Kerschantz's you had to spend some money, and credit was extended only to printers, who settled their bills regularly every Saturday. No, not even an editor-in-chief would have received credit here – so we cannot say that Finedwell was not gratified to be spending his last evening at this night tavern with its solid middle-class reputation.

He sat down at a commodious corner table, as one who is absolutely sure of himself.

It did not escape his attention that Kerschantz, a taciturn, red-moustachioed Schwabian, who measured out his wines at the counter as carefully as an apothecary his potions, this silent man now favoured Finedwell's new hat and umbrella-cane with a decidedly appreciative glance. Could he have thought that some day this umbrella-cane was bound to end up in his possession? Who can read a tavern-keeper's mind? Only customers who are broke imagine that the proprietor always has an eye on them lest they leave the premises without paying.

Finedwell asked for the bill of fare from the pint-size waiter whom the owner alerted to the arrival of a new guest with a softly spoken 'Janos!' This, too, was a first in Titusz Finedwell's experience. There is no denying it: tavern-keepers can see into the customer's pockets.

Janos crossed himself when he glimpsed Mr Finedwell at the corner table. He approached hesitantly as if he had seen a ghost.

'Sir, I heard you were shot in a duel.'

'Ah, 'tis but the music of the future,' Titusz replied with a laugh, speaking in the manner that journalists in those days adopted towards waiters. 'Yes, Janos, 'tis but the music of the future. Next time you should pay more attention when you're eavesdropping at Marich's table.'

Janos's face, unable to keep a secret, now registered even greater consternation. 'For sure, last night the printers at Marich's table were saying your life, sir, wasn't worth a wooden nickel. That you were a goner . . .'

In the inner sanctum of the arcaded tavern there stood a long table where the regulars, typesetters all, had placed a sign that read, in beautiful large lettering: 'MARICH'S TABLE'. (Mr Marich was a highly regarded typesetter of his day, who could boast of having set in type Ferenc Deák's famous 'Easter article'.) Mr Marich, a tall, dignified and distinguished-looking gentleman showed up each night round about midnight to preside over his table.

Titusz was flattered by his affair being discussed even at the Marich table, frequented by the most respected typesetters, but he pretended not to notice the excitement of the waiter who stood there slapping his own knees with his napkin as if to rouse himself from a dream.

'We have sour lungs,' he said at last, as if vaguely recalling that whenever Titusz appeared at the tavern he usually ordered this humble dish that belonged, along with tripe, in the least expensive category. Titusz always requested half a lemon with his meal, and never failed to praise the cook for taking the trouble to dice the lungs into small square pieces to make sure they were well done.

Titusz ignored the waiter's suggestion, merely muttering something about Janos planning to get him 'pickled again' – as if his stomach, profession, and whole life weren't sour enough already. 'I feel like eating a rooster!' Titusz exclaimed, after noting that this was the most expensive item on the modest menu.

'A chicken fricassee, coming right up.'

'I said rooster, didn't I, a cock that hasn't been gelded before his time, like certain incompetent editors, but remained a rooster all his life and lived to chase young serving girls and maybe even pecked at a nursemaid or two.'

Who knows how long our hero would have gone on lauding the rooster he was about to consume tonight, calling out after the retreating waiter to make sure to serve the rooster's spurs, not to mention liver and gizzard, when a red moustache appeared at the tavern's threshold.

Now there are all sorts of red moustaches. Most of them are angry, malevolent, neglected emblems of manhood, unworthy of grooming, if for no other reason than their colour. But this red moustache happened to be one out of a hundred, the red moustache that radiated good humour, cheer, satisfaction and joie de vivre, as if under that moustache the corners of the mouth were elevated into a permanent smile. This red moustache had earned the right to grow full, to be twirled to a point and often caressed like some faithful hound. Above the moustache the round eyeglasses with tortoise frames, balanced on the tip of the nose, and secured by a ribbon to the ears, belonged to that class of happy spectacles behind which the eyes always seem benevolent. Below the moustache the necktie drew attention, for although it was a hand-tied blue 'lavaliere' with white polka dots, it still had a tiepin in the form of a wild boar's head with ruby eyes.

Indeed, the owner of the pin was a dealer in venison and game by the name of Andor Aureate, a name that dated back to his days as a journalist, before he entered the profession of dealer in venison and game.

'Glad to find you here, Titusz,' said the former journalist, who frequently came to the tavern from his nearby house on Bastion Street, 'just to catch a whiff of the printer's shop' as he put it. For not even as a dealer in venison and game could he forget the scent of fresh newsprint. 'I read in the papers that you are in contact with the aristocracy, the counts, the National Casino. May I call to your attention my old *Salon Almanack*, which I edited back at a time when I tried to bring Hungarian writers together with members of the aristocracy. You know, one writer followed by one count – a poetess, followed by a countess . . . That was how I compiled my *Almanack*, alternating stories and poems with portraits.'

'Not a bad concept,' replied the journalist. 'But right now I find myself sentenced to death.'

But Aureate was not a man to be dissuaded so easily from the scheme that made him leave his house on Bastion Street so late at night. 'I don't like the path literature is taking these days. Lajos Czete, all he writes about is railway employees, ever since he created the character Adam Boor in his humorous magazine. What can he see in conductors and switchmen? It makes more sense to write about counts and countesses. There will never be a Hungarian literature as long as the literary world and the world of magnates are not on a par.'

'On a par, well put,' replied Finedwell. 'As I said, right now I stand sentenced to death. And I am drinking a "Czete-wayo".'

'See, that's precisely what's wrong,' said Aureate, editor of the quondam *Salon Almanack*, flashing his watch-chain that featured a wild boar's tusk, set in silver of course. 'The tavern-keepers named a spritzer after Lajos Czete, and not after Count Andrassy or Prince Festetics. That's why you modern writers will never get anywhere! We old-timers would have known how to steer literature in the right direction. But you have knocked the pen out of our hands, you've put us down, and here you are now, up against the Casino, up against the whole aristocracy!'

Titusz answered cynically: 'This "Czete-wayo" is a fabulous concoction. One part wine, one part mineral water, one part seltzer.'

At such pig-headedness the literary venison dealer could only shake his head in disapproval. 'I for one have kept up my contacts with the aristocracy, and never regretted it. To this day I obtain my pheasants from Count Berchtold's game preserve.'

'I never eat pheasant,' replied Finedwell like a true anarchist.

'All the hares shot at Count Degenfeld's estate come my way as I have a contract with the estate.'

'I've been doing just fine without roast hare.'

The dealer in venison and game now noticed the Tyrolean hat bedecked with chamois-beard and eagle's claw, hanging on the rack, and instantly commented upon it: 'I don't know, brother, judging by your hat one would think you belonged to genteel society . . .'

'I don't want to belong anywhere,' replied Titusz, casting a scornful look at the tell-tale hat, and at the dealer in venison.

Suddenly, without any transition, the red moustache revealed its true colours, all the insidious venom hidden in it, as in every red moustache. 'Well then, consider this visit never happened. And I came here solely for your sake!'

And the dealer in venison, fully aware of his importance, prestige and munificence, took his leave, wagging his head after seeing that his attempt at reconciling Hungarian literature and the aristocracy had failed. At home he probably told his wife all about the ingratitude of Hungarian writers towards people who want to help them.

Finedwell, too, felt a certain unease in finding himself at the corner table alone with the waiter and the pullet fricassee. Perhaps he had missed his final opportunity of making peace with his opponent . . . Who can foretell the fickle ways of fate? Perhaps it would have been better to work as an editor for the *Salon Almanack* if it meant surviving tomorrow?

'I told you I wanted a rooster,' Finedwell said to the solicitous waiter who, for lack of other customers, stood by the reporter's side and watched in apparent amazement as the dead man took one bite after another from the chicken drumstick.

Janos did not reply for he had nothing to say, so Finedwell went on, grumpily: 'You can't get good service even at Kerschantz's any more. Things being as they are, the only alternative is to stop going to restaurants. I, thank God, will have the best of reasons for staying away. Bang!' yelled Finedwell, raising a salt stick to his temple.

'Bang!' the little waiter repeated and sidled away from the customer as if he had misgivings about standing near him.

Finedwell, deprived of a conversational partner, was left alone with his depressing thoughts.

We shall not attempt to describe these thoughts but merely note that prominent among them was the image of a galloping bay mare ridden by a horseman wearing pinstriped trousers and a top hat; the inscription under the framed picture was: 'Life Flies By'. Wouldn't it be wiser for him, Finedwell, to be flying as well, instead of stepping in front of the deadly pistol barrel?

He had already kneaded a respectable number of pellets from breadcrumbs on the table when the door opened once more, again admitting visitors for Finedwell.

I seem to bring business to this tavern, Finedwell reflected, recognizing the newcomers as the two gentlemen he had requested to be his seconds. They had nothing to do with journalism but were so-called gentlemen of leisure. Seeing them gave Finedwell such a painful spasm in the region of his diaphragm that it took a determined effort to hold down the food just consumed. Every single nerve fibre seemed to be jangling, a deathly cold shiver ran over his whole body and his face froze at the sight of these two men who now greeted him cheerfully, announcing they had looked for him 'all over town', until told at the editorial office that if the journalist was not at this tavern then he must have fled the city.

'Who would say such a thing?' asked Finedwell somewhat absent-mindedly, as if beginning to think that skipping town was not such a bad idea.

'Aladar Szolyvai,' replied one of the men.

This Aladar Szolyvai had been Finedwell's perennial rival 'at the paper', who resented that the latter's name appeared in print more often than his own.

'Well, Szolyvai lied again, as so many times before!' exclaimed the journalist with a well-timed burst of outrage that restored his spirits for the moment.

'But others have voiced similar opinions,' chimed in the other duelling second. 'They say that Titusz Finedwell is not waiting out the hour of the duel but is running away from the capital. Alas, that would make no sense whatsoever, since the colonel's friends, all army officers, are obliged to hunt you down anywhere in the world and hack you into smithereens, according to their code of honour.'

The man who said this was a lanky, pockmarked, big-nosed gentleman who spoke with a Slovakian accent. In civilian life he was a painter, but his name was cited more often in connection with duelling affairs than pictures at an exhibition. He spent the greater part of his life at various restaurant tables where he entertained the assembled company by telling horrifying tales of duels. For the past two decades he had something to do with just about every duel fought in Hungary.

The other second was a most dangerous manikin with a hunchback, whose pale face with its thin black beard, ever-present dinner jacket and tall cylindrical hat, pair of double-barrelled pistols carried in his pockets, sword-cane, large hunting knife in a vest pocket, and provocative behaviour were notorious all over the capital wherever affairs of honour were at stake.

The hunchback was a figure straight out of a novel. Noticing Finedwell's umbrella-cane in the corner he eyed it contemptuously. 'One slash of my sword-cane would crack that parson's stick in two. That sort of thing is only suitable for a mild-mannered parish priest,' he announced and placed his own stick, clattering with steel, as far as possible from Finedwell's proud possession.

As regards his profession, the hunchback was a teacher of stenography, but he had little time for teaching because his friends all 'dumped on him' their affairs of honour. His name was Steepletippy, and he boasted that this extraordinary name had been bestowed on the family by Queen Maria Theresa herself.

Steepletippy took up a position with his back to the wall after looking left and right to ascertain from which direction some treacherous attack might be expected, be it an assault by a drunk, the approach of a bully, some unexpected insult, or a slap in the face. This man was always prepared for the event that some place, some time, he would get a beating. After seating himself, he pulled one of his pistols from a pocket, then the other one, and made sure they were loaded.

'We are dealing here with the National Casino, and we know that their arms are far-reaching,' said the diminutive duelling second in a muffled voice, his eyes, those of a consumptive, flashing enigmatically. 'I do not presume any unchivalrous behaviour on your part, gentlemen, but we can never be certain if some servitor, some lackey, some waiter or footman or coachman might not decide to take vengeance with his own hands, in his master's name? . . . Hm, what do you say, Loczi, am I not right? The other day that fat editor who wrote all that unpleasantness about a count's mistress was badly beaten up by street porters who hang around in the neighbourhood of the Casino.'

The pockmarked gentleman named Loczi nodded in assent, for he did not like to argue over inconsequential details. He loved discussing duels, not brawling coachmen. So Loczi, in his Slovakian accent, went on with the story heard probably more than once by Steepletippy (with whom he was seen night and day in various restaurants), a story that he had begun to tell on the way here:

'As I was saying, the wound seemed lethal. Upon my word of

honour, I wouldn't have given a plugged nickel for Count Pinchy's life, for Count Bimby's bullet had perforated the liver. The liver of a high-liver . . . Meanwhile those autumn flies never let up pestering me like mad, the stables were near the site of the duel . . . We had to go in search of a priest so Count Pinchy could die a good Catholic . . . You know I always cared about religion, my uncle was a dean in Rosemont . . . But I'm telling you those flies were unstoppable . . . '

'Those flies can be devils,' admitted Steepletippy, now that Loczi spiced up the oft-told tale with this new motif of the flies. He had never mentioned flies before, Mr Loczi, and flies do like to harass duellers.

The gentlemen were soon done with their business at the tavern, as if they had come expressly to make sure that Finedwell had not fled from town. They were not true pub-crawlers, who are content to spend hour upon hour in slow tippling and silent reverie at a tavern. No, these two were merely visitors, who went to taverns only for the sake of daily arguments, and once there, cared not a whit about what they ate or drank, minding only what was said. They would have sat around in a tavern forever, if it were a matter of relating some heroic adventure, especially if they were able to weave themselves into the ramifications of the narrative.

The melancholy journalist did not seem to be a properly appreciative audience, for he was almost uncivilly inattentive during Loczi's recital, likewise ignoring the signals sent his way by the little stenography professor's twitching, scary eyebrows. Titusz remained distracted even when Loczi at last came to the conclusion that Count Pinchy's unexpected survival was in fact attributable to the intervention of his, Loczi's, uncle, the parish priest of Rosemont, of whom it was said in the Uplands that none of those who received his extreme unction ever died.

('By the way, what is your religion?' asked Steepletippy abruptly, not without a certain suggestiveness.

'Roman Catholic,' replied the journalist apathetically.

'You could have told us earlier,' said the duelling second, with an air of mystery.)

. . . But just as the two men were making serious preparations to leave their distracted listener, the journalist exclaimed: 'Allow me to accompany you, wherever you're going' said T. F., putting on his green Tyrolean hat and grabbing his umbrella-cane as if this equipment were meant to validate his appearance in high society.

The hat and the umbrella-cane must have had some effect on the duelling seconds, because after they exchanged glances Steepletippy announced: 'Very well, my good friend, I don't mind, you may come with us. We have a meeting at the Café Orfeum with some country squires who want to consult us about conducting an affair of honour somewhere in western Hungary. So don't hold it against us if we can't keep you company.'

The city's finest hansom cab awaited them in front of the tavern, for in those days duelling seconds rode in two-horse cabs to conduct their business about town. Possibly some of the passers-by crossed themselves seeing this splendid cab speed about with the solemn-looking passengers inside, and the better-informed men-about-town right away started the guessing game about the identity of the man whose affair made Mano drive at such insane speed back and forth on Crown Prince and Vaci Streets, with the pockmarked painter sending greetings to one side of the street and Steepletippy ceremoniously doffing his top hat towards the other, even if there were no acquaintances passing that way – he made sure just in case, because the gentleman in the cab must always be the first in greeting.

But it was night now, and the two duelling seconds did not mind that the humble journalist nimbly clambered up on the box next to the driver, not wanting to inconvenience the gentlemen seated inside the fiacre. The steeds of the carriage stopped at a barely perceptible tug of the reins in front of the night café, bathed in mysterious lights as the portly doorman, clad in a hussar's uniform, rushed forth as one greeting long-awaited guests.

The air was fresh and mild even in the entrance hall, without any of the unpleasant smells associated with vulgar cafés-chantants – only a faint perfume lingered in the air as if some fashionable music-hall diva had just flitted across the hall, graciously lowering her swan's-down opera cloak to accommodate the attendants. The grey beard of the leader of the band was draped over his violin as if he were coaxing the soft, meditative French-style chansons out of his curly strands.

Formerly, as a 'budding journalist' attending 'the school of life', Finedwell had been a frequent visitor to this place, but ever since the Café Ferenci had opened, with its more relaxed and cheerful atmosphere – as Titusz 'grew older' and placed less emphasis on his clothes – he was seen less often at this elegant establishment. Who would want to don a tail-coat night after night and tell lies about all the fancy soirées he'd been to earlier in the evening? That was for greenhorns, not for an old hand such as himself, who was, moreover, about to die.

. . . For this reason Finedwell did not even enter the inner sanctum of the coffee house but sat down in the outer wing where he intended to pass the time with a bottle of beer until his friends were done with their business inside. This part of the café was where the music-hall actors played pool, and several of them were seated at one of the marble-topped tables with their hats on, as if out here the atmosphere was freer than inside in the plush world of red velvets where the band was playing.

Well, well, although I wasn't born a gentleman I will have to die as one, reflected Finedwell for the second time this evening, as he sat at the corner table, letting his eyes rest on the game of billiards played by the music-hall comedy duo of Baumann and Gyarfas, and it occurred to him that these comics would keep on playing their game of billiards long after he was gone and buried with a bullet in his forehead or his heart – depending on which part the colonel preferred to aim at.

But his thoughts took a sudden turn for the better as he was greeted in rapid succession by the following individuals.

First, a tall horse dealer, whose moustache twirled to a point made him look like a supercilious person, but here he was, contented with passing the boredom of nocturnal hours by marking, on a blackboard, the billiards score for the two comedians. Next, an equally lanky waiter with a dyed moustache who emerged from the fairyland of the café's inner regions to greet Finedwell, about whose upcoming drama he had read in the papers.

Then came Karolin Turf, the flower seller, formerly mistress of aristocrats, who now in her old age said to the journalist: 'Here, take this flower, it's my present to you.' The manager of the café, who had the look of a lieutenant in civilian clothes, bowed as deeply before the journalist as he would have for a millionaire. And finally, the keeper of the cloakroom, with a pin between her lips and a hat-check ticket in her hand, ready to take charge of Titusz's appurtenances, but not daring to touch the umbrella-cane laid across the table . . .

Returning these greetings, Finedwell realized that here he sat in the café with his hat still on, that swine-gelder's hat which had thus far worked its magic everywhere he showed up with it. In the gilt-framed mirrors he was able to enjoy several views of the hat, with the chamois-beard fanning out in the back.

Perhaps, after all, I will accomplish something in life yet, reflected Finedwell, although my life may not last another twenty-four hours, if we really think about it.

But now, just as Finedwell was tempted by glum thoughts, fate again intervened to make him forget his sorrows for another spell. It so happened that a blonde and well made-up female head appeared at the doorway that partitioned the *haut monde* from the everyday, and the flirtatious smile sent by this lady's head towards the melancholy journalist resembled those seen in the window displays of beauty parlours. On another occasion, seeing this made-up, expressionless doll's face would have brought a suitably grave expression on Finedwell's visage, but now, on this night, his fingers went to his hat and he saluted like an army officer. Seeing this, the lady stepped forth in the entirety of her splendour, as if some window display dummy at a fashionable Inner City couturier had set out, still wearing the sign 'Latest Parisian Style!' pinned on by a shop assistant. This was a fatuous and vicious female whom the journalist had known ever since the days when she had been called a scullery maid in the 'night world'. Since then she had become the kept mistress of a wealthy furniture-maker, and thus it was as a lady of fashion that she inquired after the journalist who was to fight a duel on the morrow against the deadliest shot of the National Casino. It must have been the well-informed tall waiter who had betrayed to 'Magnate' Elza the fact that the journalist thus condemned to die was here in the outer passage of the café, making the fashion-plate beauty stir from her peacock-like display stance.

The lady had for some time scrutinized Titusz's hat and umbrella-cane before making up her mind to approach the journalist's table. But Finedwell, befitting his genteel accessories, eager to assist the Grand Dame of the Orfeum in her role, stood up and stepped toward 'Magnate' Elza, respectfully taking off his hat while adjusting his stride as if he were still a student at the small-town dancing school he had once attended – he approached the lady on tiptoe, but with the right amount of manliness.

'Would you honour me by joining me at my table?' the journalist asked, as if it were someone else speaking, someone who had been, unbeknownst to him, hiding inside him all along. Obviously this could only have been Kornel Abranyi, Junior, whom the journalist had idolized in his youth. Or it could have been Gyula Deri, dubbed 'LeDeri' by his colleagues, famous for his gallant adventures with the fair sex, even though the statuesque man of letters had carried only silver coins, and those in the upper pocket of his vest to prevent theft.

'Let's have some bubbly, Mademoiselle!' exclaimed Titusz, escorting this paragon of beauty to his table where he used his hat to sweep cigarette ashes from the marble surface.

The champagne soon arrived, just as in old music-hall ditties, as the lady looked on with a waxen smile, since she was used to witnessing this ritual night after night. But Finedwell pressed his advantage: 'Tell me, my dear Elza, what do I need to do so that for once in your life you'll cheer up enough to give me a kiss?'

The belle of the Orfeum answered clumsily: 'First of all, Mr Editor, put your hat back on, before you catch a head cold.' Thus spake the swansdown-wrapped, silvery, silky and supernaturally dumb angel of the Orfeum and helped to adjust the journalist's hat at a rakish tilt. Then, with hands that idleness made as white as the flesh of a walnut, she turned the brim down, as fashion dictated it that season.

The journalist and the star of the Orfeum Café appeared to be on most intimate terms by the time Steepletippy and company returned from the café's inner sanctum to join their friend in the outer area. Egged on by Finedwell, 'Magnate' Elza had already dropped one fragile champagne flute full of bubbly to the floor, so that the janitor had to be summoned. The stylish quality of their principal's partying did not fail to impress the duelling seconds. A person carousing in the company of 'Magnate' Elza could not be a nonentity. It began to dawn on them that their principal was a man of some stature, after all.

'So you are done with your business here?' inquired Titusz in a loud voice. 'I trust it was a matter of life and death?'

Hearing this, the stony-faced female idol smiled in acknowledgement at the two gentlemen, as if she had long known them for their indomitable courageousness and heroic acts. Having downed a few glasses of wine, the pockmarked painter once more felt like launching into one of his epic tales, but Steepletippy, the dwarf, cut him short.

'We had better instruct our friend Finedwell in how to behave himself at the duel tomorrow. If only to keep him from putting us to shame!'

By now the outer area of the café was quite empty. The actors, horse dealers, and various vendors had given up and wandered off. Only one old man, a one-time stockbroker called Uncle Blau, was still sitting in a corner, waiting for some well-heeled passer-by whom he could initiate into the tricks of playing the market. Patti, the magician of card tricks who was said to be a hundred years old, had also ambled off, with his hairpiece and his pack of cards. This allowed the stenography professor, who was all worked up, to measure off thirty paces which he counted out leaning on his stiletto-bearing cane. 'One, two, three . . . thirteen, twenty-three . . . thirty; and now you advance five more steps. Please, Loczi, give the command,' the hunchback shouted from the far corner of the café.

The pockmarked artist now rose from his chair and grabbed Finedwell by the shoulder. 'Come, take your place,' he said and led Finedwell to a particular square of the parquet floor. 'You stand here and wait for the words of command. First command: Attention! Second command: Ready! Third, I will count to ten, during which interval you must fire your pistol, standing sideways facing your opponent so that you provide the smallest target. So, it is Attention, Ready, one, two, three . . .'

At this point the crack of an actual pistol rent the curtain of softly playing music. The professor of stenography, standing at the far end of the café, had actually drawn his pistol and fired a shot. One lamp expired with a crash. 'We must get this fellow used to the sound of firearms!' said Steepletippy after a pause, for he had paled at the sound of the shot. No great harm was done. 'Magnate' Elza caressed the hand of the journalist, who had returned to his seat. But then the head waiter arrived bearing a silver tray with the bill, his look resembling a highway robber's, and our Titusz suddenly realized that after paying the bill he would have at the most ten kreuzers to his name, enough to pay the janitor for letting him into his building – and even that only if he stinted on the waiter's tip. 'Magnate' Elza glided off towards the ladies' room. The two gentlemen got into their cab and shouted to the journalist from the window: 'Four-thirty tomorrow afternoon at the Franz Josef barracks!'

Under the influence of all the champagne he had consumed, Finedwell was as yet unable to fully appreciate the fatal situation he had become mixed up in. Sauntering on Andrassy Avenue, he searched through his pockets in the hope of coming across monetary units he was in the habit of hiding away, as it were, from himself. He thought it likely that he would find a five-forint coin in some pocket, hidden there when he had received his advance, as he always did whenever the happy-go-lucky journalists would hold up a colleague in the office to shake him down for the contents of his pockets . . . 'That's the life of a bohemian!' they would shout, on occasion stripping Titusz down to his 'birthday suit'. But now the quest proved fruitless; even if he did have some money left in a secret pocket, it was so well hidden that it would be found only after his death by someone selling the trousers to a second-hand-clothes dealer, when the silver coin fell out in the course of bargaining. Therefore he turned his steps towards the Café Ferenci where he hoped to find a large company who were sure to be still up on this night to discuss his life and death.

But to his great disappointment the Ferenci was empty, the journalists were gone from the round table by the cash till where they usually sat, puffed up with a sense of their own importance or else deflated by the shadow of their penuriousness. Only Olga sat in her place, in melancholy languor and utterly devoid of hope, as always, whenever dawn was breaking and another night was gone without anything happening. Sobered up, the journalist stopped by the cashier lady's throne and spoke: 'My dear little Olga, sweetheart, here is the dawn of the last day on which you may still agree to become my bride.'

Olga, who had obviously heard this before from Finedwell, showed not the least surprise. Only her glance became more melancholy as the crocheting in her hands trembled.

'My dear little Olga,' Titusz went on enthusiastically, as if wishing to forget his wasted night and squandered money, as well as his penniless present, with these gurgled words that seemed to amuse himself above all. 'My dear little Olga, I would die with a far better conscience knowing that my name lived on, even if only through a widowed woman. The widow Finedwell! Olga, that doesn't sound half as bad as you think.'

'The widow Mrs Titusz Finedwell,' said Olga and produced a pencil to write it on the edge of a cash till receipt: widow Mrs Titusz Finedwell. She circled the name as if to remember it forever.

Titusz warbled on enthused, as those men do who seize a rare occasion to speak of themselves. 'Not even a cat will be left behind, after I'm dead . . . My name will be in the papers for a day or two, and then it will never be mentioned again in this land. Not even accidentally. But if there were to be a widowed Mrs Finedwell to visit my grave once in a blue moon, I would feel ever so much better down below. People would say that Finedwell was not such a bad fellow after all, before he died he honoured the promise he'd made so often to the cashier lady at the Café Ferenci. My memory would be shrouded by a certain aura, proving that I had not lived frivolously, from moment to moment, hand to mouth, but I had some purpose in this world, some goal that I had realized.'

These sentimental words did indeed have their effect, for Olga reached up with one hand towards the brandy bottles while the other hand flashed a small glass that she made sure was clean. 'I believe this is the Passover plum brandy that orthodox Jews like to drink. The boss never drinks anything else.'

With a weary smile of farewell, Finedwell tossed back the drink. The brandy warmed his innards, and he would have liked to have talked some more. But Olga gave him a serious look and sent him home before Finedwell had a chance to be carried away by another attack of sentimentality. 'We'll continue our talk tomorrow.'

His voice hoarse with the brandy, Titus replied: 'Is that what you think?'

'Yes, I have a feeling we shall,' was Olga's answer. And she held out her hand to Finedwell.

Were the green Tyrolean hat and the umbrella-cane surprised when they arrived, after a lengthy hike, at Finedwell's quarters?

At daybreak Finedwell usually flung himself upon his bed as

if he had returned from the world of the dead, to become an infant again, lying in the foetal position under an obituary in a black frame that hung on the wall right next to the sleeper's head. This obituary – or 'funeral notice', as they said in those days – stated that Mrs Robert Finedwell had passed away at age thirty-two after a prolonged illness. This Mrs Robert Finedwell was Titusz's mother, and the obituary was his only possession. Not much of a fortune, but just enough for a sentimental man.

Shall we describe Finedwell's room? It was about the size of a hazelnut with a hole. But the keyhole, through which one might peek into the room, was always stuffed with a rag. On the outside of the door a slip of paper was kept in perpetual motion by the draught in the corridor of this ancient Inner City building. The sign said 'I'll be right back!' – but the tenant never was.

The journalist, half-asleep, had a number of visitors. First, a shoemaker's apprentice lad, clutching a piece of paper that looked dirty enough to have been with him since birth. He stood in front of the door for a while, staring at its odd message as if seeing it for the first time, before his fevered glance was attracted towards the building's courtyard, where he presently joined the procession accompanying a blind street singer from house to house.

The journalist was well acquainted with the footfalls of his tailor who kept dropping in on him like some lovelorn admirer and, if allowed to slip through the door, always began by saying that he just happened to chance this way, and he certainly wouldn't want to trouble Mr Finedwell on account of a trifling sum. The tailor's sighs practically blew through the door as he squatted in front of the keyhole and yelled all sorts of terms of endearment at the journalist: 'I only wanted to see you, my good sir, just to wish you luck. And to hear some reassurance, that sooner or later you'll get to me. Let me in, my dear Mr Editor, I swear I didn't even bring a bill with me.'

But Titusz burrowed all the deeper under his quilt, and failed to respond even to the craftiest cajoling. After all it was not for nothing that he had written 'I'll be right back!' on the door. Let the tailor wait if he felt like it.

The tailor went away, but suddenly returned and indignantly shouted through the keyhole: 'God help me I'll take you to court if you don't let me in this very instant!'

The tailor waited. But Finedwell did not budge, even though he was beginning to regret putting that fatal sign on the door.

And Finedwell (who was, after all, a decent sort) suffered pangs of guilt on hearing the tailor's dejected footfalls growing fainter, retreating from the door. He never intended to hurt the good man, but he could not make an exception of him.

But now the building started to quake with steps approaching on the spiral stairs that linked the ground floor of this ancient house to the first floor. Seeing these winding stairs Titusz had often wondered: how did they ever take a coffin out of here. The approaching footfalls heralded danger, a ferocious attack, charging towards Titusz's door as if at the very least announcing the bearer of a court summons. Merciless, feral steps, like those of a bailiff closing in on the victim.

The journalist knew the perpetrator of these steps: it was Mr Munk, the debt-collector, whose manner of dealing with his customers was as rough as sandpaper. Mr Munk was a heavy-set, red-haired man whose aim in life was to have each resident of the capital pay instalments to him. Mr Munk's laughter on seeing the sign on the door was scornful and highly audible. 'Very well, my dear Mr Editor, very well indeed!'

And he could be heard snorting and gnashing his teeth as he rubbed his sweating forehead with a large linen kerchief. 'This is scandalous!' he kept repeating, and having found a chair somewhere he planted himself in front of the door.

The journalist racked his brains trying to figure out which of his enemies could have given the chair to Munk. Possibly the building's janitor . . . or was it the midwife next door, who resented the fact that she could hope for no business from Titusz? People are wicked and like to gloat at another's misfortune, Titusz thought gloomily, beneath the obituary, as if it had been his own. He felt not an ounce of strength left to take on Mr Munk; he felt himself so helpless that it actually felt good, for at least he did not have to make the smallest effort, like a patient in critical condition yielding to his fate, at most hoping for a miracle. But no miracle would work against Mr Munk, who had settled in front of this door, and all his wheezing, hawking and belching could be clearly heard inside the room, as if Mr Munk used the time of waiting to rehearse the ways he could make himself even more repulsive. He rustled a newspaper; next he leafed through his pocket notebook, the squeaking of his pencil clearly audible as he corrected his notes. Every life has horrible moments such as these, when you are unable to shake off some exasperating burden that weighs over your heart. Mr Munk was quite a sizeable burden.

Half dead with these torments, the journalist lay in bed not daring to move, hoping that at best Mr Munk would believe that he was asleep and would not sound off that terrifying, aggressive, unbearable voice of his that he employed to drive debtors to their graves.

At this moment our journalist would much rather have faced the colonel's pistol than Mr Munk's custody. It took but a moment for the pistol to fire (as he had witnessed earlier that night), but Mr Munk was capable of sitting around for hours in front of the door. Nor was Mr Munk the least bit bored, as one would have imagined. He coughed. Softly, as city folks do. Then, in the manner of a villager who wants to find some enjoyment even in coughing. He scratched his itching parts. He scratched his palms, his head; he dug into his ears with a matchstick, an operation that made him groan with pleasure – then he rubbed his calves against each other. Some people are never bored, they always find something about their bodies to keep them busy. Munk, when he could no longer find anything else to do, kicked off his boots and sat in his socks.

Fortunately there are events that can shatter the resolve of even the most determined watchers. For Mr Munk the ringing of a bell in a nearby church constituted such an event. It was the sound of the noontime bell, which evokes special thoughts in each man, not excepting even Mr Munk. At first he started to swear *sotto voce*, then he began to bang on the door with hands and feet amidst loud curses, without any sign of letting up, as if he had decided to create a scandal at all costs on the journalist's 'last day'. But Finedwell was already sighing with relief, for he had calculated how long Mr Munk would keep up the siege. True, Munk was able to sustain the banging for quite some time, since he had considerable practice at it. However Titusz, during his long hours of torment, had had a chance to steel himself for the final assault, and knew it would be foolish to yield now, when the end of the battle was in sight. By the time Mr Munk reached the stage of uttering curses, Finedwell was already sitting up on the edge of his bed, aware that Mr Munk was close to deafening himself by his own thunderous barrage of oaths.

So Mr Munk departed, having lost the battle, but kept stopping on his way out, as if still racking his brains about doing some damage, but in the end his final footfall died away like a memory that turns out to be quite pleasant in the end. Free of Mr Munk, Finedwell now examined his hat and umbrella-cane in daylight. They were imposing objects even in daytime, although they had appeared more impressive at night. Now they revealed a certain amount of wear, for they had reposed a long time in the café's storage room. The journalist consoled himself with the thought that brand-new things are actually less valuable than used items, as witnessed by great lords having their new shoes broken in by their servants. For a while he was still lost in admiration of his accessories, until a strange and deadly anxiety enveloped his heart so unexpectedly that he tumbled back on his bed. He suddenly remembered the upcoming duel that he had not given his proper attention to because of his visitors. In the face of other troubles one may at times forget about death.

Now the thought of death did not abandon him for a second while he dressed despondently, washed desultorily, and gargled at length. Fear practically made him double over, while no matter how much he would have liked to cry, he was unable to give way to the fit of weeping that lurked within him.

'If I could only cry, I would feel a lot better,' Finedwell murmured to himself, sinking into a chair when he felt the redeeming tears near at hand. But the tears refused to materialize. Only women are lucky enough to cry at will. No, Finedwell's tears just wouldn't start falling, no matter how hard he coaxed them. He had to get dressed from top to toe and venture into the outside world without weeping.

But his luck still held, for as he entered the editorial offices he ran into the editor-in-chief, who had the reputation of being unable to refuse a request – out of vanity or whimsy, as if always trying to prove that matters of money made no difference to him – although just about every other week lawyers were procuring writs for auctioning off his belongings. Finedwell made a brave 'frontal attack' by candidly confessing that he had spent yesterday's advance to the last penny and now did not even have enough for lunch.

This 'frontal attack' proved successful – or was it the magic of his hat and umbrella-cane that did the trick? The editor-in-chief was gratified seeing his associates acquitting themselves well on 'the field of honour', and therefore he handed over ten forints to Finedwell who could now face the afternoon's events in better spirits. So he visited as many as three taverns before finding one where he found his favourite dish, boiled beef. Fortune continued to favour him when he was served a portion of 'meat on the bone' that drew envious glances from nearby tables. Generally this is the kind of restaurant dish that even the most impassive souls follow with interest when a waiter passes by carrying it on a platter. The other patrons scrutinize, measure, appreciate, and all but taste it, envying the guest who ordered it. The journalist's portion of meat was a substantial one; it had been saved for the owner who eventually decided to renounce it in favour of the unknown guest with the Tyrolean hat and umbrella-cane. To show his gratitude, Titusz ordered a double portion of sauce – which happened to be horseradish and vinegar.

As a matter of fact it was after the consumption of this auspicious plate of 'meat on the bone' that Finedwell's fortunes changed for the better, so that he is still alive to this day unless he has died in the meantime. The colonel's bullet missed. On the other hand, Finedwell's bullet found the colonel, who died of his wound like the brave soldier that he was. The cab fare for Titusz's ride back from the scene of the duel had to be paid for by the editorial office boy. There were no complaints.

(1927)

The Waiter's Nightmare

Some of you might think the tavern is called the Clock because the clock is always ticking there, as if the guests needed the passing of time brought to their attention.

Well yes, the grandfather clock with its long, braided handlebar moustache indeed keeps on marking time just for the sake of appearances – for tell me, is there a sorrier sight in a taproom than a clock that has been standing still ever since the memorable day it stopped running at some unlikely hour when no one sat in the room, no one came looking for some nook alongside the brown wainscoting where true regulars like to settle down after much circumspection, as if they intended to nestle there for their remaining days. That is when the clock would have stopped in the quaint little restaurant in a side street of the Inner City, at a moment when a fresh keg was out of the question and a single prospective customer was perusing an old menu from some ancient name day celebration when the proprietor had been a man named Lajos . . .

However, the clock in our little restaurant was not one of those that stood still, the ageing waiter had seen to that, for his greatest source of annoyance was being sent by some unfamiliar customer to go out, like some bar boy, to the watchmaker's shop window next door and check the time on the largish clock in the middle, which was reputed to be telling tales of its adventures to the smaller clocks listening in silence around it. Usually the customer had told a lie about the train he had to catch and asked merely to annoy the waiter. Fridolin therefore saw to it that the clock was always running, its pendulum flashing a coppery-reddish, dreamy glint from the encasing ebony – just in case a guest wandered into this dainty little establishment, a guest who had recently received a pocket watch as a present, and felt compelled to check it against every clock he encountered. Each Wednesday and Saturday Fridolin approached the clock with a splintered old billiard cue in hand, at an hour when the afternoon silence, in the shape of invisible guests, had settled in at one of the diminutive tables for two, tables that forever had to be pushed together (so that they fitted like husband and wife), in case a party of three arrived.

In this afternoon silence Fridolin, billiard cue in hand, approached the clock, as if now was the time when, left unobserved, he would punish it like some depraved soul would a child or a puppy. He had the peculiar habit of setting the larger hand ahead five minutes by means of the billiard cue, since his hand could not reach that high. Next he tugged at the strings, faded to a dull green, that dangled from the bottom of the clock, just like the shoelaces of an old editor who came to the restaurant every Wednesday and Saturday from the nearby printing house to consume two three-minute eggs in braised meat sauce, washed down with a pitcher of beer, followed by three 'pints' – because confirmed, sagacious regulars only ordered the first pitcher for the sake of the 'pints' to be quaffed afterwards.

The appearance of the old editor signalled for Fridolin that it was time to wind the clock after lunch. But the reason for setting the clock five minutes fast was known only to those who understand not only life, and times past, but the nature of human passions as well. The adjustment of the clock was a habit Fridolin had picked up when he was a young man with wavy-gravy hair and full of hopes, working as a billiards marker at a café. He would always charge the players for an extra five minutes when he saw that in the excitement of the game they forgot about the clock.

This tells us that our Fridolin had not always been a gawky, ageing waiter. There had been a time when Fridolin would rent a room by the month only if the landlady was skilled in ironing a tailcoat; a time when Fridolin had his locks crisped into curls both silly and daring, as befits a man of the world – whereas now he sat in a cane-backed chair placed fortuitously under the clock, his elbow cradling his weary head in the manner of travelling men accustomed to catching their forty winks in any position. On the wall opposite Fridolin hung a large pier glass, tilting forward at an accommodating angle that had something of the officiousness of tailors who invariably praise the smartness of each customer's turnout. But Fridolin, through a longstanding acquaintance with the mendacious pier glass, was well aware that its fawning posture was worth about as much as the smile on the face of the cashier lady ensconced among her little bowls of candy and sweets. Therefore he made a series of furious faces at the mirror from behind his fingers, with sputtery flashes of the eyes, like sunny-side-up eggs frying in the kitchen.

He was indeed incensed, for the only time he could be angry was now, left all by himself in the small dining room. He was irked by his bald cranium, the same that had once been dubbed 'bald as an aristocrat' by ladies of the kitchen, who were always dreaming of barons. His lengthy side whiskers had been blond as a straw hat back in those days when Fridolin seemed to be just one step away from becoming a head waiter. Yes, once upon a time Fridolin had as a matter of course had his moustache shaved in the hope that he would be serving lords of the realm; now the barber's art only added some faded tint to his prickly facial hair.

But only on Saturdays. Nor did he like his ears any more, after he had so many times tried out the head waiter's long pencil tucked behind one ear, the way some bachelor longing for married bliss might try on a wedding band. For this reason he snapped an angry flick of the napkin at the offending ear as if to chase away a fly. Then he closed his eyes, to utilize the precious moments when the absence of guests allowed a working man to catch a few winks.

Let us see, what were the dream images that chased around in Fridolin's head in this small diner that gave on to a courtyard, where only true Inner City locals found their way, locals who had long been familiar with the doorknob of the entrance pointed out by the eternal symbol of a copper hand holding a stein of foaming beer. Once upon a time, when Fridolin first appeared at this establishment, each spring-cleaning added a new layer of gilding to this hand, just to provide the regulars with something to talk about.

'See that gilded hand? Watch out, it will smack your face before your wife does, when you've had one too many,' a gentleman at the corner table would remark, back when three tables had to be pushed together for the company assembled there in honour of the noontime tap. And the guests would all stare out at the courtyard, where the golden hand glittered under the cool, draughty arcade that gave off an air reeking of janitorial ailments. Fridolin could still hear the regulars debating the cost of the gilding that had in fact never attracted a single new customer to the establishment.

'Ah yes, if only our friend Lajos served decent beer,' cried a tribal chieftain's voice that always managed to out-roar the others, while the last remnants of beer were sloshed around in the glass with the kind of motion that allows not a drop of the yellow liquid to go to waste even though all beer drinkers know that these last drops provide only an illusion for the throat, barely enough to wet your whiskers, and merely serve to create a fresh new thirst besides endowing your voice with a certain hoarse, thumping resonance that resembles both the very first as well as the ultimate sounds emanating from a tapped keg. 'Ah well, if our friend Lajos had the brains of that Toni Weisz on Kiraly Street, who had persuaded old man Dreher to grant him the exclusive rights in Pest to serve Schwechat lager, the world's best beer!' this same voice thumped out each and every day, just like the beer keg in the taproom.

But here came a new customer, a gentleman wearing a coffee-brown cape, his nose advertising the colours of old wines, whose progress towards the regulars' table generated cheer on all sides, for the newcomer was notorious for always arriving on the scene when it was time to tap a new keg.

'Bring out that flat brewski for our poet friend!' went up the shout at the regulars' table and Fridolin would spring to it merrily, although he himself could not quite fathom why.

Someone pulled out a pocket watch. 'In five minutes a fresh keg will be tapped, that's worth waiting for!' he said, and pushed his glass next to the others in the middle of the table for Fridolin to gather up and take to be filled with a fresh draught.

Fridolin knew not why he looked back even in his dreams with a certain longing towards this period in his life. Experience, after all, had taught him that unless the customer had previously stuck a cigarette behind the barman's ear, the latter would mix in the leftover beer with the fresh draught, for the owner's interest was foremost. Could it be that a waiter's life had been more amenable back then, when the beer steins still had their handles and gentlemen who were regular customers would abandon even the loveliest lady and leave her standing in the middle of Vaci Street in order to see when the next fresh draught was due 'at our friend Lajos's place'. If they happened to drop in when there was still some beer left in the bottom of the keg, out they would go for another spell of flirting on the banks of the Danube. How on earth did that ever benefit Fridolin? Yet it still felt good, in the midst of his afternoon reverie, to hear those invisible ones at the vanished table of regulars voicing their antiquated bon mots.

'It's lunchtime at the parish priest's,' they would chime in unison, hearing the noontime church bell, and the owners of pocket watches would consult their timepieces, while others cast apprehensive glances at the grandfather clock that was running five minutes fast . . .

On this particular afternoon, when the bespectacled old editor had once again consumed his two eggs in braised meat sauce and Fridolin had finished with the last of the lunch customers, while repeatedly reminding himself to wind up the clock – as ageing ballerinas will hum for themselves some melody to mark time while standing backstage waiting for their cue to sally forth – on this afternoon the last lunch guest ('a gent from the ministry', whom Fridolin had promoted to that rank on account of his pinstriped trousers) had said his goodbye in response to Fridolin's bowing and scraping (for the proprietor doubled as head waiter and Fridolin, that 'shiftless drone', merely gathered up the tips) – on this afternoon the ageing waiter forgot about the warped billiard cue as well as the dangling strings of the grandfather clock and quickly 'put himself to bed', as he referred to his afternoon nap on the chair, with his elbow on a table's edge. In fact he was so sleepy that he forgot his usual cigarette, even though several pinches of tobacco were waiting in his coat pocket to be rolled into a smoke by hand, an occupation that never failed to please Fridolin. He would blow out the bitter smoke of a cigarette rolled from butt remnants, in order to obscure his image in the mirror. Now he even forgot to make his usual faces at the pier glass, for his head drooped as if ambushed by an unusually mighty attack of weariness, and floated straight off to dreamland from this tavern called the Clock, on a side street named after a former mayor. His last conscious thought was, had he turned the key once or twice to lock a drawer in the cupboard (to which by rights only the head waiter had access), for Fridolin had secreted there a small plate of ham ravioli to be consumed by himself or else to be taken home as a present for the landlady's daughter. But in the next instant the scent of ham ravioli was blown away by the draught from an opening door, just as visions of fairytale sausages fade upon awakening.

There must have been some saint's feast day in progress in the Inner City, for Fridolin now saw such a variety of customers crowd into the room as never before. Here came the shoemakers from Parisi Street, and the glove-makers and corset-makers, who are hardly ever enticed to leave their accustomed little nooks and crannies. Fridolin had a passing acquaintance with these shoemakers: hurrying past their shop every morning he would envy them for being able to sit all day long on their three-legged stools, free of the kind of fatigue that was his lot. Why, the glove-maker could play around with his delicate leathers until they reminded him it was time for some white wine and the glove-stretcher in his hand assumed the shape of a fork that, according to the hands of the clock, should be wielded over various platters.

But in addition to these craftsmen there came other, more stylish customers, such as the gentlemen who like to sit all day in some Inner City café window seat, waiting for someone or something. At times they are simply waiting for a messenger, but waiting is really not a very stressful occupation. One has plenty of time to devote to one's fingernails, eyeglasses or pocket diary, taking a good look at oneself in the mirror, all of which are most salutary activities for making the wait more bearable. The messenger arrives and greets you as if his greatest ambition in life consisted of running a successful errand for you. Well, even these envied men-about-town had abandoned their window seats to drop in at the Clock, although men of their ilk make sure that each step they take is impeccably stylish. After every table had been occupied, every chair shifted from its place and each rack covered with hats and coats, the siege was on, the assault spearheaded at Fridolin, who stood transfixed, as if his feet had been nailed to the floor, waiting for the end of this onslaught of customers. But newcomers still kept crowding the doorway, practically all the folks in Pest that Fridolin had ever had the good fortune to meet in his thirty years of waiterdom. He saw individuals arriving at the Clock who, Fridolin knew for sure, owed so much money in the neighbourhood that they wisely migrated to other parts of town. Some had even spread rumours of their own demise, and here they were now, in the best of health, pink of cheek, barbershop-fresh, the very fair-haired people who carry most of the barbershop scents coming and going about town.

And there stood Fridolin, waiting for this stampede to subside – they must have all come to celebrate his jubilee, for each guest greeted him heartily, the more playful even chucked him under the chin. Then all at once, as if a water main had burst in the courtyard, as back in 188*, the hum turned into a roar around Fridolin.

'Rollmops!' 'Pitcher of beer!' 'Eggs!' 'Scallions!' 'Radishes!' 'Liptauer cheese!' 'A pair in gravy!' 'Fresh salt rolls!' 'Another round of beer over here!' 'Small portion of *pörkölt* braised pork, no, make that a regular, don't forget the bones!' 'Sour lungs, Fridolin, for my heartburn from last night!' 'Hot dogs and mustard!' 'Have you got any of those little blood and liver sausages I had last time?' 'Bring me some frosty cabbage in oil with eggs and caraway seeds.' 'How come there's no goulash on the menu? What got into these Inner City taverns?' 'Fridolin, I feel like a few titbits with horse-radish, you know, the usual, ears and tails and knuckles . . . ' 'How does it look for some nice beef on bone, with vinegar horseradish?' 'How are we fixed for herring? I could go for a fine Baltic herring full of milt with pickled onions that came in the same box, and not added just now!' 'What kind of cheese do you have? I want the ripe, smelly, runny kind, I'm dying for a drink!' 'Let me have a pair of Debrecen sausages, if you get 'em from a decent butchershop!' 'I prefer the iceberg lettuce and will prepare the dressing myself, after I spent all that money to learn how!' 'What, no English mustard?' 'Please bring some bread, make sure it has a crusty heel!' 'A glass of wine, same as the owner drinks!' 'Fridolin, how come that canary isn't singing? In the old Clock the bird was always singing.' 'Since when is bologna with oil and vinegar and onions out of fashion around here?' 'Might you have a little end piece left in the cooler, from that hunk of roast pork you had yesterday?' 'I'll have a double portion of consommé with long noodles, and an egg stirred in, and carrots, celery, kohlrabi, maybe a bit of cauliflower stem, but make sure it comes with a meaty bone to chew on . . .'

Fridolin, by some quirk, remembered only this last order, for it was not an easy one to execute.

'Oh yes, at your service, right away,' he kept repeating to himself half aloud, then full voice, then whispering and clearing his throat, as he escaped from the small dining room, the veins on his forehead bulging from a myriad orders the like of which had never been heard before within these arcaded premises.

The guest who had ordered the consommé occupied the table in the centre of the room where customers rarely like to sit, in full view of the public from all sides, whereas the only view they have from there is the balding gentleman straight across, who enjoys berating other guests for allegedly staring into his mouth. (That kind of elderly gent is usually easy to tell by the way he pares away the bread crust as if it were his greatest enemy.)

This guest at the centre table, a man presenting a stubborn back, shoulders set impassively, the nape of his neck radiating indifference – a man that not even Fridolin would remember after he left – sat rather peacefully amidst the infernal hubbub. His eyes aimed at the arcade vault, he waited; he wore a cape with flaps and a double row of buttons like some bureaucrat, had large rainspout-like shirt cuffs and his shirt collar was as loose as if he had received it as a hand-me-down from some fat man; in general his clothes looked ill-fitting on him. Yet his elastic-sided boots had been polished with sufficient care, even the parts that are usually covered by the trouser cuffs. But his necktie had slipped sideways, and the back of his coat lapels was sticking up as if he spent much of his time sitting bent over a desk. As for his face, to use the terminology of restaurant humour, it resembled that of a sad lobster that was left behind all alone while its companions were merrily turning red in all sorts of concoctions. Therefore let us say no more about his face; it never registered any arrogance or anger beyond the massive equanimity that would have done a camel proud, while ignoring the horseflies that pester his leg.

The guest now inspected the tablecloth, scrutinized the eating utensils, not forgetting to check the manufacturer's name before he tied the napkin around his neck. Next he shot back his cuffs, adjusted the position of the salt cellar, tested the point of the toothpick on his fingertip and placed it within reach – although it would not have been surprising to see him pull forth from a pocket a toothpick carved from a feather. At this point Fridolin arrived bearing the tureen used (provided it was on hand) for serving double portions of soup. The customer took up his spoon and for the first time it became evident that he was able to use his eyes, and was not as blind as a lobster.

'And after the soup?' asked Fridolin officiously, as if he were seeking refuge from the racket that again rose from all sides upon his reappearance, as if he were simultaneously hearing every single order ever given in this restaurant. His leg practically twitched when a stentorian voice thundered in his ear a demand to see the marrowbone he had ordered 'an hour ago'. Fridolin dared not look up in the direction of the thunderous voice – he knew anyway that the person in question was one of the regulars who always attached undue importance to his orders.

Therefore the waiter bent closer to his unknown guest: 'Perhaps you'd like something after the soup?' he implored, as if waiting for some magic word that would render inaudible all the merciless, threatening, jeering voices around him.

The guest, however, said not a word, but simply took the menu clutched in Fridolin's hands and drew his index finger down across the sheet. That's right, with one sweep of his finger he went down the entire list of vegetables, meats, pastas, cheeses, salads and fruits that Fridolin had written there in ink. Fridolin backed up one step, as if the guest had mutely commanded him to do so, and rushed off towards the kitchen, afraid to glance at the multitude of ghostly customers filling the establishment.

The guest ladled soup into his bowl flush with the level where the rim bore the burnt-in initials of some old-time restaurateur. Nay, he kept on ladling past the monogram, as if he were a man who had no interest in such trivia. He leaned over the soup bowl, having sprinkled salt and pepper in it, and added some brown drops of soup fortifier from the bottle that stood on the table for the benefit of the guest. He did this thoroughly, before commencing to stir the soup as if to rock it to sleep as he would a child he meant to devour after it fell asleep.

He dipped the first spoonful from the periphery of the bowl, after using his spoon to herd back bits of vegetables and straying, long strands of pasta. The second spoonful arrived loaded with noodles that were thoroughly yellowed by the egg that had been stirred in. The third spoonful contained carrots and cauliflower, cheerful as the smile of a plump woman. As for the noodles that dangled from the spoon, they were slurped up without a second thought and vanished after a lick of the chops and a smack of the lips. This was nothing less than exchanging kisses with the soup, innocent, youthful kisses, to be followed by love of a more mature kind.

Who knows why, on this day of all days, there was a purée of peas with pig's knuckles included on the menu? Cooks and tavern-keepers' wives have their own systems that defy the interference of laypersons. The puréed peas swam in the customary brown gravy, and the guest could tell right off that the pig's knuckles came not from some old sow but from a porker that was but a yearling.

By now Fridolin had advanced close to the unknown customer as if by his side he hoped for shelter from the storm of ghostly accusatory voices, although one or two overcoats, fashioned in the style worn by the Prince of Wales, had shifted from the rack and began to glide away as if propelled from the tavern by some invisible breeze. Hats waved in greeting and walking sticks started to walk by themselves. None the less the clamour of shouts was far from over: some guests, acting as if they had brought their own wine (for which they would be charged a corking fee), now began to thump the bottles against the tabletop. Others found superannuated beer steins on some cobweb-laden shelf that Fridolin had not even known about. Now these earless mugs were made to clink and clank in a dance that recalled for Fridolin the tin-kettle mock serenades back in Year One, when he had been a mere novice. Someone had even dug up the billiard cue that had long ago lost its rubber tip, and made menacing gestures as if he meant to exercise it on Fridolin's back. Junky candlesticks clanged and clattered, freed from their hiding place where they were stored against the event of a power failure. At this time, too, emerged all the paraphernalia that decorate the crowning of a newly elected president of a table company: paper hats and rattles, a chimney sweep's brush, and baby pacifiers. It seemed all of these were going to be used by the assembled folks to celebrate none other than Fridolin himself.

The waiter dared not move from his position by the side of the unknown customer whose protection he hoped to enjoy at least as long as he kept serving the dishes he had ordered from the kitchen. The guest's left hand was already grasping the pig's trotter, while his teeth and tongue were browsing for those titbits of meat that like to hide in the crevices of bones. Finding one of these pockets of flesh is a great boon, the equivalent of coming across a smallish purse lying in the road. In his right hand the guest clutched a spoon, with which he endeavoured to round up the remaining fugitive peas on the rim of his plate.

'Some like to eat peas with a fork,' the guest observed, 'but I don't hold with that fashion. My motto is: always act natural, no matter what happens . . . And you can't get any serious eating done without a spoon because a spoon is like a kettle that brings out the deep taste of a dish. It's regrettable you have no other greens on your menu today . . . Tell them in the kitchen: I deeply regret that.'

Fridolin, in spite of his knowledge of human nature, was at a loss how to interpret the guest's regrets. Then and there he made up his mind to find out just who exactly was this extraordinary customer, who in one swoop had ordered the entire menu for lunch.

'Well, let us see,' the guest went on, 'what other specials has the proprietor in store for us today.' Having said that, he pushed away the menu offered by the waiter, as if he preferred to be surprised. Actually he knew quite well that the vegetable dishes were followed by the roasts, first and foremost the roast duck with red cabbage. And here came Fridolin bringing the duck, guarding it successfully from the ghostly hands that reached for it hungrily from all sides. By then the customer's right hand held a fork ready to skewer a mouthful, and he had already sharpened his knife against another knife, creating an agreeable clatter. Then he positioned the roast duck in order to scrutinize it from every angle.

'The platter is far bigger than the duck,' he noted somewhat peevishly. 'Why, on the right platter the drumsticks reach out over the edge, collared with white paper cuffs, like a bouquet of flowers. On a true grilled platter the sirloin overflows, it's just too big for the plate. Still, this dish has a pretty decent shape, you can tell it dates from a time when people loved one another instead of throwing plates at each other's heads.'

The stranger aimed his fork at the drumstick now, even though in Fridolin's experience practised eaters always left the tastiest morsel for last. No, he had never seen a customer tuck into his roast duck starting with the drumstick. That sort of thing only happens at weddings, where people tend to compete for the best morsel. Anyway, this guest had pulled the plate so close to himself that it would have been difficult to snatch it away. He turned the drumstick this way and that on his plate, testing it with his fork to see if it was indeed as juicy as promised by the appearance of the meat done to a turn, in places darkened by the grill as flames like to flare up through the grate when a fatty item is roasting above.

And here the guest cried out in surprise: 'Oh don't tell me you took my spoon away? No, it won't do to start rubbing a fresh spoon with your filthy napkin. I would have preferred to keep my old spoon, the one I'd got used to, ate my soup with, and my peas, and then wiped off with a piece of bread. How can you ask me to dip a strange new spoon in this gravy?'

From this point on the unknown guest eyed Fridolin with a certain amount of distrust, as if afraid that the latter's sloppiness would sooner or later make his appetite go away, as any contretemps can ruin a man's lunch. As a sign of his misgivings he used his own napkin to give an additional wipe to the spoon before launching it into the golden gravy under the roast duck. Yes, we must confess that even though the colour of that fat had the same hue as Tokaj vintages of old used to have, the customer now cast suspicious glances over his shoulder in the direction of Fridolin, especially when he noticed the latter edging closer, into an intimate proximity.

'Please don't,' said the customer, as if shooing away some fly, and he stacked the meat sliced from the drumstick back on the platter, as if it were some Wertheim-style safe where those mouthfuls would earn interest. He left only the drumstick on his plate, intending to finish it off first.

'You work just like a surgeon!' Fridolin now whispered in awe, simply to start a conversation.

The guest carefully grasped the bone, raised it and made it vanish in his mouth so that only the paper-cuffed end of the bone remained visible under the tinted moustache. We shall never know what the teeth and tongue did to the bone within that oral cavity. From time to time the stranger himself would shake his head as if in disapproval of the crackling sounds that emanated from within. After a while the bone re-emerged, utterly deprived of all its glory. One last time the guest sucked on the bone, intent on doing a thorough job, and be done with it once and for all.

'No, I'm no surgeon, although I do have something to do with physicians,' the guest now said, in order to fend off Fridolin. 'But I happen to know how to eat. Most folks like to leave the bones for last, when the teeth are tired of all that rending, grinding, and mincing. Naturally by then they cannot do justice to the bone.'

'So he's not a surgeon, but has something to do with physicians,' Fridolin thought, although the colour of the customer's bald dome was the same rosy hue that he associated with the scalps of doctors and pharmacists, who probably used some secret lotion for the care of the complexion.

Meanwhile the guest, after the requisite dip in gravy, was shovelling slices of duck thigh into his mouth as into some storehouse, and he seemed especially gladdened by the sight of pieces of skin showing a soft layer of fat. This stowing away proceeded at an accelerated pace, with only a tentative stab or two toward the red cabbage before the eater made up his mind to balance a small heap of cabbage on his knife blade and shovel that too into his maw. The cabbage proved to be crunchy.

'We'll have to chastise the cook because she did not marinate the cabbage long enough,' said the guest with a certain severity of tone to Fridolin, who, in the manner of old-time waiters, was fascinated by each mouthful of food that disappeared in his customer's mouth.

'Maybe you'd like a little gravy on the cabbage,' the waiter ventured.

'I know that without being told,' replied the guest dismissively, as if he suspected some trick behind Fridolin's advice. Then he dispensed one or two spoonfuls of gravy on top of the cabbage, which he did not neglect to turn over with his fork, as a small haystack is turned after a rainfall. Next he directed his attention back to the platter of roast duck, after munching on a piece of rye bread as if to obliterate some taste. Possibly that of the cabbage.

Now came the breastbone of the bird, which was plump enough to prompt the following remark: 'No wonder our housewives come home from market with tears in their eyes . . . They simply cannot compete with the innkeeper's wife who'll pay any price for a fattened fowl. Waiter, tell me, how many portions do you get out of one duck?'

'Two or three . . . maybe four,' replied Fridolin hesitantly, for he did not like to divulge secrets of the kitchen.

'There, you see!' the customer gloated, as if he had caught the waiter out with that admission. But he let the matter rest, preoccupied as he was with the tasks of sucking away the last bits of duck breast and inner parts from the bone. By now the cabbage had absorbed the gravy, and his knife and fork reached for it with a certain amount of forgiveness. And this mouthful of cabbage was somewhat larger than the portion placed on his knife blade earlier.

'Quite proper, that sharp knives are no longer in fashion at taverns. They always manage to nick the mouth. According to some it is not proper to put a knife in one's mouth. If you ask me, a man has the right to eat any way he likes. Fashions may change but in the end we all die just the same. I use my knife even for the fish course,' the guest announced with a challenging air and glanced at Fridolin as if expecting some comment. But by this stage all Fridolin cared about was noting how many slices of bread the guest consumed in the operation of mopping up the gravy left after the roast duck in the platter. Here and there a strand of red cabbage lingered to be plucked up by the eater's nimble fingers.

'Only what we eat is truly ours, because once we're in the

coffin we won't be served any more helpings!' The customer announced as he took a final swipe at the plate. 'May God save everyone from lack of appetite!' he added with a touch of piety, as if he had something else on his mind beside what was on the menu.

Once again, voices rising from tables occupied by neglected patrons started to hound Fridolin, but he rushed off to the kitchen for the saddle of hare he had set aside for this extraordinary guest.

The saddle of hare arrived and drew not a single wisecrack referring to some missing tomcat, a customary remark since times immemorial when rabbit is served in a restaurant.

The guest was holding a small pocket notebook bound in linen, as if going over some calculations, the way hard-working people do even while having lunch. There must have been something wrong with the figures because the guest contemplated the hare with a certain melancholy, as if he had to consume it under duress. However he did not omit to taste a spoonful of the piquant sauce that lay under the hare, or to cut up the dumplings to give them a chance to cool down, and he even probed the saddle of hare with his fork to test if the meat was tender enough.

'A man is just like a hare. He never knows when the fatal shot will hit him as he flees. Tell me, Fridolin, how old are you?' the stranger suddenly asked, as if something in his notebook had changed his mind about Fridolin.

The waiter was startled by the unexpected query, but then leaned towards the customer's ear with an air of sly conspiracy: 'For your Excellency's information I am past fifty. But my boss thinks I am younger because no one likes to employ a waiter over fifty.'

'Why, where do old waiters go?'

'God only knows!' said Fridolin with a sigh, encouraged by the customer's apparent sympathy. 'Some of us, especially head waiters, make sure they can soak their aching feet in all kinds of footbaths, preferably in Rákospalota or Budakalász, some suburb where you can still buy a small house. You have no idea, my good sir, how badly an old waiter's feet can hurt! The pain is worse than a heart broken by unrequited love. And believe me I've seen plenty of men in love. Why, I remember "Lord Baltimore" from the golden youth of the Café Korona, each night he would march the length of Vaci Street slapping everyone because some piano tuner wouldn't let his daughter marry him.'

Fridolin himself was so amazed by what he had just said about 'Lord Baltimore', that good-for-nothing ruffian of former days, that his mouth gaped. The mysterious customer meanwhile took this opportunity to proceed with his meal: a number of dishes on the menu still tempted with the fascination of the unknown. Then he cautiously sliced away the bits of meat from the saddle of hare, careful lest a bone break, for apart from the undesirable effects of swallowing a sliver, that would keep the teeth from testing the bone to judge its hardness and age. The bones in a saddle of hare will tell you how many years that hare has been evading the hunter's weapon. But here the guest opted to change his system. He postponed the cleaning of the bone because he discovered buckshot in the meat. The bunny had received the shot in the saddle. And finding buckshot in the roast is always a welcome sight for someone who really likes game. The imagination can envision the melancholy yawn of the autumn fields where the hunter's idle wait seems to harmonize with the weather until the moment when the rabbit emerges from among the dried cornstalks that bemoan their widowed state, and the hunter's gun sounds off.

'Oh, forget about those old-time Lotharios' said the guest,

making a humorously sour face upon tasting the sauce of lemon, sour cream and marjoram spooned from under the roast rabbit. 'No use mulling over past loves. It's always the present that counts, my friend, no matter how much some people like wallowing in the past. For instance, what would you do right now, if the restaurant's owner decided to replace you with someone else, say his cousin? Every restaurant owner has a cousin in Budakeszi or one of the neighbouring villages, some cousin he is raising to be a waiter.'

Fridolin made no reply, for this possibility had not occurred to him before. He had always thought of the Clock as the place where he would grow old, with the billiard cue, the ebony grandfather clock, and the usual customers . . . The stranger seemed to guess the waiter's thoughts even as he sucked clean each individual toothpick-thin rabbit bone. It is for a good reason that women who tend the kitchen fire all day love these little bones. A good housewife gathers the bones from her children's plates on to her own, and notes with a benevolent smile which one of her children loves the bones as much as she does.

The waiter thought it was time to favour his guest with the next course.

According to the menu this should have been capon, larded with bacon, but in the world of smaller restaurants these larded capons usually appear on the menu only to enhance the reputation of the establishment. Capons like that – even if they are actually sizzling red in the oven pan, waiting to be basted by the cook with hot drippings from time to time – capons like that rarely make it to the guest in the dining room. Usually the cook will pilfer a piece or two: if she is a decent sort, she will be satisfied with the feet, neck or liver, possibly leaving the head as evidence of her honesty. Next the capon has to pass inspection by the innkeeper's wife, who will at times also covet a choice titbit: she too has to live. And the proprietor himself will neglect the tap upon catching a whiff of roast capon wafting from his kitchen. So that the waiter came back with a piece of barbecued pork that he had just had grilled in the kitchen to compensate his fascinating guest for the bird that flew the coop, probably by way of the chimney.

'Hmm,' the guest brooded, 'what in the devil's name happened to that capon, it suddenly turned into pork? Well, never mind, I've seen greater wonders. But take note, my friend: a baked potato makes the best side for barbecued pork, and you don't need to serve any bread, for the potato soaks up the gravy just as well. Some prefer home fries with onions, but *not I.* For in a restaurant one might think those potatoes have been standing for hours in the kitchen, and that is enough to discourage both the potato and the eater.'

But Fridolin, agitated by the prospect of losing his job at the Clock, no longer paid much attention to these comments about food. Flapping his napkin against his knee, he inquired with a certain amount of impatience: 'But my good sir, please tell me, what is an old waiter to do? A waiter such as myself, who has nothing and no one in the world?'

The guest now looked up, as if he had quite forgotten what he said earlier. He was using his own pocketknife to carve into the complicated terrain of the pork barbecue – it was freshly grilled indeed. 'My friend, you're probably familiar with the tarot deck, for every waiter plays cards. Well, consider the eight of diamonds, if you want to know what to do with your life. It's time to start a family,' replied the guest. 'As time goes by, waiters and guests grow old, but not the clever fellow who, say, owns the restaurant and lets the others do the ageing. You must be a proprietor, for it doesn't matter how old the boss is – for him old age simply brings more respect.'

Fridolin let out a sigh of disappointment. 'Sir, I was hoping you could offer some other remedy. How on earth could I become the proprietor when, for one thing, I have nobody and not a penny to my name.'

'This pork demands to be washed down . . . maybe with a large pitcher of beer. Wouldn't you agree, my friend?' asked the guest, rummaging around his emptied plate for loose toothpicks, crusts of bread and other detritus that is left behind everywhere in the world, no matter how neat, cleanly and orderly you try to be. 'So bring me a nice big pitcher of beer, my good man,' he repeated with a smack of the lips and a click of the tongue.

The waiter brought the requested beverage with bad grace, rather dispirited because he suspected the strange customer was making fun of his helplessness. It was a waste of time to spoil one's guests; better to just place their portions in front of them and move on, for customers are a thankless lot once their appetites have been sated. They feel entitled to some free entertainment once their bellies are full.

But Fridolin was unable to leave this table because the ghostly howls, although somewhat diminished, still rose around him on all sides, so he had to look on (although without any pleasure) as his guest wiped the rim of the pitcher with his napkin, rotated it so that the handle faced him, whereupon, after brief contemplation, he raised it to his lips and, staring at the ceiling, began to drain the contents in slow gulps as if to prolong the enjoyment. In spite of this unhurried pace he had drained about three-quarters of the pitcher before he put it down, deeply satisfied.

'It seems to me we've had a sufficiency of roasts,' announced the guest. 'The way I see it, the duck took the prize, the rest played second fiddle to that plump beauty queen – a duck, even if it is a drake, should always be considered feminine in gender.

For only a woman can pitter and patter and waddle and wallow in puddles as comfortably as a duck.'

At the moment Fridolin, preoccupied with thoughts of his sad fate, could not muster much enthusiasm for ducks. In his mind's eye he could see himself as an old, unemployed waiter walking the streets, stealthily hugging the walls, shaving only once a week, and peeking over the fence of garden restaurants to see if they needed his services, only to find odd jobs here and there as extra help at Easter and Pentecost, when in his unhappiness he would drink up all the remnants of beer and wine and seltzer to muster enough energy for going home. The devil himself must have steered this weird trencherman his way to engender such melancholy thoughts. The best thing was not to think any more, to rest one's brain and feet and await tomorrow's disasters with equanimity.

The customer had yet to unbutton the lowermost button on his vest, and now cast an expectant look at Fridolin. 'And what about some cheese, my good friend? A piece of cheese is a must at the conclusion of lunch, even if some people believe that cheese is for dinnertime. God only knows why they think that. *I certainly don't,*' concluded the guest.

Fridolin came back with the desired comestible, but by now he began to have deep misgivings about this customer who refused to be sated. This one surely deserved to be called a glutton. Then again, possibly he was consuming so much because he had no intention to pay the bill of fare and was only waiting for the right moment to slip away through the door marked 'Exit' for the benefit of honest, paying customers. But this one showed no sign of ever intending to use that 'Exit', and now it seemed that he was in a conversational mood at last.

'My profession compels me to seek out cheerful occasions that make me forget the nature of my activities,' the guest now announced and Fridolin, formerly a waiter at grand cafés, smiled cannily deep down inside. He had known all along that sooner or later his guest would turn talkative, if you gave him a taste of the gruff treatment. Most customers preferred an amicable footing with the waiter who serves them. Baleful looks from one's waiter were not conducive to good digestion.

So Fridolin listened with polite attention, for he was a cosmopolitan waiter.

'Not one man in a thousand would guess that I am an undertaker by profession.'

'Upon my word of honour, I would never have guessed, judging by your appetite, sir,' said Fridolin, exultant that he had at last found out something about his guest's private life. He had had few opportunities to meet undertakers who, because of their solemn profession, rarely appeared at restaurants and coffee houses. He had heard about a restaurant near the cemetery where all the undertakers of the city gathered on a certain day of the week to discuss recent and upcoming funerals. Now Fridolin understood the reason for the dignified bearing of his guest. His business had to do with the dead, whom one handled with grave respect: you do not slap a dead man around, because if he hits back, you are a goner.

But Fridolin was after all a waiter and as such the financial aspects of the undertaking business fascinated him. 'Tell me, sir, is it true that dead people leave all sorts of jewellery behind? Rings that cannot be pulled off a swollen finger, amulets that the dead person wore around her neck all her life, and the family members did not dare remove? And other such *tchachkas*, that end up in the undertaker's hands?'

'Oh certainly, we end up with elderly widows on our hands, women we are expected to marry off!' the customer replied, raising his voice. 'In truth, I am the last friend of the deceased, the others having all abandoned him as he lay dying. No one else remains by the dead man's side except the unfortunate undertaker, who has to shed tears along with the orphans and widows, and must comfort them, take them by the hand. Once I even had to act as godfather to a child born after the father died. Oh, mine is a difficult occupation, my friend, no wonder we look for a bit of cheer on days when there are no funerals. The only thing that helps in my profession is good manners. You can't imagine how much coaxing it takes to persuade a family member to permit the dearly beloved's belly opened in order to fit him into a coffin.'

'His belly?' Fridolin echoed, shaken. To his amazement the guest continued to wreak havoc among the toothpicks. They all kept breaking between his teeth, and another had to be used to push the broken piece through the ramparts of his teeth. This man clearly knew how to keep busy after lunch.

'My dear friend,' the customer continued solemnly, 'you are quite mistaken if you think that these blood sausages, rump steaks and pork chops you serve to the citizens of Budapest are carried by your customers to the underworld, just so they can discuss the food served at the Clock. *No, sir.* We must slit open the bellies of fat people to fit them into the wooden box that carpenters refuse to make in larger sizes, no matter how many fat men one sees running around in the city. Carpenters are a stubborn lot. They do not change the rules inherited from their fathers and grandfathers regarding the dimensions of their clients in Budapest. That is why we must have some acquaintance with the medical profession, so that we can improve on the carpenter's botched job. A dead man must be laid to rest gently – as if he were asleep.'

Without giving Fridolin a chance to put in a word edgewise, the guest, like some professor, went on with his lecture. 'But we are left with the widows, helpless women who, after a successful funeral, and especially if people they like are attending, will remain in a corner of the funeral parlour to discuss each and every detail of the ceremony that took place and expect comforting words just the same as when the departed lay in state.'

'I have heard, my good sir, that jewellery is usually hocked at the time of a funeral, and that undertakers tend to be the pawn-brokers,' said Fridolin, exercising the impertinent wit of old-time waiters, but this was to be the last flicker of his brilliance.

The duplicitous patron went on at such lengths about those widows who relied on him to find them a new husband in Buda or Pest that Fridolin truly began to think great prospects awaited him if he got to meet one of these helpless widows.

'All you need is a photograph, and a fifty-kreuzer tax stamp!' the guest advised.

'I have the photograph, although it is ten years old. But why do I need a tax stamp?' Fridolin inquired, barely hiding his excitement.

'Well, my friend, you know how these widows are . . . They don't believe anything unless the paper has an official stamp on it. So accommodate them. Go buy a stamp at the tobacconist's.'

While Fridolin had gone to buy a stamp, the customer naturally skipped out without paying the bill. Which way did he go? How could he have disappeared like that? Who knows?

At this moment Fridolin awoke from his afternoon dream and found himself in the darkening nook of the diner. He glanced at the mirror. His flushed face was streaming sweat, as if he had just returned from the netherworld. He was certain he would lose his job at the Clock.

As soon as he was himself again, Fridolin noticed that the clock above his head had stopped running.

That damned clock is the cause of it all, because I forgot to wind it, he thought, with the bitter self-reproach of ageing men, and rushed off to get the billiard cue. But for days after he had the lingering feeling of a man who had been cheated.

(1927)

The Landlady, or the Bewitched Guests

Being the wife of an innkeeper, Aranka was acquainted with all kinds of men.

As she approached forty, she had gotten into the habit of scrutinizing a man the way she would a goose or rooster, just short of actually hoisting him up to estimate his weight.

One acquaintance of hers at this hostelry not far from the Central Terminal happened to be a certain Mr Paszmati, who had introduced himself as a dealer in hogs. Mr Paszmati always arrived very early on one of those trains scheduled so that provincials from distant parts could go about their business in the city without wasting an hour. These trains brought passengers with mud-encrusted boots rarely seen in the capital, enormous crooked staffs for warding off stray dogs, fur coats that had been on the road for a hundred years, and suitcases that had grown old after many a long night at some godforsaken train-stop listening to the jingling bell of the telegraph office. And of course there came wallets stuffed with every kind of banknote, bills that were wrinkled, greasy and rancid enough to have passed through the hands of every citizen in the land.

'Anything ready to eat in your kitchen?' inquired Paszmati as he came in from the winter fog through the glassed front door of the restaurant.

The glass panes were steamed over, the floor already bore the tracks of snowy boots, and the guests sitting at the tables covered with colorful cloths had their overcoats and knapsacks by their side, this being only a taproom.

But sitting at the cash till was Aranka herself, hair freshly curled, cheeks recently rouged, arrayed in silk like some Balkan princess, for she had struck a deal with her husband: the takings from the taproom in the morning hours were to be hers. Therefore Aranka did not mind sitting in at the till where at other times a wilting manageress sat wearily handling the bills. Aranka needed the money – as we shall see, she needed it quite badly. So she made a show of special delight when receiving the hog dealer as he removed his fur coat and scarf.

'So, lovely lady, what's cooking in your kitchen?' Mr Paszmati inquired again, approaching her with the waggish crow-like steps of a faithful old regular. (There are men who, other than shaving and twirling their moustaches, disdain showing off for the benefit of the female sex but will display a preening strut. The hog dealer's crow-steps were meant to convey calm confidence backed by a stuffed wallet.)

From behind the cash till the woman's tantalizing smile aimed straight at the merchant's belly. 'Why, we have Mr Paszmati's favourite: peppered pork stew prepared from a young pig, and not diced into small pieces, but sliced into pieces the size of a child's palm, which is the tastiest way to make this dish.'

'Hmm, pork stew, you say? With potatoes or noodles?' Paszmati soliloquized. 'And plenty of gravy, I hope? Whew, we certainly have had some rotten weather. A blizzard hit us past Nyíregyháza and the train slowed to a crawl so that all the hip flasks were depleted. When we got to Püspökladány the cafeteria had only stale food, without any taste or aroma. They served a watered-down goulash. Instead I opted for just a mouthful of fog, knowing I'd find something freshly cooked here.'

The hog merchant fawned on the proprietress.

'It's fresh all right, you won't be disappointed in that, Mr Paszmati. My staff rises at the crack of dawn, and I myself watch over them as they prepare breakfast.' Saying this, she motioned towards the kitchen, where the response was immediate. The blue-aproned bartender left the tap to fetch a sizeable platter of pork paprikash from the kitchen, and placed it, unaccompanied by a bowl or a plate, on the table by the cash till.

'Bring some bread, and make sure it's an end piece' ordered Aranka from her perch by the till.

Paszmati examined the promising hunks of meat that had their share of fat and bone, turning them in the gravy so that the bonier pieces would reveal themselves. It was not a suckling, but a young porker none the less that had gone into the making of the stew: the landlady had spoken the truth. Paszmati took out his long pocketknife to probe the bonier pieces. 'I wish you had some green pepper for me!' sighed the hog merchant.

Aranka smiled again, as if she had foreseen her guest's thoughts.

'We have no green pepper this time of the year, but we do have sweet red peppers from the Serbian gardeners in Zugló. Hey, Anna!'

The serving girl placed a portion of red peppers in front of the guest.

Paszmati took one of them and turned it in his hands a few times. 'Looks like this one's going to have a bite – but I can bite back.' He used his pocketknife to slice slivers of pepper into his stew. 'Whew!' He exclaimed after the first bite. 'That train should have come faster, with a dish like this waiting for me.'

The woman gave him a conspiratorial smile. 'Why, my husband and me, we'll do anything for you, Mr Paszmati. We purchase pork directly from the villagers, who deliver it here in their carts. We buy all our supplies from the villagers, even our peas, and not from storekeepers or market vendors who have a way of adulterating everything they touch. The villagers know us by now, and when they have a fine goose or a shapely pig, they know they have a buyer in us. Why just yesterday I bought a cartload of cabbages from a man from Szentendre, and this afternoon we're going to pack them into barrels.'

This news made Mr Paszmati perk up. 'Hmm, so this is the day of cabbage-trampling! Well, that is always an entertaining activity.' With that, he went back to his pork stew, for eating can be fairly amusing too.

The fatty, delicately boned pieces of meat, the well-cooked bits of skin, flesh, tendon, in addition to the thin flank – all of which goes into the making of a righteous pork stew – with the help of the pocketknife and a piece of bread, all found their way into Mr Paszmati's maw, much to the rejoicing of his molars that had had nothing to sink into all night long but smoky fog and a cigar-holder carved of cherry wood.

One's tongue acquires a strange taste after travelling all night, gulping coal smoke. The gullet forgets it ever had a palatable mouthful. The occasional shots of brandy the traveler consumes here and there – provided he is knowledgeable about where to obtain the right kind of brandy – merely lull the stomach for a brief while, like a fly-by-night impromptu affair. Accordingly, Paszmati took his sweet time with the chunks of meat in his stew. Coming across a tougher piece of skin, he gave it a try, but abandoned the effort with a shake of the head, for his teeth were past fifty years old – although he had had only one of them pulled, by a rural dentist on a day when he could not allow a toothache to affect his bargaining ability at a regional fair.

He was at the stage of cleaning up the platter using small

pieces of bread on the point of the knife – speared lightly, so that they can be turned over easily – when he returned to the earlier topic: 'So this is the day of cabbage-trampling . . . And pray tell, who will perform this by no means everyday task requiring considerable expertise? First of all, the layers of cabbage must be evenly formed and adequately sprinkled with black peppercorns. Often, folk wonder what went wrong with the barrel of winter cabbage, why does it give nothing but a bellyache and a pain in the middle? It's because the cabbage-trampler was not a man of sufficient weight.' Saying this, Paszmati involuntarily squared his broad shoulders and gave the landlady a devilish smile.

She replied with averted eyes: 'Cabbage-trampling, as we all know, should be performed by the master of the house. Cabbage is a masculine type of food – womenfolk can get by very well without it. But my poor husband is so busy that it's unlikely he'll have time this afternoon to trample cabbage.'

The hog dealer's reply was nothing less than splendid. 'And take care not to let just anyone cut the cabbage cores. You can't use some young chit of a girl whose mind's always on other things. You need a mature woman for cutting cabbage cores, just as you do for shearing sheep or washing intestines for sausage-making, because an older woman knows how to find enjoyment in that kind of painstaking work.'

Now the landlady leaned closer from her high perch and inquired, not without flirtatiousness: 'Mr Paszmati, would you by any chance be interested in trampling my cabbage?'

'Why not?' the hog dealer replied. 'Today my clients are still away at country fairs all over the place, so I won't be meeting any of them at taverns and cafés before tomorrow. I was planning to visit the baths this morning, anyway. So I'll take a turn in your cabbage tub this afternoon.'

With a conspiratorial air, the landlady and her guest parted company. Who knows what kind of hearty acquaintanceship this afternoon's cabbage-trampling may lead to?

Paszmati took off for the baths in Buda to get his feet soaked most thoroughly. Meanwhile Aranka stuck to her post until the time when, above the clatter of plates from the restaurant fronting the courtyard, her ears registered the sweet sound of a guest tapping the tip of a knife against glass, which was most likely the drinking glass in front of him.

'Here come my customers at last,' Aranka said to herself, glancing at the clock that showed 11.30 – the same time, to the minute, as the train station's clock.

Aranka liked guests who came early because they brought appetites that were not picky at all. These were the men with so much business in the capital that for breakfast they had to make do with a small glass of booze – grappa or slivovitz – before they sped off in a frenzy, as if they meant to get a lifetime's worth of work done that very morning. So it was natural that, well before the stroke of the noontime bell, their minds' eye started conjuring up steaming bowls of soup and red-brown roasts swimming in dark gravy, to quicken their faltering steps.

Among the early lunch crowd, Aranka's most notable customer was a Mr Bombai. His hamster-like countenance featured a moustache like cat's whiskers over big buck teeth that looked capable of devouring a roasted ox in its entirety. This Mr Bombai had a greying set of side-whiskers that he liked to arrange and groomed with back-and-forth strokes of a small brush when bored, until it suddenly occurred to him why he was here and he vehemently rapped the wine glass with his knife.

Aranka arrived in answer to his summons and this seemed to further incense the provincial attorney. At this point a 'real, live waiter', heading his way with his bowl of soup fresh from the kitchen, would have been a sight far preferable to all the fair damsels in the world. But good manners have not been forgotten in the small town Mr Bombai came from to visit Budapest.

'Busy day,' Aranka opened, lowering her colorful woolen shawl over one shoulder. Wednesday lunch would be unimaginable without Mr Bombai.

The lawyer, who was most likely a dignified figure in his home town, chose to reply in a disingenuous manner: 'Well, even a village lawyer such as myself is kept busy, regardless of what his Budapest colleagues may think. All the vexation I get back home. And then the runaround at the offices here in the capital: Court of Appeals, Supreme Court, Ministry of Justice. No, my dear lady, our humble rural existence is not quite as enviable as it appears to the distant observer. But at least at home we are used to eating lunch on time. When the noontime bell rings and soup's still not on the table, here in Budapest it seems we must relinquish even this small pleasure. Say, Fritz, where's my soup?' the lawyer exclaimed, seeing a waiter appear at the far end of the room, whereupon the waiter fled in terror.

Aranka lowered her hand and rattled the bunch of keys on her hip, a manoeuvre to distract her guest. 'You as a lawyer are well aware it's best not to rush matters, better to wait until things ripen. Those old fogies at the court of appeals or those ancient Supreme Court judges aren't going to strain themselves no matter how much you would urge them.'

'Oh yes they will,' replied the lawyer with a no-nonsense, countrified tone. 'I happen to have connections, acquaintances just about everywhere, for at one time my father was a member of the National Casino. The old man gambled away plenty of money but at least he acquired some useful friends. And then again, my dear lady, getting judicial matters accomplished is after all not the same thing as preparing a cutlet.'

'But they are not all that different' said Aranka, placing her hand on the back of the guest's chair. 'Why sir, what would you say, if you did not receive the same conscientious service here that you give the clients in your office? Here, too, everything must be done exactly at the right time, to the minute. As long as the jury is out, and the lunch is still cooking, everything is on hold. We won't let a half-baked dish leave our kitchen.'

'So this is the fate of a hungry man who wanders into this inn, to his peril,' replied the troublesome lawyer, as with a certain amount of resignation he broke apart a Kaiser roll and dabbed it in salt and paprika. 'I know this will harm my appetite.'

'Perhaps you'd like a glass of our home-distilled brandy, or a glass of beer,' suggested Aranka.

'That would send me straight to the hospital. I have an execrable stomach. At night I can drink a barrel of wine, but during the day I can't stomach anything beside solid food.'

'How is that possible?' Aranka stared with wide-open eyes at Mr Bombai, who leaned back, shrugging his shoulders as if he found his own case utterly bewildering.

'It's because I used to have a stomach ulcer. Take it from me, that's a wicked affliction, guaranteed to make your good humor go away further than a stork migrates. Why, it even makes you hate your own work. What's the use, when your stomach rejects all the food you send down your throat? Even the sight of others enjoying their meals is noisome, seeing them consume their portions with a healthy appetite is enough to make you nauseated. The dyspeptic man looks at his dish with dubious eyes, looking for any excuse to send it back. You no longer even enjoy having money, no matter how easily you make it, because it won't buy you anything you would want to eat. Well, Martin, I say to myself, at this rate pretty soon we'll have to close up shop and stagger off on pilgrimages to holy shrines; if the lame and the halt get well there, why shouldn't I, with merely a stomach ache . . . ?'

'Were you colicky?' interjected the proprietress.

The guest's response was prolix. 'Yes, that too. But mostly my problem was a constant nausea that attacked me after every mouthful I swallowed, be it consommé, my all-time favorite, or smoked ham, the kind that is supposed to help even the sickest person. And I could not allow my stomach to bully me at will, because then I wouldn't have been able to eat in public, whereas, being a bachelor, I was obliged to take my meals at restaurants.'

'We like to cure that kind of affliction with a glass of fine brandy!' said Aranka, with an implication of regret at not having known this worthy gentleman at the time of his stomach ailment.

'Oh, I tried drinking brandy before lunch, after lunch,' he said, with a wave of the hand. 'But by then it was no use, because those late-morning snacks and beers, and the lunches missed on their account, succeeded in wrecking my stomach so that nothing helped anymore.'

'What about your doctor?'

'To tell the truth, I didn't dare consult a doctor because, first of all, I was afraid that he would reproach me for neglecting my illness; if an educated man, a lawyer, behaved like this, what could he expect from a simple peasant? And then again, I am convinced that every man is his own best physician. Only he can feel what ails him, and how; it is futile to try to explain that to a doctor. How could he have understood that the instant I swallowed a mouthful of finest potato soup made with fresh cream, it would come back up? Believe me, I was ashamed of having become such an invalid; I thought the cheerful, sociable time of my life was over. I could hardly wait for night-time, to try to lay down my ever-aching stomach into some position where it would stop tormenting me, and let me get some sleep. I tried lying on my right side, but that usually gave me a cramp in my lower left calf. Then I would shift to my left side and for some reason, God only knows why, the corn on my right little toe would flare up as if the weather was about to change. Finally I had to settle on lying on my back, like a corpse in a coffin. Lying supine like that has the unfortunate side effect of depriving one of air, so that I'd wake with a coughing fit, as if I was about to suffocate.'

Feigning constantly increasing amazement, Aranka heard out the gentleman who had been so seriously ill at one time. 'One can't imagine the suffering that goes on in this world.'

'I couldn't have been any sicker if I'd lived on a diet of frogs, snakes and lizards. I was always thirsty, so I began to drink wine, but in the end even wine started to lose its taste. I said to myself, this is the end, my friend.'

'But eventually God helped to heal you,' opined Aranka.

'Yes, because I wanted it so badly myself,' said the guest, quickly tying the napkin around his neck as he pushed his plate forward and seized his spoon, upon glimpsing Fritz the waiter and the steaming cup of consommé full of long noodles. (This was a tavern of the old school, with porcelain soup cups bearing the same monogram as all the plates and eating utensils.) The guest stirred his soup, sipping at a spoonful of broth then slurping up a long ribbon of noodle that was left dangling.

'So how did you go about curing yourself?' inquired the proprietress, as if the subject was of burning interest.

Bombai, having successfully disposed of the first spoonful of hot soup, began spooning it up heartily. He measured out his words between spoonfuls:

'I fasted, and kept on fasting even when I felt a twinge of appetite. I fasted like a dog, like a Hindu fakir. Like Succi, the Italian hunger artist who makes a living starving himself. My abdomen became flat, my intestines shriveled up, for I even stinted on my intake of water. I became so weak that it was too much of an effort to go from one room to the next. I longed to stay in bed all the time, for that's where you fast best. Then suddenly I started to eat again. It happened while they were trampling cabbage next door – for even during my illness I refused to shut myself away from enjoyable sights. I watched those cabbage-tramplers and imagined the happy folks who would eventually eat that cabbage, cooked or stuffed, or even raw, as sauerkraut. And as my starved eyes looked on all that cabbage being trampled, I noticed a little girl who was cutting out the cabbage cores with a curved knife. She playfully offered me a cabbage core – Here, try one, mister, you've never tasted anything this good. Well, I ate that cabbage core and haven't been ill since.'

'Mr Bombai, this is your lucky day, because we're doing our cabbage-trampling this afternoon. You can have all the cores you want.'

Bombai, having disposed of the soup, was in the process of inspecting both sides of his veal cutlet before squeezing a liberal dose of lemon on it, and looked up with a far more cheerful expression. 'And pray tell, what will you give me if I show up as your cabbage-trampler?' he inquired flirtatiously.

'Ah, we shall to see about that,' replied the proprietress with an air of mystery, before directing her steps toward the kitchen. The strokes of the noontime bell signaled that her customers were arriving in the restaurant.

In addition to the restaurant and the taproom, where Aranka's approach in her colorful folksy outfit always caused even the most toothsome forkfuls to pause on the way to gaping mouths, just as beer mugs halted midway to the most inhumanly parched throats, beer mugs that were drained to the accompaniment of satisfied hiccups, belches and groaned comments as soon as the door slammed behind her blue-trimmed skirt – as I was saying, in addition to the restaurant and taproom the inn also boasted a café that was frequented mostly by gentlemen who for some incomprehensible reason preferred to stay in the vicinity of the cash till, even if it was tended by some old maid who only wore white stockings because that made it easy to pick off a flea. The gentlemen who leaned against her throne never drank anything but slivovitz and the like, accompanied by the requisite hawking and harrumphing; they smoked cigars and reused the paper holders, and discussed herds of black swine feeding on beech nuts and acorns in distant woods or stallions whinnying in even more distant paddocks, in tones that made you believe these beasts were next door, ready to be inspected by the potential buyer. But when Aranka's blue and white checked shawl, spread over her shoulder, hove into view, even the far-flung thoughts of these gentlemen reverted to the immediate present as they observed with keen interest the way she counted out sugar portions as rapidly as if they were eggs on top of the cash register.

After the proprietress cast an expert glance over the account book she joyfully exclaimed: 'Uncle Friedmann, I see you keep your moustache in good trim even in these miserable hard times.'

'I've got no complaints, *'as long as it's my brother-in-law's hands that tremble,'* came the reply from a small round table that was pushed close to the cash till as if it were a stove where a freezing man could expect some warmth.

Uncle Friedmann was an old-time broker who nowadays rarely left his nook, the corner table by the cash register, from where he contemplated with an ironic smile the waves of good humor or coarseness breaking around him. Every once in a while he would inquire after the price of springtime lamb's wool that was shorn by hired women who knew their business. Only wool did he deem worthy of attention among all the goods that were traded. He knew just about everything there was to know about wool production in Hungary, and for this reason he entertained a deep cynicism about the rest of the world's affairs. He was an old man with a grizzled moustache who held a deep grudge against every young broker who entered the café with a pipe clenched in his jaw. He claimed that pipes had gone out of fashion long ago and nowadays a man could only smoke one at home in the bosom of his family. At a coffee house, a decent person ordered cigars, and let the head waiter make a little money on the side.

'So, Uncle Friedmann,' began Aranka, pulling up a chair at the grim old man's table. 'I hope you have no stomach complaints?'

'I should think not,' replied old Friedmann. 'For one thing, it's not my habit; for another, I take great care about what I put in my mouth. Today for instance I had a mushroom omelette, but first I had the mushrooms brought in from the kitchen to make sure they did not include one that might cause trouble.'

'Why, Mr Friedmann, do you know mushrooms that well?' the landlady asked with enthusiasm, as if she had never heard this ancient story before.

'Oh I know mushrooms, all right,' said the old broker, solemnly sucking on his cherry-wood cigar-holder. 'I know which are the best mushrooms brought to town by peasant women who pick them after the rains on the slopes of Schwab Hill, where the road takes a sharp turn. That's where you find the tastiest mushrooms, because many an amorous little miss takes cover in those bushes to put her clothes in order, out of sight of her swain.'

'Why, you old rascal!' fluted Aranka in a cajoling tone, picking up the porcelain match-holder and turning it in her hand as if she had never seen acorns and hearts like the ones painted on it.

'My dear Madam, in my life I have seen so much, going back to the collapse of the firm of Deutsch and Haas, that nothing surprises me anymore. Mushroom and eggs! Just the right nourishment for an elderly man who mustn't burden his stomach with bean soup and pigs' knuckles or sauerbraten in gravy. It's of paramount importance that the eggs be fresh, laid preferably the same morning. I'm not a believer in so-called "candled" eggs. That's why I usually bring my own eggs in a paper bag, bought at a reliable grocer, where I can be certain of their freshness.'

'The eggs that village women bring us are quite good.'

'Oh, those villagers are the biggest scoundrels!' cried Friedmann, his face reddening with angry indignation, flying into a passion as many older men will when touched to the quick. 'Why, those village women who seem to flounder so helplessly on the streets of the capital, like waterfowl lumbering on dry land – they will adulterate everything from red paprika to sour cream, when it's not for their own use but for sale outside the train terminal at prices cheaper than the grocer's, so the brainless wife of some office clerk will be happy to buy it and save a few pennies. That kind of customer will never realize she's eating brick dust instead of paprika.'

'We get our paprika in Szeged,' the proprietress countered, in a wheedling voice. 'If you'd like to see, I can show you the box our paprika comes in.'

But Friedmann was more interested in expounding certain principles that preoccupied him. 'My poor wife, God rest her, would never buy anything but goose, and that only because we had a cousin who dealt in geese and was afraid of my fists, so he always gave us the best quality. But what could a woman know about buying horseradish, for instance? How would she know that in a village called Phtrugy, beyond the River Tisza, they grow a horseradish zesty and powerful enough to rouse a cataleptic from coma? Well, I've been to Phtrugy and bought a suitcase full of horseradish that I still use for my salads.'

The landlady stared at him with wide-eyed docility that implied she would remember each word for the rest of her life. 'We usually serve grated horseradish on the side with our frankfurters, or pickled in vinegar, with our boiled beef.'

Friedmann nearly tipped over the table. 'You mean to say you don't know how to store horseradish in jars along with pickled gherkins, green peppers and beets? Prepared that way, by midwinter it acquires a flavour to make you feel at peace with the whole world. I always maintained that you don't understand how to run a proper kitchen here, even if the innkeeper runs from cellar to attic all day. That's why I come equipped for every contingency when I eat here. In one vest pocket I've got dried chili peppers to mince with my pocketknife into every dish that you serve: these peppers are hot enough to improve even a dish that would make your stomach ache the day after. In this other pocket here I have a young red onion you can decapitate at one bite, but I won't tell you where I find them because the whole town would be there the next day. Also in my vest I have an authentic clove of garlic from a dealer I know personally, who purchased it in Makó. And I always carry some imported black pepper without which kidney and brains would be unthinkable. In my coat pocket there's a small jar of mustard, the kind you can't find in a restaurant where the owner refuses to take the trouble to go to the best stores. What's a poor widower to do when he has to rely on restaurant meals? He must bring in his pocket all the condiments that add true savor to food and life itself. For I've got all the time in the world to observe how the population is being poisoned by adulterated spices.'

'Now, now, Uncle Friedmann, you mustn't view the world through such gloomy glasses,' said the landlady in a conciliatory tone.

But Friedmann refused to be disarmed: 'My poor sainted wife

liked to stay in bed late, so I'd go marketing in her place. Yes, I took the shopping bag and walked to the market halls to find something that would please me and I could look forward to during my day of work. For it's quite another thing if a man can anticipate a wonderful dinner when he comes home tired after a hard day's work. Although it's true that towards the end of my married life our meals began to be somewhat burned, but that wasn't my wife's fault. It was because we had a lodger who demanded that his kidney and brains be served in bed. Ever since then I haven't been able to stand the sight of kidney and brains.'

The landlady contemplated the toe of her shoe for a while – she liked to wear comfortable 'sensible' footwear at home for running 'up and down the stairs all day' – then she leaned forward, emanating the warmest friendliness towards the broker, who shrank back like a hedgehog.

He feared that this sudden warmth presaged some kind of trouble, for he was a man of considerable experience, and for this reason he quickly exclaimed: 'Madam, can you tell me why there is no barley flour to be found anywhere in town, the kind that goes with potatoes into that wonderful black bread?'

'I have some, and I'll knead the dough myself just for your sake. But first I have a great favour to ask of you, Uncle Friedmann. This afternoon we'll be trampling cabbage here, and I'm still a novice at it, because until now we always bought our sauerkraut from the grocer. I would like to ask you, Uncle Friedmann, to come and supervise.

'Supervise? Why, I'll jump in and take a turn in the tub myself. Just yesterday I went to the Rudas Baths for my weekly visit,' replied the broker with real enthusiasm, so that Aranka walked away from the table near the cash till as delighted as if she had received the greatest present.

⋆

The inn had a cellar that was reached from the courtyard, through an arcade where large, empty hogsheads were kept, too large to be rolled away unobtrusively, as smaller casks might be. Past this arcaded porch lay the actual wine cellar, the keys to which never left the innkeeper's side, but the vestibule was part of his wife's domain.

There stood the celebrated tub, made of oak, recently brought back from the cooper's workshop.

'Don't you have some brawn that has the tastiest cartilage, liver and kidney chopped up in it? That's the kind of winter food that goes with cabbage-trampling, rasped a voice under the arcades. The green cabbage heads were heaped there as if they had been laid low in some great battle recently fought against a gardener or scarecrow. The rasping voice belonged to Mr Paszmati, who showed up at the cellar entrance carrying himself like the men who used to roam the countryside with bunches of copper hoops dangling on their belts and at whose approach the black-bristled boars about to be unsexed would flee with ears pointing at the sky. Hearing this wintry note, the proprietress looked up from the stool on which she sat among the cabbages, sharpening a curving blade on her husband's razor strop.

'But where is the obligatory man from Tyrol, wearing a broad-brimmed hat with a tuft of mountain goat hair in his hatband?' Paszmati jested.

But the knife-sharpening woman was ready with her reply: 'The Tyrolean who'll slice the cabbage is sitting in the taproom, recalling old wartime memories with my husband.'

Reassured, Paszmati removed his leather jacket and hung it on a wooden peg that had been inserted into the drystone wall by means of God knows what sort of devilish trick. Seating himself on a three-legged stool, he contemplated his feet shod in comfortable elastic-sided boots, above which one caught a glimpse of the fine, snow-white footcloth, like the tip of a handkerchief peeking from a dandy's pocket. The landlady's eyes also came to rest on Paszmati's feet.

'I never wear socks,' announced Paszmati in a solemn, one could say ceremonious, tone, very different from his everyday livestock-trader's voice. 'My feet happen to be too sensitive to stand anything but the finest footcloth.'

'The kind great lords wear,' countered the woman seated on her stool, as she picked up a cabbage. 'For unlike socks, the footcloth must be changed frequently.'

'In the summer I use floss paper to wrap my feet in, simply the best antiperspirant there is,' said Paszmati, still absorbed in eyeing the feet in question. Maybe his chin even nodded at them. 'But in wintertime, flannel is still the best. True, it tears easily, and it doesn't whiten well in the wash, but it makes the best footcloth because it doesn't let the melted snow seep through.'

'That's right, melted snow can be the death of many a good man,' added the landlady, while her curved knife blade cored several cabbages. The sound of coring cabbages is comparable to that of cutting reeds, and invokes winter scenes shrouded in mist, in which expert hands set fire to bundles of reeds at the edge of a thicket, while deep in the thicket of reeds fishermen catch little black loaches under the ice, tiny fish that can add a matchless flavor to cabbage soup.'

'In my youth, when I cared more about my appearance,' said Paszmati, 'I used to cut up my former lovers' shirts to make footcloths, and every time I squeezed my foot into the boot I would say to myself, "Take that, bitch". For by nature I was too tender-hearted to lay a hand on a woman.'

To which the landlady had this to say: 'Whereas, believe it or not, Mr Paszmati, some women just beg for a good thrashing, they think it's medicinal. Some women are unimaginable without a thrashing – they look good with black and blue spots on their faces. It's seems to restore their lost honour. I tell you, Mr Paszmati, I never feel sorry for a woman whose husband lets her have it. There must have been a good reason.'

'Why, does your husband beat you?' Paszmati inquired in a low voice, as if the question addressed to the hefty matron had not come from him but from someone a good distance away from the cellar entrance.

'If he dared lay a finger on me, I'd use a knife on him. I'd put out both of his eyes and blind him for life,' declared the woman seated atop the pile of cabbage heads, and her sudden flare-up implied there was much more she could have added on this topic.

Then the Tyrolean, in his grass-green knee breeches and shirt-sleeves, plus his commanding goat-hair-trimmed hat, appeared on the scene and giving his mustache a twirl, appraised the cabbage pile. 'We'll be done in an hour,' he announced, and casting a Lothario glance toward the pile of cabbage, picked up his cutter from a corner, like a singer his harp, before launching into his performance.

The landlady was still shaking her head while cutting the cabbage cores, as if she couldn't get over Paszmati's earlier question. The Tyrolean seated himself on a three-legged stool in the manner of someone about to play the accordion.

Paszmati lifted his head in discontent: 'Why don't you toss me a cabbage core, it's been twenty years since I've had one.' He already had his pocketknife out, all set to slice.

While Paszmati was munching, the landlady and the Tyrolean discussed the ways she intended to prepare her cabbage for the winter. She wanted to keep some slices intact, in the Transylvanian Szekler style, for that way the cabbage remains cool in its pickle juice, and most suitable when served with certain roasts and barbecues. But she planned to pot some cabbage cut into long thin filaments, an absolute must for everyday kitchen needs. It was also essential to have some core pieces mixed in with cabbage cut into squares, for it is a great delight for the cabbage eater when the exploring tooth bites down on a real chunk of cabbage instead of a piece of potato. Furthermore, regarding the outer leaves of cabbage for potting and the cores left in their entirety for pickling, the innkeeper's wife had enough detailed instructions for a lifetime's supply.

Now Paszmati chimed in with his two penny's worth: 'As for me, madam, I can only say this,' he began in a voice as solemn as if he were transacting a business deal, 'as for me, I must state that as far as stuffed cabbage goes, I would never trade a small roll for the larger kind. For this type of stuffing you don't need those large leaves that cover the outside of the cabbage. The lesser, inner leaves are just fine, they are far tastier and juicier than the outer ones. Once during my travels, as I recall it was at the Nyíregyháza train station restaurant, yes, at the "resti", that's where I had a stuffed cabbage where each roll was just enough for one mouthful. One can eat much more of this kind of stuffed cabbage than those huge rolls that somehow end up not being cooked through and through.'

At this point, the proprietress rose from her stool where she had been rather comfortably enthroned. She rose like some corpulent lady who wishes to air herself a bit. She stepped over by Mr Paszmati's side and bent down to whisper in his ear: 'My dear Paszmati, you know very well that next to my husband I like you best of all the other men. And from now on I'll like you even more, if that's possible.'

Before Paszmati could think of a worthy reply to these friendly words, Messrs Bombai and Friedmann arrived in the courtyard. As long-time customers of the inn they already knew each other by sight. They did not quite approach arm in arm, the way invited guests do sometimes, clinging together even if only to share the blame for being late. These two were deeply immersed in a discussion of the finer points of cabbage-trampling.

'Pickling cabbage is best left to men with stomach ailments who on account of their illness wouldn't even dream of actually tasting the cabbage to be potted for the winter,' observed Mr Bombai, the provincial attorney who still professed the opinions of a man suffering from stomach ulcers, even though by now he was able to eat a normal diet. God knows what it is about the philosophy of stomach ulcer patients, a grievance that lingers throughout their lives, as unhappy lovers are haunted by songs they had sung once upon a time for their own consolation.

Mr Friedmann questioned the commercial aspects of the matter: 'I hope the woman wasn't cheated; did they sell her a decent lot of cabbage? I believe the best cabbage comes from Szabolcs County, but it's never sold in quantities under a wagon-load. One, two, or three wagons ... I doubt that the innkeeper had the gumption to purchase a whole wagonload. Oh, people are so petty.'

Discussing such matters, the guests invited for cabbage-trampling approached the cellar entrance, but pulled up with great consternation on seeing Paszmati in waistcoat and trousers rolled up to his knees, standing barefoot in the cabbage tub, taking two steps back, two steps forward, at a leisurely pace – almost meditatively – as one who is fully aware of his calling.

'There's that hog dealer,' said Friedmann to his companion.

'I know him,' the lawyer replied. 'They say he's made a fortune in pigs.'

'This man I wasn't expecting at all,' groused Friedmann, for the old man had a jealous streak; it pained him to hear someone else's lip-smacking gusto near his table.

Paszmati, installed in the tub, cast furtive glances towards the newcomers as if they threatened the success of a sizeable deal he was about to conclude. He gave them the cold shoulder as they greeted the innkeeper's wife and wished her all the best for the cabbage-trampling.

'I just hope all this won't spoil,' fussed Aranka, sounding anxious, and looked into the tub where, pretending to adjust a layer of cabbage leaves, she gave Paszmati's calves a squeeze that made him tread with renewed vigour.

The lawyer Bombai, who tired easily, slumped down on a small stool by the cellar entrance and began to mop his brow at the mere sight of cabbage-trampling; Friedmann, however, bustled about the tub (he even inquired how much it had cost), then around the Tyrolean, who, on account of the pipe clenched in his jaws, was unwilling to give a comprehensible reply, and next around the proprietress, who was concentrating on cutting cabbage cores as if her life depended on it.

'Ah, where are they now, in what distant lands, the travellers who'll one day get to taste this cabbage!' Friedmann exclaimed, since Paszmati's steps were still sprightly and deliberate, as if he had practiced cabbage-treading all his life.

'Those travellers aren't all that far away' replied the innkeeper's wife, in the midst of her cabbages. 'I happen to know for sure that the first time we tap that barrel to let the sour juice out, Mr Friedmann will be the very first to ask for chilled sour cabbage with peppercorns and caraway seeds, because that is the best appetizer there is.'

Warming up, the lawyer Bombai waved his hand: 'Better stay away from these sour appetizers and heavy digestive tonics, they are for drunkards and trenchermen, whose stomachs can digest anything. The one and only justification for raw cabbage is serving it with Baltic herring, because its flavour is in splendid harmony with herring and onions, beets, and pickled peppers. Better leave that raw cabbage alone, Madam, because now I'm certain that was what caused my former dyspepsia.'

Hearing the lawyer's lament, the innkeeper's wife stood up from her stool and, like some voluminous butterfly, fluttered over to his side. 'My dear sir, my cabbage will never harm you, I'll swear to that. Tell me, do you feel like trampling a little?' she asked, with a smile never seen before by the provincial guest.

'But of course!' cried the lawyer, who was already unlacing his yellow Bergsteiger boots that had a triple sole: a layer of cork (to absorb moisture), a layer of leather, and one of rubber, for back then only the intelligentsia wore rubber-soled boots in the countryside.

At a gesture from the landlady, Paszmati desisted from his back and forth movements in the cabbage tub. His look of solemn determination vanished and with a mild condescension he asked: 'Have I earned that glass of wine I've been thirsting for so long?'

With fleet steps, the landlady headed for a nook in the cellar entrance. Tantalizingly, she clanged the wine glass against bottle. The glass beaded with dew and the wine had that true taste of dawn when its task is to wash away smoke, soot and annoyance from the traveller's palate.

'I have really and truly earned this,' said Paszmati, having downed his wine and gently cleared his throat. 'This tastes even better than at a livestock fair,' he added, carefully disembarking from the tub.

The lawyer stood at readiness in his socks that were as loose as those pulled on the feet of a cadaver. Off came the socks, flying, and the lawyer clambered into the tub with considerable struggle. But his glory was not to last for long: trampling soon left him short of breath; starting to cough, he had to grab the rim of the tub so that he was merely marking time.

Mr Friedmann cast mocking glances in his direction and pressed the toe of one shoe against the heel of the other. 'I knew the shyster wouldn't last long – what does he know about trampling cabbage, anyway? But fortunately I am right here to show him how.'

The retired old broker sneaked an ardent glance at the landlady. She leaped up and hummed her way over to the side of the old man who was removing his shoes and whispered in his ear: 'Dear Mr Friedmann, of all my customers, you're the one I love the best!'

(1926)

The Undead (A latter-day Szindbad tale)

. . . Once upon a time Szindbad died under peculiar circumstances.

He was visiting his sweetheart, because from notes pencilled in his pocket diary he was able to positively confirm that he would arrive at just the right time to see Terka – a divorcée, a windblown leaf. (It is a sign of youthful folly when a grown man, like some poet scribbling love lyrics, lists in a notebook the number of amorous kisses exchanged, for perusal in later, solitary reveries . . . Women also like to note down the dates of their affairs, but according to evil tongues this is for another reason.)

So, like some long-awaited Christmas package, Szindbad arrived at Terka's once again and settled in next to the roast apple-scented stove, just like an older man who plans to spend his remaining years sitting by the fireside. Granted, at times the stove resounded with the crackling and whooshing of acacia trees that stand by the meandering roadside, sounds that remind the listener of travellers' songs in the distance. And yes, the rustic afternoon somnolence was at times underscored for Szindbad by the music of jingling bells from sleighs heading to some fair or wedding, the drivers' souls warmed by wine and their flanks by the hefty wife. Frost seals women's mouths so nobody knows what they're thinking about when they glimpse a snow-covered wayside crucifix or the manly hat of some scarecrow jutting up through the snowy blanket of the fields.

Although Szindbad was still deeply interested in the thoughts of womenfolk, no matter how lowly their station in life, for once he paid no attention to anything but the patter of Terka's slippered feet. Sounding like Christmas buskers in the village, those slippers pitter-pattered during the first hours after his arrival, scurrying, like a woodpecker on a shingled roof, up to the attic to select the choicest winter pears and apples for Szindbad, or down to the root cellar for the kohlrabi and carrots Szindbad had to have in his soup ever since he had learned he was suffering from arteriosclerosis. Yes, those slippers rushed down the warm-in-winter steps into the dank murk of the cellar to tap a cask of the unpretentious local wine favoured by Szindbad, while the candle atop the neighbouring barrel (that was the deacon's) guttered in peaceful complicity . . . Those same slippers clickety-clacked to make the eiderdown bed in case Szindbad felt like lying down after his journey – but for now he preferred to sit by the stove (for which reason a serving maid whose bare feet were turning blue received two quick slaps out in the courtyard). After that the busy slippers slowed down, and came to a standstill on the threshold.

'Tell me, why won't you lie down? What's the hurry? Is your wife waiting up for you?'

Szindbad waved a sad hand. 'It's been a long time since my wife waited up for me.'

'If you love her so much, why do you still come to see me?'

Szindbad tried to dismiss this with a laugh: 'I can't die without saying goodbye to you first.'

When Szindbad let this jest slip out he did not realize that truer words had never been spoken.

Round about twilight time Terka, sitting by the fire, launched into her usual fairytales, fables of times when Szindbad had loved her and her alone, legends of woodlands the two had roamed together, and the time when, sitting on an anthill, red ants swarmed over her legs. Now her words warbled of tulle-drape mirrors where their eyes had met once as if posing as a twosome at the photographer's studio in town, on a day when this lady, with the fate of a wind-blown leaf, would be called 'Sweetheart' by Szindbad. Tears welled in her eyes as she spoke of the room they had once shared at the Hotel Kuria in Vac on a market day, when they registered as husband and wife. Her voice assumed an otherworldly air recalling the Mariabesnyo shrine where Szindbad had recognized her, Terka! among a thousand pilgrims simply by her legs and her walk. This is where Szindbad began to nod off like a man in his cups who by far prefers dream visions to tales told by a mortal.

'Don't tell me you came here to sleep!' cried Terka, changing her tone of voice, for at her age she still appreciated manliness and courtesy in a paramour.

'Stop preaching!' riposted Szindbad as if shooing away a fly, or reacting to his wife at home.

'You know one kind word from you is enough to get me to do anything, why are you so rude?' said Terka teary-eyed, her hands grasping the pipe stem Szindbad held on his knee.

Now Szindbad committed the gravest affront of his life. He spoke as in a waking dream 'What a lousy village! Not even a decent inn where a man can have a good time!'

The woman reared up, as she had in her youth, when her first husband would give her a hard time. 'Why, you big lummox!' (This, in a voice that would have made anyone but Szindbad sink into the ground in shame.) 'Are you still dreaming of tavern maids with cracked heels? If you don't want me, why don't you go back to your lawful wedded wife, that old hag Cezarina, just waiting to scratch out your eyes. At least I won't get to die of shame watching you drink a toast out of some bar girl's low-cut shoes.'

And she slapped Szindbad in the face. 'Off to bed with you now, go and get your sleep.' Terka, in her emotional state, utterly failed to wonder why Szindbad did not knee her in the belly, as he always used to, in former scuffles . . . Instead, to demonstrate her love she wrapped her arms, muscular from kneading bread, around her man and tried to drag him off to bed, but to her amazement failed to budge the dead man.

And yet Szindbad was perfectly aware of everything happening around him.

He could see anger flooding the woman's face, as if she had just discovered her favourite rooster lying dead in the henhouse, then he saw her start to sniffle like a little girl whose doll had broken. Next she sent up a groaning sob and clapped her hands together repeatedly, as if trying to escape some nightmarish dream that kept hounding her even after she had woken . . . The howl that left her throat now came from the gut, and was comparable to the screams of uterine spasm or giving birth – their authenticity beyond doubt since midwives can be as notoriously heartless as the dead. This howl of anguish frightened the grey and white speckled hen, kept in the kitchen, into inquiring with frantic clucks what was happening in the house. Next a cow started lowing in the stable; cows have had an interest in domestic events ever since New Testament times. Outdoors in the snow the dog ambled to the middle of the yard to watch the soul in its flight towards the sparkling stars, and howled her own canine funeral rite.

Terka, hearing these signs of sympathy from her domestic animals, gradually eased up her howls, eyeing the dead man dreamily, hoping he might still be swayed from his stubborn determination and come back from the other world, back to this familiar eiderdown bedding, back to the company of Terka who smelled of fresh ham, bacon and sausages at a pig-sticking feast, and help her solve the secrets of lucky or ill-omened dreams in the silence of the night, and scrawl lottery numbers with charcoal on the wall – even though the Temesvar lottery had been discontinued long ago . . . Could his promise really have come true, that one fine day he would fall asleep and never come back from that other world one mostly visits in dreams? . . . Men are so weird – you can't believe them even when they're dead. . . And who knows, perhaps Szindbad up and died just to be free of Terka.

'At least you could have waited till morning, then it would have made more sense,' she muttered, and her face already clearly indicated that she wished the dead man out of her house.

'Now what is she going to do?' wily Szindbad wondered, for he loved to second-guess women, just as he loved to predict the lowest prices at the market.

Terka went outside as flustered as on laundry day, ready to distribute the required number of slaps. She kicked the backside of the dog howling in the yard, and looked into the henhouse to see if her rooster was cock-a-doodling out of sincere mourning for Szindbad or merely to announce a weasel's presence.

Szindbad used to get around without a coachman, on a two-wheeled cart well known to the landladies at taverns far and wide. The rickety old cart creaked and rattled out its own song; most of the time it was 'I'll Be Glad When You're Dead, You Rascal You . . .' – the very tune those landladies liked to hum into the driver's ear.

That rattle-trap lay waiting in a corner of the yard now, just like some partner in crime, holding the bag. The whip stood cocky and romantic, stuck upright in its holder, as if at a wedding

– evidently the owner left it there expecting plenty of occasions for further use.

Terka headed towards the stable where Szindbad's coppery dapple turned a cunning head from the feed-box to eye her.

'It's only me!' – she reassured the equine who was famous for having spent her years as a filly in the service of an itinerant circus and was known far and wide for her unusual colours, in case anyone had a mind to steal her. Oh, how often Terka had felt like interrogating this ten-year-old mare about the places she had taken Szindbad!

Occasionally Terka would find ribbons of pink or other frivolous colours braided into the horse's mane, and with a flick of the whip she would chide the horse, 'You're just as flighty as your master!'

But now she approached the animal with a certain amount of sympathy and untied her from the feed-box for she was familiar with the tricky knot Szindbad liked to employ, the same which was on his own apparel.

'You'll have to take your master home,' she instructed the mare as she harnessed her to the cart, just as she had on dark winter mornings when Szindbad felt like another forty winks under the eiderdown. 'Take him back to his old lady.'

She led the horse and cart to her door as noiselessly as if she were a thief in her own home. . . Then, mustering all her strength, she hauled Szindbad from the room by grabbing his yellow boots. Dragging him along the floor made Szindbad's hair tousled like the feathers of a drake, but he arrived in the yard without injury. Then came a miracle only a woman is capable of: Terka hoisted the dead man, just like a sack of straw, up on to the cart. She propped him up, tied the reins to his hands, and hissed at the horse just as she had so often heard Szindbad do. The clever little horse turned towards the open gate and headed out, carrying Szindbad on the familiar road into the winter night.

So the dead Szindbad travelled on . . . seated on the same old cart that took him to his rich but aged wife Cezarina, to hefty, buxom Terka, as well as to other wenches here and there whose legs he deemed desirable during his lifetime.

Had he been truly dead, he would have fallen off the rickety vehicle; but this way, in suspended animation, he may even have listened to the usual creaky song of the cart. At any rate his head kept nodding as the wheels bumped and lurched along the rutted road.

Now he rode without stopping, past the ratty bushes at crossroads and the apathetic roadside acacias waiting for some wayfarer to hang himself on a branch, whereas formerly Szindbad would pull up at these spots to check out the messages left by wandering Gypsies who tied all sorts of colourful rags on the twigs. Was it under that tree that some road-weary tramp stretched out his bunioned toes for the last time, glimpsing angels in his final dream as he froze to death with a smile on his face? And by the side of that ditch there is that an old, useless ownership paper tossed away by disheartened horse thieves whose business came to naught – or was it a letter carrying someone's entire life story, until rain and snow obliterated all such vanities . . .

Neither did the creaking cart stop at those outlaw-frequented taverns Szindbad could never pass by without inquiring from some old sheep-herder's wife if anyone from these parts had been taken off to prison, or had a new son or daughter, or had been beaten to death the week before. Behind the small, barred windows of the wayside tavern the regulars heard the familiar creaking of the cart, but nothing doing; the bagpipe player looked up from the cinder heap, his eyes, red as winter sunsets, strained in vain; as for the tavern keeper, he might as well have sealed his long beard to the table with candle wax . . . The bedsprings of roadside inns would no longer groan under the weight of Szindbad in his cups – and womenfolk seated on iron-clad trunks riding to the fair would now be left in peace. Never again would Szindbad torment them with questions about the number of petticoats they had on for the winter journey.

Crickety-creak went the cart carrying the dead man, but no farmer with a young wife to guard grabbed the pitchfork at the approach of the wayward gentleman . . . Yet here and there light still streamed from the small rooms of a house in some hamlet, like the eyes of young girls kept open by curiosity even at night. Surely there were women gathered somewhere for an evening of quilting, feather-plucking and story-telling, where Szindbad had once listened reverentially, only to sneak up on the storyteller and give her a thorough tickling. And he would carry away with him scents and aromas that Cezarina could instantly peg as coming from a peasant home . . .

Arriving in a dark yard, the well-trained little mare came to a stop and whinnied lustily. Cezarina, in a sheepskin waistcoat, grabbing a stable lantern, stepped from her doorway like damnation and hellfire . . . Even in a state of suspended animation Szindbad still trembled at the sight of this woman who was as sharp and thin as a capital letter printed in a book of psalms.

'Well, looks like he's a goner . . .' Cezarina pronounced after a brief scrutiny. The widow of a poultry-breeder, after a fowl plague she could assess at a glance the damages entailed by the fallen roosters and hens. (Pullets didn't count for much, they were a dime a dozen, like any fledgling. But Szindbad had been a useful old rooster . . .)

Without lamenting, or indeed creating much of a fuss, she

quickly decided what to do. She gave two or three slaps to the former circus mare eagerly trying to head for the stable, checked to see if there was a knapsack or other valuable in the hold of the cart, and pulled off Szindbad's short fur jacket, for it was lined with lynx, and still handy for some deserving man . . . After brief hesitation she even took Szindbad's astrakhan fur hat, for she herself had bought it for him at a shop in Miskolc.

'Well now, go on back to your girlfriend, to your Terka. I sure won't bother with your funeral, seeing as how you didn't die at home,' she said, depositing her husband's things on the porch.

As the cart carrying the dead man was about to roll out through the gate, she caught up with the two-wheeler and yanked out the stylish whip-handle from its holder.

So now Szindbad and his cart proceeded on the familiar trail back to Terka's house. The clever little horse stopped in the yard and whinnied. But whinny as she might, Terka had not the least intention of opening the door. She pretended to be asleep, but surely she must have been cursing under her breath . . . However, at daybreak, when the cold turned nippy, she heard Szindbad's voice in front of her door: 'Open up, woman, I'm freezing out here!'

(1925)

The Apostle of Heavenly Scents

As I recall it was one of those virginal, snow-flurried early spring days in the year 19** such as the editors of the *Farmers' Almanack* never dare to predict, seeing as how the kisses thrown by snow-flakes are rung in by the tweet-tweet of those little birds of March whose whistle, frozen silver, proclaims the certainty of fair weather around the corner. None the less, stepping out through the front door one still pauses for a shake of the head before deciding to set out on the daily rounds. Hmm, you think, it's still too soon to don that new hat purchased in honour of the spring of 19**. Once again you are obliged to dress like some itinerant college student about to set out on a long journey, whereas with spring just around the corner one would like to entertain all sorts of different notions. – That's how my thoughts ran, for I am a solitary man, without anyone to direct my wandering mind towards pleasant valleys or glittering mountain peaks.

That was when, as I stood under my window, I glimpsed in front of the house a strange-looking man I had never seen before, a man whose appearance I believe would have astonished persons even more experienced than I am.

He was in the process of clambering down from a village cart equipped with little bells that were still swaying, as if to broadcast a message far and wide about their sad state of being lost.

Here was a man whose gleaming white beard and long hair

made him look like St Peter, but it did not seem likely that he would climb on the roof and fly off to Madrid. His bent, yet fairly tall frame was wrapped in some sort of monk's habit, such as a simple-minded sacristan would wear on the saint's feast day at some shrine in our region, in order to inspire children and even old women to kiss his hand. He carried a pilgrim's staff topped by a copper cross that no doubt enabled him to perform all sorts of miracles within reach of smoked meats left hanging in the chimney. He wore a variety of amulets and medallions pinned over his chest that must have brought good luck to others, but were unlikely to improve this old man's lot. No matter how many rosaries he draped about himself, death trailed not far behind his back. His worn and faded boots had long forgotten to whinny like freshly tanned horsehide. By now, especially around the knees, the worn tops of these boots had become quite loose, as if there were no more maids and young wenches needing a hug and a squeeze in this land. These boots were looking forward to their last ride, on the hearse drawn by St Michael's steeds, demanding no further effort from them.

He climbed up the front steps of the old house as if he had been here before, and spoke in a voice one hears resounding in a barrel-maker's workshop: 'I am Nyergesujfalusi, apostle and missionary. I would like to stay here in this house because it is conveniently close to town.'

Nyergesujfalusi was by no means one of those smelly old vagrants who, in their twilight years, still trail every stench picked up at various stations of their lives. On the contrary, he paid great attention to cleanliness. Although he had travelled just about everywhere, there was about him not a hint of the Püspökladány train station's aroma, redolent as a caravanserai, a melange compounded of smells from the eastern and north-eastern parts of the country. No, Nyergesujfalusi brought not a whiff of sheep pens and horse stables that folks from the lowlands can never shake off, which follow them like an invisible swarm of flies no matter how fast they drive the dogcart. Neither did those gamey, smoky and sooty nomad Gypsy aromas from Transylvania waft into the house in his wake, as I had feared at first. No, our guest lacked even that close and stifling air that inevitably accompanies flat-footed pilgrims who waddle like ganders on the highway, sweating and raising a cloud of dust, camp out in the shade of a wild pear tree, and sit in a thicket to study the movements of ants, ladybirds and stag beetles under their noses, meditating on the wonders of nature. . . Rather, Nyergesujfalusi emanated the tallow candle smell that strikes the nose on passing the door of a church which has been shut down for a while. It was the scent of the confessional booth where the priest rests his weary head on his palm while hearing out a penitent's tiresome and monotonous list of sins. Illuminated altarpieces have this scent when the faithful humbly address the holy icon, always trying to justify their acts and thoughts. (But of course all rationalization is in vain; the view from the altar is clear into the hardened and blackened hearts of sinners – as well as into the hearts of lost sheep.)

Thus Nyergesujfalusi, whose appearance, behaviour and beatific prayers had convinced the womenfolk in the building that his presence would doubtless prove providential, since he knew herbs and cures for children's illnesses, and the right spells to keep trouble and strife away, as well as spiders, mice and the sneak-in thief, had at last made himself quite at home. (Strange, how we lived back in those days: we gladly welcomed the unexpected guest.)

'So, my good sir, you asked to hear what brought me here?' began Nyergesujfalusi one fine day, noticing that boredom had begun to spin a cobweb around my mood, making the occasion ripe for speaking up. 'Well, if I didn't know I was dealing with a man of learning, I could say that I'd read in some ancient tome about a ramshackle house hereabouts, inhabited by kind folks – the sort of thing tramps used as their excuse upon arriving at a strange town they'd never been in before. No, I won't even claim I had been here before, three or four hundred years ago when other tenants lived here: hermits, holy friars, lizards and trees with medicinal properties. It could be that I too lived here once upon a time, wearing the crimson cloak, but no one would believe that. Therefore let us stick to the truth. I have reached this place because I happen to have a most talented nose.'

I took a closer look at the apostle's nozzle, which resembled a pig's snout: surely it must have luxuriated in all sorts of putrid, titillating or voluptuous smells, ranging from the ever-intriguing aroma of garlic all the way to that of cesspools, which some noses find delectable.

But the apostle went on: 'I repeat: thanks to this most talented nose of mine, even in my dotage I still know something of life. My eyes have betrayed me – nowadays I couldn't find those lines of the holy Scriptures that atheists and heretics professed as their truths, nor could I tell the work of counterfeiters, fairground magicians or pickpockets. The fog of old age covers my eyes; I sense the movement of that tree's leaves but I barely see the leaves. But that hardly matters, for even the completely blind – musicians for instance – are still able to enjoy life. As a matter of fact, certain shy women prefer a blind man to one who can see. My hearing, too, is not what it used to be: I can no longer hear what robbers in the woods say behind my back, and I must guess what whisperers whisper into each other's ears. In the old days I could have told you what two women spoke about lying in bed side by side. Don't think their talk is always godly. As for my sense of touch, it's gone! Maybe I could still tell if I touched a leg in a plaster cast, that happens more frequently to women, for who knows what reason. But I can no longer find at a single touch the slit in a skirt – sometimes it's on the side; nor can I tell by touch the vest pocket that hides the fat wallet of the vendor or horse dealer at a fair. And I cannot tell by palpation any more whether the baby is going to be a boy or a girl. My sense of touch is worthless, while formerly even my big toe knew more about journeys prosperous and evil, fortunate wanderings, auspicious encounters, promising thresholds and stairways than your door-to-door pedlars who spend their lives on the road.

'And the same goes for my sense of taste . . . The tip of my tongue can no longer tell sweet water, fine wine, good bread. In my heyday one mouthful was enough for me to describe with my eyes closed the woman who prepared the dish, the yard where the rooster strutted or the hen scrabbled for worms, or the hunter who shot the game in the woods, or the bird-catcher who brought the squab. These days everything I eat makes me imagine some old hag roosting over the pot, drying the juice of the meat, parching the marrow in the bone, and withering the tender garden sorrel, while a single pea rolls away from her cursed hand, for peas are autumnal . . . All I have left in life is this most talented nose of mine.'

Here I took another good look at our visiting apostle's organ of smell, which, while under discussion, seemed to be so powerfully aware that it kept changing its appearance, just like a person at various stages of life. Right now, Nyergesujfalusi's nose looked like a foppish bridegroom facing a variety of joyous tasks in the offing, setting out with high hopes, attracted by pleasurable scents . . .

The apostle went on as follows: 'I owe my nose everything, just like the Caesars of Roman antiquity, who, as we know, owed their popularity to those fine, prominent noses that looked so good on their coins. Just take a good look, sir, at the set of this nose – it can express both dignity and humility at the same time . . . This nose is capable of making you sad or glad . . . There never was a more grateful nose in the vicinity of kitchens; but this nose knows how to be witty, too, if the conversation so demands. But those are merely external aspects of my nose that are as easy to master as twitching the scalp, wiggling the ears, or squinting . . . It is the inner qualities of this nose that are priceless. For instance, my nose also happens to be my pocket watch. In the darkest woods in the thick of night one whiff is enough to tell what time it is. I admit there are other noses capable of telling apart morning from afternoon, day from night, for each part of the day has its own smell. But I ask you: where in this province will you find a nose that'll tell you exactly when the hands of the clock stand at a quarter to two at all those inns, monasteries and parsonages where they truly care about lunch and about post-prandial reflections?'

For a moment I was at a loss as to Nyergesujfalusi's meaning, so I glanced at his omniscient nose, which once again had changed its appearance, like a faithful servitor, in complete harmony with the master. The nose now assumed a shape resembling a rotund blood sausage simmering in its rich broth in a pot on the kitchen range, having risen from the bottom and turning its colour at a touch of the cook's wooden spoon. Now I could see this nose transfiguring itself at lunchtime . . . The apostle was showing off his nose as complacently as a woman her new hat.

'Just think, can anything remain a secret from such a gifted nose passing in front of a hut, trudging past a godforsaken village, or pausing to take in the scene in front of the little houses of a small town? As I approach advanced old age, having learned a thing or two about my fellow man, I have come upon one bit of true wisdom: lunch is the most important thing in a man's life.

More important than anything else – wife, health, fine boots or a beautiful sweetheart. A man who has not eaten lunch does not amount to much in this world. He cannot be sure of his business, of what he says or what he does. He is certain to err on a day without lunch.

'Well, this is why I was always intrigued to see what people had for lunch. My nose was never too haughty to stop in front of some solitary hovel where a lonely man was cooking his meagre soup consisting of water, flour and salt . . . But my nose still preferred the scent of those small-town lunches that are cooked so that the whole neighbourhood is aware of what's on the menu. Then I would stop and linger in front of the door to meditate on the woman bustling in that kitchen. If it was springtime, then the scents of parsley, winter turnips and saffron at once made it clear that the woman tending her kitchen range, waking that morning, had not entertained thoughts that would keep her in bed, musing about the cut of her brother-in-law's moustache, or the style of the young schoolteacher's trousers, but jumping from bed her first thought was: what to cook for lunch?

'Would the butcher have fresh meat with the right proportions of muscle, fat and bone? Would the stall-holder have tender young sorrel or would we have to resort to last year's tomatoes? (By the bye, I must add: the fine aroma of sorrel sauce on a table in springtime signals a woman with a green thumb and a gift for domestic work. By hook or crook she finds a bit of sod, even if an antique travelling trunk must be sacrificed for this purpose, to plant some of her best friends and nearest kin, those spring vegetables. Many a woman has a sibling relationship with tender green onions, even if she won't eat them, concerned about the sweetness of her breath; she is more likely to indulge in her cousin, the red radish – even if at times she must step outdoors after enjoying them; she is a loving auntie to her parsley, sorrel and all those spring vegetables that lead feminine lives, that is to say, are loveliest in springtime. I must also add, my good sir, that carrots, kohlrabi, cabbages and potatoes should be considered masculine, for even though women like to grow them, they are consumed mostly during the masculine months of winter. As for Savoy cabbage, not even my nose has been able to decide whether their sour smell is masculine or feminine.)'

I took another peek at the apostle's nose. This proboscis now resembled a corncob stuck by children into the face of a snowman, a corncob that would guard the winter yards and gardens and ward off the hooting tramps . . . By now the apostle's nose had become engorged with blood and appetite, and showed its age, as if stewing in the vapours rising from some invisible soup. Meanwhile his nostrils filled with the scents of all those springs and winters that he would soon have to leave behind. But let the apostle speak:

'As I was saying, my nose's favourite haunts were those houses where the aromas streaming out were a melange of feminine undergarments laundry-fresh on Good Friday and the scent of the feminine springtime garden vegetables. Obviously in those kitchens the woman of the house washes her hands after chopping garlic, and is mistress of her garden with which she converses intimately when alone. The domestic animals understand her words, so that the dog, an unclean beast, stays outside the door, wagging his tail, and dares not let on where he's been roaming . . . Equally obvious is the fact that a woman busying herself in that springtime kitchen has taken care to wash her feet and waist, in order to add some of her own fine bouquet to the food she is cooking. Let's take, for instance, the aroma of a meat broth . . . We can immediately sense what kind of woman boiled the water, since water, as it flows through a woman's hands, instantly picks up her scent, just as it does the tang of minerals in a mountain. And don't the noodles that go into the soup similarly betray the entire inner life of a woman, thus her innermost scent? A woman's hand takes especial care with the noodles that go into her soup. While she shapes, lengthens, flattens and cuts it into squares or ribbons, her mind watches over the pasta, even if she happens to use a rowel shaped like a hussar's spur. The shell, the dumpling, the matzo ball, as it takes shape under a woman's hands, is able to command the nose's attention, or to repel it. I dare say, my good sir, that only soups possess truly individual smells in this province. I can tell immediately if the soup was cooked by a parish priest's housekeeper worrying about her future, or some little housewife who pins the vagaries of her fortune on a single button or tree or stake. But all things considered, the best scent emanates from soups cooked with the intent to arouse love or prepared for a guest who comes as a suitor. I always thought that for a soup of that kind a woman will not hesitate to add a pinprick's worth of her own blood.'

I took one last look at Nyergesujfalusi's nose. It was wrinkled, crooked and rigid like the trunk of some cursed beast that races all over the world with suppressed panting or loud howls in order to hunt down smells it had dreamed of, air currents whiffed from afar, odours sympathetic to its nature. Here comes this snout rushing, clad in the trappings of a pious pilgrim, accompanied by princely lies, as is the custom of old men who in their dotage would like to embrace every single bowl of soup in the world. In view of the fact that at the time several inexperienced young females were staying in the house, I had to send Nyergesujfalusi packing.

(1926)

Betty, Nursemaid of the Editorial Office

Sortiment (who amongst you still recalls that name?), editor of a Budapest weekly, was fated to track down poets and writers in their haunts behind the red windows of taverns where he would never have set foot on his own account, preferring to avoid premises where wood shavings litter the floor. The story of his chronic stomach ailment was the story of his life. Yet all his livelong days he was obliged to bolt down the braised *pörkölt* gravies, soupy goulashes and watery broths bathing the slabs of boiled beef served up by tavern kitchens everywhere. Let us take a closer look at but one day in Sortiment's life, and get to know, as a lesson for all of us, the man turned pub-crawler by happenstance – when by all rights he should have been resting, clad in a hospital gown, sipping herbal tea in a cool sickroom under the care of an old aunt.

The trouble started when Sortiment had to change from bedroom slippers to street shoes, following night after night of nightmares in which the next issue of *Sunday News* was prevented from appearing because of a lack of manuscripts from poets and writers. Therefore he was forced to pull from under the bed his shapeless boots with the uppers loosened by all the footcloths stuffed inside, and down at the heels, just like the boots of bar-flies who spend their lives wearing down tavern thresholds. Mr Sortiment was not very good at bending over, being one of those men with sensitive stomachs and increased bodily girth – especially around the waist. For this reason, while pulling on his boots, Sortiment cursed the ruddy-nosed, dissolute-looking, goateed editor who, in a neighbouring street of the Inner City, like himself put out a weekly rag. Sortiment believed his greatest enemy to be this skinny man who apparently had nothing better to do than chase hot-blooded dames on Franciscans Place, while Sortiment had to hustle and sweat to find authors with manuscripts. But at long last the boots were on. Editor Sortiment's footwear was of a cut that made left and right interchangeable.

Mirror there was none in Sortiment's room, for he had no desire to see himself ageing daily in pursuit of the godforsaken business of his weekly paper. This explained the hit or miss brushing he gave the hair that bristled above his ears, hair that felt to the touch like the hog's bristles on his desktop that he used for wiping his pen. From time to time Sortiment observed in a shop window's reflection that under his black, broad-brimmed, severe Calvinist hat his hair seemed to be greying mightily, but he always dismissed these evil thoughts, for he had to assemble the next issue of the *Sunday News*.

Now, as he picked up his black-sheathed umbrella cane (a contraption at the time still a novelty in Pest, where only the priest of the Elizabethtown district had one like it), he gave no thought to his own appearance, but a sudden gust of anger made him grit his teeth when he remembered the Petőfi-style beard of a jaunty writer of stories who, wearing neatly pressed salt-and-pepper pantaloons and a blue and white polka-dot bow tie knotted into a butterfly bow, some weeks ago had extorted an advance for a story that never got written . . . Sortiment conjured up the writer's physiognomy, his dyed moustache twirled to a point, his pomaded hair parted in the middle ('just like some haberdasher's clerk'), those slyly twinkling eyes and the sizeable

Adam's apple bobbing up and down thirstily above the broad, rigid shirt-collar, until Sortiment handed over the desired cash.

This vision made the editor slash at the air with his umbrella cane: 'Let's find Ligetsarki!' he growled as he began in advance to gather some choice invectives to hurl at that illustrious founding member of more than one literary society.

A grey pigeon squatted on the hands of the church-tower clock that showed ten in the morning when the editor Sortiment stepped out of the ancient Inner City townhouse on whose first floor baggy-trousered editorial associates with bunions on their feet had just begun work on the forthcoming issue of the *Sunday News*. Where, oh where, was that swindling short-story writer to be found at this hour? Perhaps at the barbershop, having his thinning locks brushed forward over the ears, to lend his face an appearance of respectability? Or more likely at the tavern where he receives a discount for devising Hungarian-sounding names for items on the French menu? Sortiment decided in favour of the tavern, for he himself rarely visited the barbershop.

In the tavern he only bothered to look in the room where the tablecloths were red and blue, for experience had taught him that his acquaintances frequented only these rooms in restaurants. Writers of short stories sat down at tables laid with white cloths only around the first of the month, when government pay cheques arrived.

Seven Owls was the name of the tavern, a circumstance that maddened Mr Sortiment, who sensed a blaring plagiarism here. According to his lights, Seven Owls was the name of a former rooming house for students where the landlord Szendrey, father-in-law of the poet Petőfi, rented out rooms by the day to single young men – whereas this Schwabian tavern-keeper who named his establishment after the Seven Owls had nothing to do with the said Szendrey . . . Sortiment happened to know that the present proprietor came from a suburb of Buda and had started out as a red-haired waiter answering to the monicker Seppl.

'Will you be having something for brunch?' The query came in a voice redolent of cabbage smells, just as Mr Sortiment was sitting down at a corner table that offered an ideal cover to ambush the unsuspecting short-story writer. The editor did not respond, being huffily preoccupied with finding a shelter for his umbrella cane and churchwarden-style hat, in order to secure them against the thieves who, as everyone knew, were rife in the restaurants of the city, and who would leave behind some tattered hat on the peg in place of the fine headgear they'd lifted. The umbrella and hat found their place on the rack right above Mr Sortiment's head – a brazen thief coveting that hat would have to steal the head first – when the editor at last bothered to look up. In front of him stood a sleepy, wrinkled, unshaven young waiter who had obviously spent the previous night serving rambunctious drunks, before the police put an end to the revels by removing the rowdies to the cells, leaving the intimidated waiter to catch his forty winks by laying his weary head on a table in the emptied taproom . . . Sortiment eyed the shopworn fellow with the superiority of men who have had their restful sleep.

'Let me have a menu and we'll see!' he replied morosely.

'Would you like something to drink? A beer, or some wine?' The melancholy voice again inquired, like the woeful refrain of some bibulous song resounding from a side street.

'After I've had something to eat!' Sortiment replied, and looked right through the waiter as if he were invisible.

He turned his attention to scrutinizing the tavern's interior to form some notion of which poets and writers would be contributing their work to the next issue. As yet his eyes, swollen with red-cabbage hues and ashen grey emotions, did not detect a single writer or poet – the good-for-nothings were late risers – but he did identify the district chimney sweep at a neighbouring table (in civilian clothes, of course). The man was famous for spending all day in taverns while his journeymen scraped away at the chimneys of the Inner City. Sortiment wondered what this experienced tavern-goer had ordered to eat and drink before hearing out the cook's complaints about her smoking kitchen stove.

The district chimney sweep had ordered 'lights' – sour lungs doused with gravy and served with two rock-solid dumplings and a double portion of lemon slices on the side. This dish was a favourite brunch of men whose teeth had been set on edge by wine, and for this reason the lungs were diced, or sliced into ribbons to make them more easily digestible. Of course real 'lights' were prepared using pig's lungs, thought Mr Sortiment, trying to find fault with the way the chimney sweep was spooning up the sour lungs while dunking into the gravy small bits of bread sliced by a penknife drawn from a vest pocket.

Remembering his gastric problems, Mr Sortiment turned his eyes away from the chimney sweep just as the man was starting to squeeze lemon juice over his dish . . . The editor's doctor had forbidden him to indulge in foods containing lemon.

But at this moment a resplendent figure appeared in front of him. This was Mr Mozel, the head waiter of the establishment, who, as a sign of the popularity and respect he commanded, was always referred to by his last name, and deservedly so. For he was the finest among the various Messrs Tiltsers, Petanovics's and Klivenyis who scurried around the patrons of Inner City restaurants. Greeting the editor, Mr Mozel presented a radiant visage such as one sees on a fat suckling pig just doused with boiling water in the kitchen to liberate it from superfluous bristles. You could tell from a distance by the cut of his tailcoat that it was not bought at a flea market but was custom-made to fit his voluminous figure. Neither did the pockets of this coat swell with various wallets that head waiters were wont to carry for keeping apart banknotes of diverse denominations. No, these pockets were lined with deerskin, so that the coat kept its form-fitting shape. Hidden out of sight under the tails of the coat were the change purses, and Mr Mozel was famous for being able to hand over the exact change at a single pinch, never making the patron nervous by fumbling for change. Mr Mozel was like a splendid menu, the cover of which carries a bouquet of water-fowl, hares, boar's heads, pheasants, fat grouse and ox heads, as imagined and drawn by some starving artist. Mr Mozel's ever-present smile seemed to say that there was no such thing as gastric ailment and that people had only one desire in life, to sit down at a comfortable table in a restaurant and eat their way through the items listed on the menu. Mr Mozel stepped up to Mr Sortiment's table with the respectful greetings due to an editor, and an air of officiating at a ritual involving matters of life and death . . .

'We have wonderful "lights" today. I've already had some.' Thus spake Mr Mozel to Mr Sortiment, while the latter was toying with thoughts of a spa in Bohemia next summer, for the sake of his health.

'"Lights"?' Sortiment echoed, terrified.

The head waiter's answer was lip-smacking, solicitous, full of promise: 'Oh yes. Sour lights. Served today for our best customers.' He spoke, and clicked his tongue.

The editor cast a glance in the chimney sweep's direction. The latter was in the act of sopping up the last remnants of gravy on his plate by means of a piece of bread stuck on the point of his pocketknife, sweeping the last drops on to his spoon.

'Oh well, let it be, I'll have the "lights",' said Mr Sortiment with a touch of listlessness. Then he added, with a flicker of animation: 'One must have a bite for brunch, after all.'

'And a mug of Kobanya beer, freshly tapped, to go with it?' suggested Mr Mozel, and gave the table a few slaps with the napkin he carried under his arm, as one who is most gratified by the results thus far.

The sleepy waiter now reappeared with a basket of croissants and Kaiser rolls. The dyspeptic editor found himself deliberating with the utmost care which Kaiser roll was most fully baked, done to a russet shade. Furthermore, he cast a glance at the salt rolls – even though his doctor had proscribed salty food – before settling on a Kaiser roll extracted from the middle of the heap using the finger with the green signet ring, the finger he deemed cleanest.

But here came Mr Mozel already, with the promised delicacy, smiling at the editor from a distance as if he were the bearer of glad tidings. In one hand he held the plate of sour lungs swimming in brown gravy that was surely the product of the finest beef ribs or pork chops. The dumplings were made with pig's liver and vegetables, so that their cannonball hardness would not upset even the most sensitive of stomachs. Slices of lemon, split at the ends, were affixed to the edge of the plate, and there were three of them, one more than the chimney sweep's portion (which the latter instantly noted).

'I brought you the last portion we had,' confided Mr Mozel. 'The best-cooked pieces, from the bottom of the pot. Even though the Father Superior of the Franciscans had just sent a message asking for a portion of sour lungs to be put aside for him . . .'

He served the plate of food as if it were some miracle-working drug for Mr Sortiment, followed by the glass of beer held in his other hand, luminous in the late autumn sunshine glinting on Franciscans Place. The glass of beer, golden, fragrant with the scent of hops, and adorned by a paper collar, would have made even a dying man reach out for it – while our Sortiment tried to keep the thought of death as far away as possible, if only for the sole reason that his weekly had to appear on Sunday . . . The editor stirred the gravy with his fork and strove to find some pleasant prospect to occupy his thoughts, other than devious writers of short stories or uninhibited canines on the street corner.

So his thoughts turned to his youth, when, coming from an Uplands village, he had arrived in Budapest as starved as a runaway wolf pup. With only small change in his pockets he had ordered sour lungs in an arcaded, smoky Inner City tavern where the patrons were far more corpulent than he was – as if the tavernkeeper's ambition had been to gather every man of some girth in the city in order to exhibit them as living testimonials to his tavern. The gentlemen who sat there had beefy necks, buffalo statures, and all looked like butchers. They kept casting envious glances at each other's plates, just as the chimney sweep did at his plate now . . .Those old-time tavern patrons' necks bulged like blood sausages above the backs of their collars and their bald pates sweated profusely from the spicy food laced with paprika, pepper and garlic, while their faces assumed the colour of earthenware pots glowing red, left too long on the kitchen stove. They paused in their feeding only long enough to wipe away with a moistened napkin the remnants of spilled soup and sauce from their vest or jacket. For only the most experienced among them had the presence of mind to tie a napkin around his neck before plunging into the comestibles, the way a barber ties on a sheet before a shave. After the editor had recalled these old-time tavern guests with their enormous appetites, he looked around the room to see if he could find a patron eating in that appetizing manner of old, and whose example would make him forget all of his dyspepsia as well as his accursed editorial existence.

His glance at last found one patron who resembled those former tavern customers, but alas, this man had not ordered sour lungs, but a platter of boiled beef, for by now the hands of the clock had progressed past eleven.

Who was this man who had ordered boiled beef?

Sortiment, who knew just about everyone in the Inner City, realized he was looking at the shoemaker from Parisi Street, the man whose chief interest in the calendar was keeping track of the national holidays. Naturally, the shoemaker held the country's first king, St Stephen, in highest esteem, for on St Stephen's Day every gentleman worth his salt dressed in his best, including appropriate footwear. (This shoemaker also kept tabs on the anniversary day of Franz Josef's coronation, although as regards boots, this day could not vie with St Stephen's Day.) The Parisi Street shoemaker looked like a guild master, tall, with a twisted salt-and-pepper moustache, and a bearing that was always solemn, as if taking the measure of some baron's foot (by means of little paper ribbons). He liked to rub his hands together, as if preparing to hold the hand of one of his titled customers. This shoemaker took it for granted (he barely nodded his head) when the sleepy waiter served him a portion of beef so enormous that Sortiment at once regretted becoming angry at the rumpled fellow whose exterior made him unsuitable for service anywhere but in the cellar of the Seven Owls. And in any case the sour lungs he had pre-empted from the Father Superior of the Franciscans did not turn out to his liking, and his conscience was troubled about whether he had done the right thing. The dumplings were especially hard to swallow, and he feared they would prove difficult to digest. He might have nightmares about the *Sunday News* never again appearing in his lifetime.

Therefore he directed all of his attention at the Parisi Street shoemaker consuming his meal, and inwardly cursed the chimney sweep who was on his way out, toothpick in mouth, reaching for his hat and many-pleated coat.

For here was truly a splendid portion of beef. Gourmands dream of such cuts of beef when they arrive past their usual lunchtime at the tavern they frequent, only to see the boiled beef crossed out on the menu as if exiled forever by the waiter's pencil. And so Mr Sortiment's covetous eyes (eyes that at times betrayed his true nature) kept reexamining that colossal slab of meat, which must have been cooked to a state of utmost tenderness in the kitchen that morning. That cut of beef may have included a part that patrons of taverns liked to call an 'end piece', while the enormous bone that crowned this prize portion of meat testified that the Parisi Street shoemaker's was truly a regal helping of beef, no doubt due to favouritism on the cook's part. (The maker of footwear obviously must have bribed her with a pair of slippers.) Sortiment envisioned the steaming hunks of meat, fatty parts and even bits of tallow that hung so appetizingly from that bone, all going into his own mouth. And his carious teeth craved the rich fare, although his doctor had advised him against fatty foods.

The shoemaker, you had to hand it to him, really knew how to deal with such regal spoils, so rarely attainable for the restaurant goer. First of all he made sure to tie a napkin around his neck. Next he lined up the salt and pepper shakers and even the mustard jar within easy reach, even though it was unlikely he would need the latter, given the plate of horseradish in vinegar served up, alongside the beef, by the sleepy waiter. The shoemaker certainly did not spare the salt. He used it liberally over the bits of vegetables that partially covered the meat, paying especial attention to the slices of potatoes, carrots, celeries and Savoy cabbage that came with the soup, always a favourite of cobblers who work sitting on three-legged stools. He salted the meat and turned it over to inspect it from the bottom with hungry eyes, as if he were checking out some female from head to toe. And he even salted the horseradish.

Hmm, reflected Sortiment, pushing away his half-consumed dish. This shoemaker is a bigger rascal than I would have believed . . .

Whereupon the shoemaker, grabbing the fork in his left hand, stabbed it into the meat so that the juice spurted, and started to slice it up into small pieces with his knife. By then Mr Sortiment had made up his mind. He was only waiting for the shoemaker to taste the beef, to decide by the expression on the man's face . . . But unexpectedly the shoemaker seized a spoon and dipped it into the broth remaining in the bowl. He slurped the hot broth which obviously must have burned his mouth; none the less he went at it again and again (after seasoning it with a pinch of paprika), all the while shutting his eyes in pleasure or pain. . .This clinched the matter for Mr Sortiment, who suddenly recalled a bachelor friend of his, a retired judge, who liked to lean on his umbrella and speak slightingly of the world, his philosophy being that only what we eat is truly ours. Mr Sortiment was convinced that the judge would approve his next act . . .

'Mozel,' he began in a deliberate drawl, when he saw the waiter shaking his head in concern over the half-finished plate, 'tell me, Mozel, might there be in your kitchen some bone about the size of a child's fist with a few bits of meat left on it?'

'But of course!' replied Mozel, his face brightening. 'And if there isn't, we'll see if we can make one.'

The editor gestured to explain: 'You know, it shouldn't be too big, just a nice little titbit that will still leave room for lunch.'

Mozel nodded, and directed his legs enveloped in loosely

fitting trousers (which he must have pressed every night) towards the kitchen. Meanwhile Mr Sortiment kept an eye on the Parisi Street shoemaker. That individual was now dipping the tip of his knife into the horseradish in vinegar, and, removing a small heap from the abundant supply, placed it on a pre-selected mouthful of meat – part fatty, part sinewy – then balancing the meat on knife and fork, shovelled it into his mouth. A single, but all the more satisfied, movement of the jaw followed, as if a millstone had shifted inside the mouth, and the knife was already heading towards the horseradish, while the left hand broke off a piece of bread and held it in readiness over the table.

And now here came Mozel with a meaty bone resting on a double platter. Hmm, the shoemaker's was a finer piece, obviously he had ordered first, thought the editor, eyeing the meat that was lined by a feathery, thin layer of fat . . .

'Who is your butcher?' he inquired absent-mindedly.

'Dubovetz, on Lipot Street.'

. . . Before the editor launched into the appropriate rituals preceding the consumption of his beef, he cast a sudden glance at Mozel, who stood on his left, in a pose of almost worshipful attention. 'Now what?' inquired Sortiment, withdrawing the knife that was on its way towards the salt cellar. 'Are you having second thoughts about bringing me *this* particular piece from the kitchen?'

Mozel gave off a tremendous sigh: 'If my father were alive and came to have brunch at the Seven Owls, I couldn't have given him a better portion. But the poor old man cannot be with us, because he rests in the cemetery in Vac, since a scoundrel named Kupriczky persuaded him to use his talents for the production of counterfeit five-forint bills . . .You see, my father had been assistant photographer to Professor Ellinger . . .'

'Well, how did the bills turn out?' asked the editor, sucking his teeth.

'They only managed to produce a single five-forint bill before the police apprehended them, and the judge sentenced my father to ten years – for one lousy fiver, such as big spenders who have had one too many sometimes use to light their cigars with. A single fiver!' Mr Mozel added after a pause and involuntarily reached under the tail of his coat to rattle the change purse concealed there.

The editor, too, envisioned a five-forint bill, with its depiction of nude mythological figures wielding spades, hoes and rakes in a green field. These were the bills the editor used to pay for poems and stories – he kept the money at home in a desk drawer, the banknotes neatly folded between the pages of a cookbook written by Aunt Rezi. And oh yes, Ligetsarki had wheedled from him two of those bills as an advance for a story that was still 'forthcoming' . . . This thought soured the editor's mood once again, so that he began to notice that the meat was rather stringy, in other words, not the real thing, certainly nothing like the shoemaker's – who was just at that moment reaching the stage in his meal where he started to round up the leftover pieces on his plate and from the bowl, fishing with his spoon in the remaining broth for bits of vegetables that he steered with a piece of bread, and capturing slivers of meat on his knife, to be advanced towards his slurping, opened mouth. Yes, they say it is precisely these last mouthfuls that nourish a man. – Ah, how splendid that helping of beef must have been, when even its wreckage was consumed with such passion!

'Surely one five-forint bill is not worth ten years,' murmured the editor without much conviction, for his vanity was flattered by the head waiter lingering near his table while there were other guests in the establishment.

Mr. Mozel responded: 'Actually the ten years wouldn't have been so bad. Anyway the old man did no more than three, before he died of consumption. But he left behind a girl, a stepdaughter with whom neither my wife nor myself can seem to do anything. She's in her twentieth year and she's already worked as a milliner, seamstress, tobacconist . . . But she just wants to be another Mariska Simli. She's crazy, I tell you, totally crazy.'

'Mariska Simli?' snorted the editor.

'You know,' Mr Mozel said in a conciliatory tone, 'the poetess who tours the country dressed in a priest's cassock. And a top hat over her hair which is cut as short as a man's. You wouldn't believe how one crazy woman is able to drive another one just as crazy. Betty, ever since she ran across Mariska Simli, spends all day writing poems, and is dying to meet Mr Sortiment . . .'

Although Mr Sortiment was listening to the head waiter's words with great attention and the appropriate ironic smile, suddenly his attention turned elsewhere . . . to an occurrence that seemed extraordinary. The Parisi Street shoemaker came up with something that, for the moment, outdid all the Mariska Simlis of this world. For the shoemaker discovered that the bone remaining on his plate actually consisted of two pieces, similar to one's elbow, bound together by muscles and ligaments. He grabbed the bone with both hands and, after considerable exertion, broke it in two, whereupon, sweeping knife, fork and spoon away from his side, he started to gnaw on the bone in such a spectacular manner that even a dying man would have hung around long enough to see the shoemaker finish picking that bone clean. You had to hand it to him, he was really grinding away with his teeth while pulling, tugging, sucking and picking at it with his fingernails – so that Mr Sortiment lost all his appetite for meat, and he, too, wanted a bone now, even though he no longer had the same faith in his teeth as once upon a time . . .

Indeed, fate decreed that on this late autumn day the editor Sortiment should have his bone, convinced as he was that this would assuage his dyspeptic stomach. It so happened that the puny corset-maker on Franciscans Place – whose shop window containing wax figures and other sights compelled passing women to stop – this corset-maker had come forth from his store that was full of whalebones, straps, hooks and fasteners, all of which served to make the women of Budapest as svelte, if that was possible, as Queen Elisabeth herself.

This corset-maker now entered the taproom of the Seven Owls, and made an extraordinary request of the head waiter, Mr Mozel, who hurried to greet him: 'Last night I dreamed I was eating a marrowbone with toasted little slices of Kaiser roll and a tomato salad. Would your kitchen by any chance have a marrowbone for me?'

Mr Sortiment's eyes bulged at the temerity of this man who left his prosperous business where ladies were trying on all kinds of corsets, in order to eat a marrowbone at a tavern . . . Even the Parisi Street shoemaker seemed to pause in his gnawing on the bone, although that sort of thing is not easy to leave off. But Mr Mozel the head waiter was not the least bit amazed. He cheerfully carried his rotund belly, decorated by a watch chain with a commemorative coin, in the direction of the kitchen, as if a long-awaited guest had just arrived. And in a trice he was already back, holding a steaming dish more beautiful than a cookbook illustration, and with the proud smile of a lucky prospector who had struck gold, placed it in front of the sickly corset-maker. Why can't he dish out his Betty to that corset-maker? was the disgruntled thought passing through Mr Sortiment's brain.

But the head waiter stayed by the corset-maker's side, awaiting the forthcoming ritual. The corset-maker used his knife to trim the meat remnants from his marrowbone and, having applied paprika, salt and pepper to them, one after another he shovelled them into his mouth, all the while keeping his eyes on the bone, as if it might run away from him. Tilting his head left and right he peeked into the ends of the marrowbone, as if spying something delightful through a keyhole. Look at the grin on that fellow's face, thought Sortiment with surprising agitation, and pushed away his dish, plate and eating utensils, as if suddenly mad at the world.

Meanwhile the corset-maker, under the lively scrutiny of the entire clientele, grasped the marrowbone in his left hand, and making a fist with his right, vigorously tapped his left wrist. This blow caused an avalanche of marrow to pour forth upon the hot plate in such abundance that this had to be the finest marrowbone served in the entire city today . . . But the corset-maker, that impertinent fellow, was not satisfied with this windfall: he looked through the marrowbone (as if to stare at Mr Sortiment through a telescope) and, sticking his fork into the hollow of the bone, twisted it two or three times, thereby producing a few more slivers of marrow.

By now Mr Sortiment had had enough, so he half turned his back on the corset-maker and propped his chin with his elbow on the table, like some outlaw at a country tavern. 'Head waiter, I'd like some beer!' he shouted, to interrupt Mr Mozel who was still enthusing over the exceptional contents of the marrowbone, eagerly rearranging the salt and paprika cellars to be closer at hand, for as soon as marrow sees daylight it cools off.

Hearing Sortiment's voice, the head waiter turned and floated over to the editor's table in shoes as soft as glove leather. 'A glass of beer, you said?' he asked, but Sortiment, with darkened brows, merely nodded.

By the time Mozel returned with the glass of beer, Mr Sortiment had somewhat relented, for he had noticed that the corset-maker did not know the proper manner of consuming marrow from a bone, and was spreading it like butter on large slices of bread, whereas you were supposed to place it on small, bite-size pieces of toast. Neither did he see a steaming bowl of hot consommé that had been placed in front of this ignorant customer, although everyone knew that as soon as the marrow sees daylight it must be placed in piping hot broth . . .

'I feel like having a marrowbone,' the editor announced out of the blue, when the head waiter placed the glass of beer in front of him. And Mozel was already on his way to comply with the request, with an alacrity seen only in footmen who adore their master; his corpulent figure practically flew, waving his napkin from afar, signalling the kitchen. His fair, balding pate was bedewed with perspiration when he returned with a bone twice the size of the one the corset-maker proved unable to do justice to. Mozel had also brought a bowl of hot consommé to accompany the bone, as well as toasted slices of Kaiser roll that were indeed no bigger than bite-size. Mr Sortiment triumphantly looked around in the taproom of the Seven Owls, receiving truly respectful glances from all sides. Once again he tied the napkin around his neck and condescended to address the head waiter who was mopping his brow: 'All right, why don't you send your Mariska up to see me during office hours this afternoon . . .'

'Please sir, it's Betty,' rhapsodized Mr Mozel.

'We shall see if the girl's any good at writing poems. But let's make sure you have authentic Szeged paprika here, before I taste it . . . I have a sensitive stomach.'

Mr Mozel raced off again, and returned with the container of paprika to assure Mr Sortiment it was the authentic stuff from Szeged.

*

During the afternoon office hours Mr Sortiment usually soaked his feet in a basin of hot soapy water after all the running around he did during his mornings. This is what he was doing now, seated behind his ink-stained, slim-legged, rather feminine smallish desk; his aching feet comfortably immersed in the warm water while his associates busied themselves around him. Vacsok, a short man who resembled an overweight hamster, was assembling the Miscellany column, pasting in news items about thirty-storey skyscrapers in America. He liked to inform his readers at least once a year about the tallest tower in the world. Murocski, an individual who looked like a ladies' tailor, was taking care of the Puzzle column, working at random, devising a rebus. He was a world-weary man whose wife had left him, and he could hardly wait for the evening, which he spent at some outlying tavern sitting at a table all by himself. Bosnyak was a former captain of infantry, who, despite his very modest salary, was secretly building a 'villa' on the outskirts of the capital. He had the red face of a habitual drinker, but it stemmed from his military years, for he had not touched a drop since becoming a civilian . . . He always wrote about the army as if he had served in every single regiment of the Dual Monarchy. And there was the picture editor of the *Sunday News*, Mr Palotai, pen and ruler in hand, sitting at a desk with many drawers; he was a hunchback, his shoulder and waist bent like some misshapen tree. He had a predilection for publishing pictures copied from foreign periodicals. All around, pens were scraping away and blotting-sand being squished over the pages filled by the scribblers. Mr Sortiment, editor-in-chief, was musing over his life, something he was not in the habit of doing . . .

The door opened and a young miss wearing a red hat advanced into the room.

The lively noise of the outdoors intruded into the room

through the doorway along with this otherwise rather unremarkable young woman. Instead of a priestly cassock, she wore the inexpensive outfit of a laundress, over which she had thrown a little cape resembling bat wings. The fingers of her grey glove had been darned more than once. The young lady sported a kiss-curl over one ear . . .

'I was told you needed a nursery maid,' the girl in the red hat announced with a merry laugh, and stopped in the doorway.

All the old co-workers in the office raised their heads and were cheered by what they saw. But when they noted Mr Sortiment's gloomy visage, they, too, turned serious and assumed an air of indifference, although they kept their ears open.

The little miss stepped forward: 'I am Betty. I was told I could be nursemaid at this office . . .'

Sortiment looked the girl over, and spoke in a somewhat forced tone with a touch of humour that conveyed authority and was the equivalent of a pay raise: 'Mr Vacsok, do you by any chance need a nursemaid?'

The editor of Miscellanies gesticulated with stubby fingers in a defensive way, but before he had a chance to utter a word, the girl, without removing her red hat or her bat-wing cape, spun around and landed in Mr Vacsok's lap, seated as he was in his armchair stuffed with newsprint, and put her arms around his hamster-like neck. She spoke in a wheedling, breathless, irresistible voice: 'Oh yes you do, please say you need a nursemaid, my life depends on becoming a contributor to *Sunday News*. My guardian is a head waiter who spends his earnings in a gambling casino each night; my stepmother is a laundress who sends me out to pick up dirty laundry from the customers . . . What else could I be, but your nursemaid, when I feel such a strong poetic vocation?'

Before Mr Vacsok, the editor of Miscellanies, had a chance to reply, the editor-in-chief with the diminutive desk spoke up again, but this time as if with a touch of bitterness: 'Well then, let us proceed in order. Mr Murocski, grand master of puzzles, for whom there is no insoluble puzzle in the world, what would you say to a nursemaid? Captain Bosnyak, our military editor, do you feel the need to have your nappy changed by a nursemaid? And you, Mr Palotai? Speak up, tell us if you need any help to handle the picture captions.'

While editor Sortiment was saying the above, the surprising young lady immediately leaped on the lap of each gentleman addressed and began to caress his hairy neck . . .

'Yes, yes, say you need a nursemaid!' she entreated, whispering then shouting into the ear of the gentleman called upon, so that her bat-wing cape seemed to flutter. At this moment the door opened as if some everyday visitor was about to enter, and in came Ligetsarki, the swindling short-story writer, just like a character on stage, on cue.

The editor's voice sounded hollow by the side of his little desk: 'At last here is someone who is qualified to decide whether we should hire Miss Betty as nursemaid of the editorial office – or should we look for an older woman?'

The short-story writer looked around in confusion, until he glimpsed the enthusiastic young lady, who cried out in ecstasy: 'Ligetsarki, you cannot tell me to be a laundress like my stepmother. You are the noblest soul in the land, I have been a reader of your unsurpassable works for a long time. Oh, all those anonymous letters I wrote you after reading a story of yours!'

The writer looked at the editor, awaiting Sortiment's response.

And Sortiment replied with a laugh, in a firm voice: 'Ligetsarki, I still owe you for your last piece. Here is the money. Do me the favour of interviewing the young lady about her past, her goals and plans, before I hire her as nursemaid for our office. I recommend the patisserie on Franciscans Place for the purpose.'

The short-story writer, who had expected to be thrown out by the quick-tempered Sortiment, accepted the five-forint banknote and offered his arm to the young lady.

'Please wait one moment, my dear author,' said the prospective editorial nursemaid. 'I still have to sit in the lap of the editor-in-chief . . .'

'That won't be necessary,' replied Mr Sortiment, and once more began to rub his foot, this time the left one, with the right. He cast a benevolent, smiling, congratulatory glance at his old co-workers, who were all seized by a sudden urge to dip their noses into the inkbottle to placate the boss.

After all of this, who can explain why Sortiment, editor-in-chief of the *Sunday News*, put on his tail coat around midnight in his small room on the ground floor, and shot himself through the heart that very night, when on the previous day seemingly everything had gone to his liking?

(1926)

The Green Ace

The Edifying History of How a Soul, Lost in a Jug of Wine, Was Found

I

What the pitcher said to the wineglass in Golden Rooster Street

Mangy fox collars, ghastly tattered overcoats, trousers ready for the spindly legs of scarecrows, faded moustaches resembling dripping drainpipes dangling from old thatched roofs, conscience-bitten, thinning beards, blinking, cobwebby eyes, heads of hair knotted by autumn wind and fog, buttonless vests, neckties shrivelled up like withered leaves, and hollowly resounding cellars of the moth-eaten old Tabán district in Buda: this was the setting of the miraculous pledge made by Kuvik, the vendor of street song broadsides: he would never again, of his own free will, allow another mouthful of wine down his gullet.

Old Tabán, with your chimney smoke like so many sighs stuck in the throat, subterranean groans like those of a narcoleptic, sobs drowned by the whirr of a sewing machine, treacherous dreams born of moonlight that rapidly age and turn helpless in daylight, nameless, forgotten sorrows, aimless loiterings and even more aimless sessions of sitting around! – this is where it came to pass that Lenke Mariancsics, who was as blonde as the new moon and whose sky-blue eyes had for years been casting glances into the leafy arbours of taverns as well as through the window-panes that tremble with the hum of monotonous song, in order to rouse sleeping acquaintances from their spellbound damnation in the corner nooks of wine shops and introduce them to that long-forgotten merry cup of wine that would make them burst into song . . . One fine day this same Lenke Mariancsics renounced taverns forever, and announced that wine was both stupid and without taste.

Oh Tabán! With your streets winding uphill towards unknowable dead ends, doorsills that only make one stumble, ailing doors that are ready to fall off their hinges at the touch of an unpractised hand, furniture that had been new in the days of your grandmother and before, sofas wasted away to a painful thinness, arthritic armchairs, mirrors that had lost their quicksilver and reflect only former faces, teapots with spouts like dog tails, glasses yellowed by medicines, antique icons depicting children, squatting crones harbouring fleas unused to hopping; desperate, limping ancient roosters, courtyards that moulder into dust at night like decaying graveyards, deathly tired oil lamps, female topknots that had long ago forgotten their famed beauty and the compliments they drew, blouses yellowed with apathy, swinging on fraying clothes lines, mynah-birds that had long ago lost their ability to talk, women shrunken into ornamental initials in prayer books without ever having known the magic of a night of love, men cursed in childhood and aged into crotchety old freaks, goldfinches and blue-throats that never sang a note, not even in springtime, virgins that did not take care of their garters even when they were in convent school, marriageable, barren girls whose dreams of running water never delivered their promise, and aged janitors who wrapped their blue uniforms in ghostly winding sheets – all in old Tabán! – where it once happened that a portion of the populace, among them the gingerbread vendor and candle-maker Guguli, the town scribe Arkus, Poturicsics, the captain of ships, and Weinsong, the 'landlord', one and all made a pledge to stay away from wine and other alcoholic beverages, as if the devil himself had cast a spell to make them all want to end their days in open-eyed sobriety, without trembling knees and twisting ankles, without vests torn away in frenzy and with their belts in place, and not like those miserable drunkards found dead in Tabán, hanging from a withered tree in the orchard or from a hook in the cellar or else collapsed in the back of the house, on the dung heap, or in ditches, with gaping mouths not even stray dogs deign to lick. The bright sun of Indian summer sermonized against alcohol over the Serbian orthodox church on Greek Street that marks the boundary of the Tabán, and one abstemious man was seen climbing uphill on Golden Rooster Street where since time immemorial no one had walked in a sober state, and without first tearing away a piece of wood from a fence, railing or palisade in drunken defence against the myriad arms reaching up from underground.

Wineless (and wordless) men trudged past Foamwhite's tavern where the owner himself was so crazed with wine that he had to be locked up in a room (from where he occasionally escaped, and returned days later bloodied and lame, as if he had been forced to dance in a quarry), leaving old women to 'manage' the tavern – two, three or four or five of them – friends of the tavern-keeper's wife who served up the wine for the guest, and mistook the grape seeds left in the wine for fleas.

Wineless (and wordless) men passed scornfully by the wine cellars where the hair of tipplers grew long and turned a dull mould-colour, for your true lush never has time for a haircut, at most he'll give an emphatic twirl to the moustache, to keep it from soaking up wine intended for the gullet. Meanwhile the nose turns red, no amount of frostbite ointment will help, the nose will not relinquish its bibulous crimson, and through borrowed eyeglasses the nose appears ever more misshapen in the mirror where a moment before the tavern-keeper's girl had been eyeing herself. A true lush will not sacrifice good money for eyeglasses but would rather borrow a pair from some superannuated old man, through whose glasses the world may appear more permanent and contented, and happier . . .

As I was saying, suddenly you began to see men sobered and spruced up, reeking of incense, walking the streets of Tabán, men whose ears remained deaf to even the most table-thumping songs that winos locked in cellars like to wail out to attract someone, anyone to bring news of what was happening outside in the world at large. (Only Sasadi was afraid of news from the outside – it usually meant another child of his was dead, after stretching her arms in vain towards the absent father. 'Veronica!' screamed Sasadi from the cellar whenever he thought of his dead children and pangs of conscience made him feel like crawling inside a wine barrel.)

2

The thoughts of girls who walk a beam of moonlight to the window when someone knocks on the pane

Surely something must have happened, if certain folks in the Tabán district now started to notice on some days the cloud-white sheen of the nanny goats grazing on the hillside, mildly maa'ing in the absence of the bearded billy goat. Yes, even without wine folks noted how bright certain spring days can be, days when the junky old cupboards and dressers creep out, as it were, on their own to keep company with the wheezing old men in the courtyard, and a little bird alights on the picket fence to sing a few songs for those who lately heard only the caterwauling of some heavily made-up tavern chanteuse, although the old men emphatically deny this. The song sparrow and goldfinch warble a different song from that of the wine-cellar songstress. And Countess Brunszvik, leader of the teetotal movement, surely must have understood what the birds were singing, for how else would she have been able to speak their language?

Miss Brunszvik lived in a two-storey house on White Eagle Place, the same house where, a century earlier at the time of the Martinovics conspiracy, the brides, fiancées and female acquaintances of the captured conspirators had gathered to confer, to pray and to endure – as described by His Worship the titular Bishop Fraknoi in his book (and a bishop is naturally more accurate writing about the adventures of young women than poets of the same period, who tend to mix up the hair colours, and never see clearly in matters of the feminine heart). For this reason, ever since then this two-storey building had a 'feminine' aura from which, according to some imaginations, emanated the nightingale-like strains of woeful women's songs and plaintive chants.

The Countess Brunszvik had a major role in liberating the men of Tabán from the influence of wine, and consequently from the magic spell cast by the flashing eyes of Gypsy women, the cockeyed smiles of tavern floozies, and proprietresses of taverns who are always ready for a fling. This Countess Brunszvik was a clean-living human being of the feminine gender, a candidate for sainthood whose miracles not even the wine-sellers' complaints could diminish.

Since the Countess was a newcomer to Budapest (with only a single relative here, a maternal uncle, a colonel, who now reposed in the military cemetery of the Watertown section of Buda), it was all the more remarkable that her endeavours succeeded without any effective intervention by her family.

She was a petite lady quite amply endowed in the region of the heart, and seemed to be one of those women born for love. Yet Countess Helen confuted the opinions of poets who, mostly counselled by wine, considered such *petite femmes* as the most desirable for their embraces. In fact Countess Helen was a living example of the saying that the smallest peppercorn packs the mightiest wallop. And fortitudinous she was indeed, at least in her heart and soul, for even if she did hear out the confessions of men who confused the ecstasies of wine with true love, and on moonlit nights loitered around her silent house on White Eagle Place, straining their bloodshot eyes at the cast-iron grille of the ground-floor windows, or at the balcony above while straining their feebly crooning vocal chords and capering ankles in expectation of a glimpse of the Countess – who, even if she did give ear to the spiels of these men who kept coming, under tattered clouds like warriors stuck in cellars back in the age of the Turkish wars, kept coming like rebel songsters about to put the reed of the shawm to their gap-toothed mouths, coming, like so many idle twangers on guitars, good-for-nothing strummers on the lute, moonstruck serenaders – even if she did give ear at times from her ground-floor window, left open by chance, or from her lookout on the upstairs balcony, to these sickening confessions of love (which Countess Helen thought should have been addressed to some parlour maid cornered in a dark corridor, or to a wandering witch with loose morals), she, Helen, paid no mind to these nocturnal vagabonds. And it wouldn't have occurred to her to call on the night watchman in his musty cape for protection, for protection against the caterwaulings of these gallants on the night watchman in his musty cape. Let Sasadi howl until he gets tired. And she had the same opinion about the other candidates who, in the old Tabán tradition, emerged around midnight from taverns, heartened by wine, song and companions' chivvying to venture forth and 'ensnare' the hearts of sleepless womenfolk.

It is possible, even probable, that before Countess Brunszvik's arrival here, there were one or two little misses who kicked off the eiderdown quilt and tiptoed on a moonbeam to their window when they heard the heroes of the tavern bawling out in the piazza. There might have been some misguided little girl whose fingers reached out between the slats of the shutters if her hand was small enough. Some of these hands might have received a ring or a bracelet; others, a love note scrawled in tears, wine, or blood – or else her knight might have offered a live calling card, to be grasped by the female hand like some whip handle in a dream where she is in the driver's seat, urging the magic steeds of passion. There were gallants who covered with hot kisses these hands reaching out from the windows of Tabán at night, without giving thought to the unhygienic acts these hands had been performing in the dead of night.

But Countess Brunszvik had never given her hand. It is equally true that she had never done what old crones in the Tabán like to do with the full chamberpot they keep on hand: toss the contents out the window at the mouths of minstrels singing down in the street.

So what did Countess Brunszvik in fact do, this early riser with her pink nose, her cheeks freshly washed with soap, her droll little mouth always hiding a secret smile, her melancholy brown eyes, her heart-shaped face, her blonde hair spun from songs and imaginings, and her soft voice – how did she manage to improve the world around her, without actually bestowing her heart and soul to reward reformed men?

3

Rimaszombati, who has devoted so much time to love

Miss Brunszvik targeted Mr Rimaszombati.

This gentleman, quite likely past seventy years old, was the undisputed ringleader of the drunkards of Tabán.

Rimaszombati, who retained his light-rye hair colour, was a gentleman who throughout his life preferred to look out at winter storms from underneath the tavern eaves, for which reason the snowy whiteness never quite conquered his head, although his coevals, the men seen mostly around churches, if at all, were model greybeards who had become sainted in their lifetime as they neared the nether world.

Rimaszombati's customary tone of voice recalled that of a merry traveller on a morning in early winter at a roadside inn where he has stopped for a few shots of brandy.

He was a man of compact build, with a beard in the imperial style, whose nasal septum sprouted three hairs, until this was called to his attention. His mouth had never pronounced the name of a respectable woman; his fairly numerous remaining teeth were always grinding out the names of those dubious ladies whose role in life is bestowing happiness on men. Otherwise, he devoted most of his pronouncements to the subjects of love, wine and song, as if a man's life was to be spent mostly in taverns, passing judgement on bar maids, as one judges various wines and comestibles. It happened that fate had allotted seventy years and more to this gentleman who rolled his words, twirled his moustache, jauntily wore a monocle on a string (at first he had started sporting a pince-nez mostly to facilitate his amorous conquests), and knew by heart nearly every poem penned about the ecstasies and excesses of love.

Even past seventy fortune had allowed him to retain an office job – true, only as part-time clerk, but it was at the Royal Hungarian High Court of Justice, where he was not well known, but this position brought him respect and sympathy. When he set out in the morning, clad in his lynx coat, a remnant of times past, he coughed and hawked to let the world know, both pedestrians and drivers of carriages, that he was on his way to the office. But in the afternoon, with the taste of lunch still lingering on his palate, he proceeded to a tavern in the Tabán, where the first words he uttered were: 'Boriska, Mariska, Juliska!' as if each woman whose name left his lips was his lover, to say the least. He quizzed them about the events of their recent nights, their experiences and adventures, because, he claimed, he never read the papers and relied on the hearsay of tavern girls to find out what was happening in the world. This ancient ragman had tied up into a bundle all the tales told by cashier ladies, for they confessed everything to him, knowing full well that they would find absolution. Having heard out all about these women's romantic afflictions, ailments and love affairs, he next examined their skirts, aprons and garters and handed out free advice even about details such as how much rouge to use on their cheeks.

'You're saying that Galgóczi hasn't been seen in three weeks?' Mr Rimaszombati inquired on that certain autumn day as the girl at the Green Ace set down his afternoon carafe of wine in front of him. (Rimaszombati drank it up as if it were medicine.)

'And we'll never see Galgóczi here again unless the Green Ace starts serving goat's milk,' replied the girl who was called Jolan Foamwhite, like so many other girls in this world, except that she was perhaps somewhat more emotional, sentimental, tender-hearted than other Jolans in general. Even though she wore a short skirt so that anyone who likes to scrutinize tavern-keepers' daughters could have a good view of her ankles, and she had permitted the sacristan at the nearby Serbian church to place his hand on her hip, Jolan's narrow forehead showed a certain mark displayed by women who live to suffer the torments of unhappy love. In her heart of hearts she was surely awaiting some stirring voice that would have caressed and warmed her, and her face would invariably flush whenever men in their cups began to explain the nature of the feelings they nurtured for her within their hairy chests.

'So Galgóczi hasn't been here in three weeks . . .' Mr Rimaszombati repeated. At the age of seventy he still considered making friends with men through the agency of women to be a better way to success than all that useless office work. 'One must get involved in love somehow!' Mr Rimaszombati was wont to state whenever he noticed an incipient attraction between a man and a woman. To spoil or to heat up the affair was all the same to Mr Rimaszombati. Therefore he was most surprised that Galgóczi, 'without a word to anyone', had stayed away from the Green Ace these three weeks.

In any case, he hurried to reassure the tavern-keeper's girl, whose torments had given her a cast in one eye, while her reddened eyelids spoke of midnight floods of tears. 'I'll make sure to find him for I do not tolerate unfaithful men among my friends.'

'Ah, unfaithful!' repeated Jolan, snapping up the word like a chicken does a hemp seed, for when a woman is unhappy, sometimes she can't find the simplest word until someone says it to her.

'Unfaithful, unfaithful,' she hummed to herself while doing her chores, alternating between tears and anger. It must have been market day in the Tabán because more people were clinking their glasses at the tables than usual.

For this reason, after a while Rimaszombati felt it advisable to offer a few words of comfort to the flustered girl: 'We don't know for sure that Galgóczi's been unfaithful.'

'Unfaithful!' replied Jolan Foamwhite, as if she would never relinquish this word that said it all.

When the waitress turned to go, Rimaszombati had to admit to himself that he noted a medicinal smell, such as the scent that surrounds a corpse. Could his wine have lost its taste? Outside, on White Eagle Place, the October sun shone red and jaunty.

'I think I smell an outlaw!' snorted Rimaszombati, as he did whenever he wanted to please some female acquaintance who saw in him only a harbinger of manhood who had lots of fine words to say about those who had sent him as their herald, while he himself had for quite some time been *hors de combat* in matters of serious masculinity.

'I smell an outlaw coming,' Rimaszombati repeated and huddled into the cobwebby bay window as if trying to catch a distant glimpse of the outlaws whose scent had preceded them on the wind.

4

The fate of those who drink too much wine

On White Eagle Place two hanged men were being carried away, in the very state they had strung themselves up.

We have seen large crowds gather to see the various guilds march forth with their huge flags aflutter, and religious banners also attract followers when paraded about in a procession. Even a police detachment marching with truncheons may draw many onlookers. But in the entire history of the Tabán district there has never been a multitude of the size that thronged White Eagle Place on this autumn day to accompany the two hanged men, Bitchkey and Botchkay, on their last journey.

Bitchkey, in his drunken stupor, had hanged himself by means of his belt on a crabapple tree, and his bodily attire, footwear and foot-rags hung down and trailed from his stiffly extended legs, just as they had when the crabapple tree was cut down to the roots. Now the dead man was being hauled away to the place where suicides are buried, together with his tree, for nobody dared to cut down the hanged man's rope. (Or possibly no knife could be found to cut the sturdy belt.)

At the same time, another procession turned up from a side street, lugging the door with its hook where Botchkay, a bosom pal of the above-mentioned Bitchkey, had hanged himself, also in his drunken doldrums, by means of some packing string that he had carried about in his pocket for days, cuddling it like a lover. Superstitious folk dared not tempt fate by touching the suicide so they removed the heavy door and used it to transport the body to the place of burial for suicides in the Tabán.

The two deceased men were loners who had not a soul in the world other than each other. Not even a lover could be found to accompany them, to weep for their miserable fate. Rimaszombati had seen events more remarkable than the wilful demise of these two orphans who had obviously decided on a mutual pact, but he still huddled wordlessly for quite a while at the window that opened so seldom to air out the Green Ace, watching the boot heels and slippers on the feet of that mass of humanity – men, women and children – shuffling past White Eagle Place. This malevolent spectacle so discombobulated him that he found himself striking a third matchstick to revive the half-smoked cigar he had thriftily saved. 'I knew that fellow!' he pronounced with a shrug, seeing Bitchkey and the crabapple tree taken away. 'Well, I'll be damned!' he muttered when he saw the brown door, with its upper part still showing traces of the letters C + M + B some parish clerk had chalked there on Epiphany day, now passing by the window, with the dead man strung up on the hook.

On occasions such as this old crones come forth from all kinds of stove pipes and dusty old tomes and put on black robes and jackets of faded green, airing underskirts that not even fleas bother to visit any more, in honour of the ill-starred pair of lushes; after them came in their blonde and autumn-gold gowns the younger women (who always manage to show up no matter how closely they are kept under lock and key), stepping past the dead men and their still live memories with an unfathomable indifference, blithely ignoring the fact that they were in part responsible for the demise of those two. Then darkness fell and one could hear those invisible people stopping in the streets, these who, ever since the world began, like to discuss the events of the day. One voice stubbornly saws away like some woodsman on a sawhorse, and his companion grunts periodically, just to say something; another unseen one enthuses, planting his back against the mouldy wall of a building, unwilling to move before fully expounding his detailed opinion on suicides; a third one has a voice that creaks like a key grinding the lock of a gate in the evening, a voice to make the hair stand on the back of your neck while its owner passes judgement on the hanged men. These invisible men, these windbags who stick their noses into everything, were muttering in the darkness outside the tavern that now it was Rimaszombati's turn, he was the next in line among the town drunks to hang himself in an outhouse (so they opined).

'I'll let the lovers go first!' was Rimaszombati's courteous reply to these invisible ones who really start to speak up after the third or fourth cup of wine, when the bibulous man begins to commune with his soul.

5

The manners of divas, both foreign and local

'I think I'll let the lovers precede me in the order of hanging!' declared Rimaszombati, afraid that he had not quite got the words right, concerned as he was, as an affiliate of the Royal Hungarian High Court of Justice, always to employ the correct terms of expression.

'In any event, Jolan, let's get spruced up and go to Countess Brunszvik's soirée, as long as we've been invited,' he said to the tavern-keeper's daughter who, in spite of her unhappiness, loved to attend social gatherings.

Mother-of-pearl buttons adorned Jolan's grey, so-called 'coachman's' cape with wings that made her look like some foreign lady who had wandered into the Tabán by mistake. This same coachman's cape could have been seen in metropolitan Vienna. A fragrantly scented soap had scrubbed away the onion smell from her hands (that not even the most exquisite of tavern-keepers' daughters can escape). A red velvet beret strained to contain her spray of blonde curls, those tendrils having an ardent young life of their own, untamable by human hand. 'That's right,' quoth Rimaszombati, 'the young lady's mane is like a horse's tail. There's no crupper that will keep a filly's tail from slapping you around.' This bon mot was intended by Rimaszombati as a compliment to Jolan's hair and we only mention it in order to give some idea of the rest whispered into her ear as he, the proper cavalier, escorted her to the house on White Eagle Place while managing not to be flattened by the autumn wind or the coughing fits that seize you by the throat when you venture forth from the hothouse air of a tavern. Jolan's black velvet shoes fluttered their butterfly wing laces to the tattoo rattled out by her heels. 'I'd like to stay by your side until the end of the world!' stammered Rimaszombati in solemn devotion, hanging on to the girl's arm for dear life.

At the town house on White Eagle Place the guests were greeted by the wedding march from *Lohengrin*, as at some church wedding. Countess Brunszvik artfully rendered the tune on a reed harmonium, always so soothing for the soul.

Next on the programme was Mrs Kornicky, former alto soloist at the Bazilika, now performing only at Sunday musical masses at churches in Buda, yet still pursued by jealous intrigue. Even the mildest choir masters became incensed by the wild and unbelievable rumours her colleagues circulated about Mrs Kornicky, although down in the nave one would like to believe that only angels dwelled up there in the organ loft, behaving angelically. Well yes, they did sing like angels, especially Mrs Kornicky and her like, who had studied with Károly Noseda or at Kanitz's school, but beyond that their activities could not be called angelic. At the town house on White Eagle Place this alto diva sang her heart out, lavishing all her vocal treasures in the cause of teetotalism, while her aigrettes quivered like the head-dresses worn by horses drawing a funeral hearse. At the end of her song the singer spat, following the custom of foreign divas performing at the Budapest Opera House.

After the vocal rendition the indefatigable Helen Brunszvik and her harmonium accompanied a violinist. The player was a local music teacher who only a day or two earlier had been one of the most inveterate drunkards of Tabán, comparable in the amounts of liquor consumed to the bassoonist of Krucifix Street, whose apartment even on the tenth anniversary of his death yielded up secret bottles of brandy stashed in the cupboard. But our music teacher, pimply-faced, tentative-handed, hoarse-voiced, scrawny and tubercular-looking, had been converted by Countess Brunszvik, and now played a movement from a Mass on his violin, the piece he had once played for the Bishop at the cathedral in Veszprem, when he had been in love with a fat soprano about whom all he remembered was her tight-fitting yellow skirt with a hand's breadth of blue ribbon edging. That skirt had driven him to excessive drinking, and in return for his conversion Helen Brunszvik had promised to find a similarly attired lady for the musician. Was there anything that this blessed creature would not do to make a talented man give up the drink that leads to an early grave?

This performance by the singer and the violinist had a beneficial effect on the audience whose delight in entertainments for the heart and soul was all the keener when the admission was free.

Among those attending were some who had taken the pledge earlier, such as Guguli the gingerbread-maker whose shop had been in the same location for the past century and a half, with the sign on the door reading 'Apprentice Wanted' these same 150 years, until Guguli came to realize that his business had had one flaw all this time: namely, that his earnings got left behind at the taverns that were found in such abundance in the environs of both Buda and Pest, especially at the fairgrounds and in the neighbourhoods frequented by Guguli while peddling his merchandise. He had as many adventures as any stall-keeper, but as a rule he never remembered how these ended for at each fair he managed to find the booth that sold the best wine and there he would forget all.

Among the takers of the pledge was Arkus, the borough council clerk, whose constant inebriation at last forced him to decide between office or tavern, and he opted to become one of Countess Brunszvik's little lambs – although no one would have believed this possible for a man with such a tremor, wine-reddened nose, face and neck, and teeth that were starting to fall out.

The situation was quite different in the case of Captain Poturicsics, who had tried just about everything in his long career as a ship's captain along the Danube, both up and downstream from the Iron Gate. An ocean-going ship's captain who is away from his family for months at a time will easily join any kind of 'crew' with whom he can while the time away. So now he joined a 'crew' where the chief entertainment was reviling wine-drinkers left and right, day and night. The captain thought he might as well join this 'crew' as any other.

As for Weinsong, the Tabán landlord, he was only a titular landlord, so for him it was all the same what office he accepted, since there weren't that many to choose from.

Among those present we should single out Lenke Mariancsics, who probably had weighty reasons to wear 'half-mourning' in order to forget her past. This blonde young lady, commonly known under the monicker 'the angel of Tabán', could be seen until recently in just about every local tavern where wine was drunk, prank followed upon prank, life was always seen in its friendly aspects and the only thing patrons dreaded was loneliness. Nor did Lenke like to be left alone with her grim and emaciated mother, whose stories she had heard hundreds of times; she longed for the company of males who always had something new and entertaining to say (even if they lied) – that is why, after all, they were men.

Now men were to be found mostly in two places: in barracks and in taverns (for those praying in monasteries do not count, for the most part). Lenke preferred the taverns, where she always ran into some acquaintance who fully empathized with the difficult situation of a 'lonely gal'. A poor, solitary girl abandoned by all to wilt away here in the Tabán, awaiting her twentieth birthday when her shoes will have worn away, all her clothes will have gone out of fashion, and she will have forgotten what it was to be young and to give men a taste of her nails, scratch-marks that seemed to please them to no end . . .

The taverns of Tabán never lacked for understanding souls who were truly gladdened when a young lady at their table announced that she liked her wine as much as any man but for the sake of decency could not slake her thirst except in small glassfuls, for which she apologized. 'The angel of Tabán' always had a mellowing influence on men huddled at a corner table with one hand over the heart to keep it from bursting out of the vest and the other hand clutching the glass to gulp down the medicine with due urgency whenever the pain became unbearable. These men had acquired their injuries here and there in the course of their lives, mostly in those feminine places where males acquire their incurable wounds. Nor could it be said that Lenke

Mariancsics had ever sent a man with a 'hollow leg' packing; anyhow, such men are usually reluctant to rise from the table for fear of breaking a leg after taking a step or two. Thus Lenke was no miracle-worker – but could a girl from the Tabán be blamed for that?

So here was Lenke Mariancsics greeting Mr Rimaszombati with a nod from far off (she believed in greeting men first), at the same time also acknowledging her friend, the tavern-keeper's daughter. She would have liked her acquaintances by her side, but this was not possible, especially since she stood in a window bay all by herself like a weeping willow, exposed to glances from the audience that seemed to blame her for all the wine-guzzling in the Tabán – whereas she, poor thing, as we have pointed out, had acted only out of charitable intentions towards men.

Mr Rimaszombati and Jolan found shelter by Mr Sasadi's side, in the 'Sasadi corner', as the nook occupied by Sasadi in any Tabán tavern was generally called. He had a handsome Hungarian face, red-brown and hawk-nosed, with a large moustache and melancholy eyes, a real Hungarian hunk of a man in spite of his Schwabian German heritage. For it is well known that the Hungarian braves in former days had always visited these German villages around the Buda hills for the sole purpose of harvesting wine and women. By this time Sasadi lived the life of a ghost, dwelling in the old Tabán graveyard, a chieftain, as it were, of those homeless men who had for years persisted in the district. (There was a number of such men in the Tabán, who took their naps in taverns, disappearing for a while when the place was cleaned, for they had no other home.) Sasadi did have a home but preferred to be near his little daughter's grave whenever a longing for the nether world seized him. It was this journey that Countess Helen Brunszvik intended to prevent.

'No wonder the Countess objects to drinking wine,' said

Rimaszombati, after a single glance at Countess Helen's rosy nose. 'The Countess has a kidney condition that makes her abstain from alcohol.'

At times Rimaszombati emitted surprising comments like that, as evidence of his worldly experience. But now the music ceased and the Countess stepped up on the podium. Such platforms, usually seen in schoolrooms, may be found in certain private homes where matters of consequence are solemnly discussed.

'The other day I happened to notice that somebody at the Black Dog had a little boy bring him a penny's worth of writing ink,' the Countess began, as if about to tell a tale. 'But never in the course of my sojourn here have I seen anyone ordering a penny's worth of wine from Poldi's, or from the Green Ace. And yet writing ink is at least as precious as wine – for one thing, it will never drive you as crazy as wine does.'

Having begun her daily sermon in this manner, Countess Brunszvik continued with a witty and fluent diatribe against the drinking of wine.

As she stood there on the podium, short of stature but long on courage, glancing without any embarrassment at the masculine audience, all eyes staring at her, at first she gave no sign of the hidden talents inside her. She held forth, but then most womenfolk who are not easily intimidated are good at that. But as she warmed to her topic she became ever more fascinating because of what she had to say. If nothing else, it became apparent that here was a young lady of refinement opening her heart and soul to the affairs and troubles besetting the petty lives of her audience. She came at last to the case of Bitchkey and Botchkay, the two suicides by hanging.

'Surely they could have become useful members of society had they been able to give up some of their inveterate habits.

For example, by apportioning their addiction to wine into smaller instalments, say by expending one portion of their passion by indulging in an afternoon hike in the hills of Buda, devoting another portion to the reading of books, and a final third, possibly, to love – of which they could have had their share since they were still quite young. This way they could have divided up their lives into portions, instead of escaping into suicide in the manner of those who had grown tired of it all. What good is it to die without having first lived? What good is it to go underground before one has had a chance to look around at this beauteous world stretching into endless distances, unimaginable for those who sit by a bottle in a tavern and trouble themselves only to count the number of glasses consumed?'

'They started the same way as everyone else, by drinking toasts to the fatherland and the king!' Mr Rimaszombati interjected in his creaky voice, concerned that Miss Brunszvik may not have noted his presence since she had not bothered to chide him.

Yet for some time now Countess Brunszvik had been keeping an eye on her 'nemesis', this short-statured gentleman of the Tabán whose ambition, everyone knew, was to make a livelihood by brokering 'romantic relationships' in the district, to which end even forbidden passions were gladly facilitated by him as long as there was something in it for himself. Oh yes, Helen Brunszvik was well aware of Rimaszombati's presence but refused to acknowledge the 'opposition' because she considered his escorting the tavern-keeper's daughter from the Green Ace to be highly inappropriate. She could not ask him to leave, for the event was open to the public, but she consistently looked the other way whenever Rimaszombati launched into his characteristically ostentatious coughing, as he would in a tavern when he wanted to make a new acquaintance.

Therefore Countess Brunszvik went on with her monologue

about the glasses of wine that some men made it their lives' ambition to keep track of. Although, truth to tell, people use all sorts of excuses for drinking in taverns, for the devil makes tavern-keepers and their customers fiendishly inventive. For instance, just think of the kind of women that drive men to drink! The tavern-goer does not drink on account of the poor woman abandoned to worries and cares, all alone in her home night and day, but instead drinks because of those females who have it too good, better than they deserve. Bibulous men like to drink to such women precisely because thinking of them is no skin off their back, because these women are always seen as carefree and smiling, ever cheerful, even in retrospect. So they drink to such ladies, may they keep smiling and stay happy ever and anon, like harp-playing angels in the world to come, awaiting the righteous. And naturally not a glass is drained to toast the one sighing and crying and praying at home all by herself. No, they never drink a drop to toast their sweet, silent, faithful wives.

'Whoa! What kind of world would it be if every man in a tavern were only allowed to drink to his wife!' exclaimed Rimaszombati, who, as a widower, was not exactly a concerned party.

The alto singer, most likely with reasons of her own for curtailing any further discussion of the affairs of women toasted by tavern regulars, now stepped forward to the platform and asked the Countess's permission to perform a gospel psalm sure to have an effect.

The Countess, who had no intention of starting a debate with Mr Rimaszombati, who had arrived arm-in-arm with the tavern-keeper's daughter, yielded to the singer's call and settled down by the harmonium. Soon the congregation, under the guidance of the lead singer, was indeed chanting a sacred hymn.

6

A wretched man inquires about the suicides who perished because of wine

After the song ended a knocking was heard on the wall. Since nobody moved in the room, yet the knocking continued, it had to come from a neighbouring room.

Inhabitants of the Tabán district usually don't scare easily when hearing a knock coming from the wall, the cellar, or even from a cupboard; residents of this ancient neighbourhood hear ghosts all the time, and that includes the terminally ill making their pact with death as they prepare for the world to come. Dying is merely going out to the local cemetery on a gloomy day and not coming back.

'I am at home to any man of good will!' was Countess Brunszvik's response to the repeated knocking.

The door to the adjacent room opened and for a moment only the sounds of the autumn wind could be heard, the autumn wind that furtively enters the Tabán at sundown, and by night makes itself at home in the zig-zag side streets, whipping around corners and houses built in such a variety of styles, penetrating all nooks and crannies and, given room, is sure to gust forth with a mischievous whistle through an open door or window. Yes, you must know the Tabán wind if you wish to make head or tail of the knocks in this world.

The wind sobbed and hissed as if to give notice that while here, indoors, sacred hymns were sung, it had arisen out in the street and taken charge of the shop signs and gas lamps, buffeting anyone caught outdoors.

Over the howling wind the rain could be heard as well, just as the rattling of a drummer who nods off, then snaps awake to add an occasional drum roll to the evening sounds, so the rain selects a roof or a wall to drum out its own song before moving on with a halting chuckle, having doused the palisade fence. This kind of weather, so common in the Tabán during late autumn, is said to benefit tavern-keepers.

After more than a minute with all eyes on the dark doorway, a figure at last appeared in the opening.

'Galgóczi!' went one lady's heart pit-a-pat under the coachman's cape, and all three hairs on Mr Rimaszombati's nose probably would have stood on end, had he not shaved them off earlier that week.

A female heart was set thrumming, then choked up, incapable of any further action. All the more reason for Rimaszombati to watch out, and so he removed the pince-nez from his near-sighted eyes and began to rub the lenses with a piece of chamois he had acquired at the Exposition of 1885 when he worked as a guide showing provincial visitors the sights of the capital.

Galgóczi had once been a cavalryman, with dark complexion shaved to a bluish hue, his moist lips always pursed ready to whistle. But now he looked like a cadaver that had been laid out in a coffin for the past three weeks.

'Maybe he's really died and returned to haunt!' Jolan later recounted at the Green Ace, recalling the moment of Galgóczi's appearance in the doorway.

Miss Brunszvik made a hurried move towards the guest, as if to help him enter the room with his unwieldy, windblown cape, wild hair and head tossed back. As Galgóczi's lanky, sagging frame entered the room it became evident that he was too thin for ready-made clothes; his emaciation would have bedevilled any tailor. His neck, that fine and statuesque neck, now showed a round hollow the size of a fist, like the imprint of some wasting illness. His pipe-stem arms would have suited a scarecrow and his overlong hair seemed to be tugged by the invisible hand that tugs at the hair of those who drink excessively.

Miss Brunszvik pulled up a chair for Galgóczi, who did not look as if he had the strength to remain standing. Even so he averted his eyes and looked down in such bitter shame as if he meant to part from them forever, never to look another human being in the eye. He appeared so helpless that, had his mother been alive, she would have picked him up in her arms and cuddled him as she would a baby. 'Why can't I just die!' he sighed, apparently without any appetite for life, and sank into the chair.

That's how badly our Galgóczi was done in – and no one dared to say a word to him, for what can you say to a man who was the cause of his own illness?

Now the violinist collected himself, to his credit: this ragtag musician raised his instrument and started to play the aria from *Robert le Diable*, for that was the first thing that came to mind. Miss Brunszvik, mild as an angel from heaven, accompanied the melody on the harmonium as well as she could.

Meanwhile Galgóczi opened one eye to look around: 'Where is my friend Bitchkey?' he demanded, whereupon the violinist began to ply his bow more fortissimo, while the questionable alto started to wave her hand as vehemently as if Galgóczi had uttered some sort of blasphemy.

When the music paused Galgóczi spoke again. 'And where is my pal Botchkay?' echoed his sepulchral voice, such as the dead use to query leaves fallen on their graves.

'Both promised to be here,' continued Galgóczi, looking around with a sadness so profound it nearly petrified bystanders.

Surveying the room, Galgóczi's eyes moved past Jolan of the Green Ace without pausing to look at her, indifferent beyond indifference. (Jolan's heart froze in that instant, while her eyes remained fixed straight ahead.)

Galgóczi just kept staring, his aspect growing desperate, as he received no response from anyone.

Seeing that folks instinctively began to back away from Galgóczi, Rimaszombati, just for old times' sake, placed his hand on his friend's shoulder: 'We're still waiting for you at the Green Ace! Why don't you come?' He might as well have asked a deaf man.

Listless, Galgóczi swung his droopy head, unable to reply.

At last Miss Brunszvik spoke up. She urged Galgóczi not to exhaust himself and, taking his arm in the manner of a practised nurse, led him from the room. At the threshold Galgóczi turned around once more as if still searching for Bitchkey and Botchkay in the assembled crowd. Jolan of the Green Ace stuck out her tongue at him, the only revenge she could think of in her sudden bereavement.

7

Concerning one about whom songs are written

By now it had become obvious that Miss Brunszvik was holding in captivity the man formerly known as Galgóczi, the man who had aroused so much hope in the Tabán. It was still unknown whether Galgóczi had willingly entered or had been forcibly swept into his current situation.

Kuvik, vendor of popular songs, a penny a dozen, who sold broadsides of his love lyrics at fairs after crooning them in the voice of a fairground barker, and thus maintained certain contacts with feminine hearts in the Tabán (as well as other parts of town), dropped this casual comment between two songs: 'Galgóczi'd be a goner without Miss Brunszvik's support.'

But several off-duty chambermaids now arrived and Kuvik resumed singing a song he had written, in a voice as heart-rending as only he could produce. One had to wait for another pause before Kuvik could be questioned further: 'Doesn't Galgóczi have anyone else to care for him?'

'No one gives a damn about a man when the liquor in him catches fire. He's got to burn down by himself,' replied Kuvik.

At the Green Ace, Galgóczi's peculiar state was much discussed. It caused no surprise among the patrons to see Jolan circulating in a black skirt and black stockings, or to hear sobs coming from the room where the tavern-keeper's daughter retired for quarters of an hour at a time. Only a woman who truly suffers can weep like that within the four walls of her room and then emerge to face humanity after having cried herself out. Mr Rimaszombati sat gloomily twirling a toothpick between his fingers while he waited for these fifteen-minute sessions to end. If the sobs lasted a few minutes longer, he was moved to approach her little bedchamber, listen at her door and rap softly. 'Jolan, that's enough for now. Leave some for later,' he admonished, as if the amount Jolan was allowed to cry 'at one sitting' in memory of her lost love depended on this gentleman who so willingly busied himself with matters feminine.

Did Jolan take Rimaszombati's advice? She did, for in the midst of major bereavement it feels good to know that someone cares about how much we can weep without hurting ourselves. She obeyed, if for no other reason than to give the lie to those who predicted that after Bitchkey and Botchkay the tavern-keeper's daughter would be the next to hang herself. (In those simple days Tabán folk thought the only way of doing yourself in was hanging.) Jolan powdered her face and, using a brush sprinkled with water, did her hair up starting at the nape, the way depressed women are likely to, and emerged from her little room very pale in the face, circulating among the guests silent as a martyr resigned to her fate. Snippets of the song-peddler's stanzas floated in from the outside: he was singing about a girl of good family who squandered her love on an unworthy man. Possibly Kuvik wrote this song with the present case in mind, but we cannot be entirely certain.

8

Which skirt to wear if you want to have your way

Not everyone mourned alongside Jolan of the Green Ace.

In the Tabán it was mostly the oldest matrons who dyed their single suit of clothes black, and only when they had abandoned all hope of wearing any other colour. Younger women liked to show off their flair for colour, for a simple girl without means can best show that she has taste by wearing colours that express her character and mood. The Tabán had its share of deep-blue fabrics, the finer kind that make you look so distinguished, provided the cut is right. Likewise the Tabán had its share of green and lilac outfits, springtime skirts worn in late autumn, as well as those russet fabrics skilfully tinted by the dyer's art so that few can tell the original colour of the dress.

Jolan soon realized she had won no admirers with her black skirt, black stockings and black beret (which sometimes stayed on her head even in the restaurant). Men's eyes, looking out the window, are more likely to be snagged by a yellow skirt (not to mention a red one) than a black dress. Not even Jolan could have wished the jackdaws on the tower of the nearby Serbian church cawing forever about her black apparel, even if a few men did praise her black stockings, chiefly Rimaszombati, who wouldn't dream of a lady's legs without the black stockings that so faithfully reveal their shapeliness. Jolan deliberated at length about what outfit to wear next. Should she appear in the long blue skirt with white polka dots, the one that those prankish gentlemen frequenting the Green Ace from the Pest side had already proposed to cut up and wear as neckties, or else the red one with white highlights that she had long ago promised to Mr Rimaszombati, who wanted it as a souvenir? In the end she opted for a fawn-coloured skirt with cute Tyrolean pockets to thrust her hands in when conversing with a man.

'Hm. So this is how long we mourn for a fiancée?' Mr Rimaszombati asked abruptly, after scrutinizing, through his spring-loaded pince-nez, Jolan's mountain-climbing skirt and especially the green stockings that went with it.

'I wasn't aware that Galgóczi and I were engaged.'

'But I know very well that you were,' replied Rimaszombati. 'How can you imagine that I would have helped bring about an unlawful liaison? How could anyone who knows me think that? I respect the law more than anyone else in this land. No one can say anything black or white about me and that's the truth.'

Jolan was thunderstruck hearing the old man say this, for no matter how you cut it, the social order of the Tabán to this day still demands respect for the older generation.

'You don't like what I'm wearing?' she asked, dropping the matter of the engagement, for truth to tell, she had on more than one occasion confessed to Mr Rimaszombati intimate details about long walks in the Buda Hills, visits to the Watertown cemetery, complete with fights and painful silences that occur all the time between young women and men. Jolan had time off from the Green Ace only on certain afternoons, the fate of all girls whose parents run a tavern, and those afternoons rarely went by without a lovers' tiff. Jolan had a quick temper, while Galgóczi wasn't one to abandon a notion once he got it inside his head – he would stubbornly insist on treating Jolan as his intended (to say the least), whenever their walks led to the more abandoned paths in the cemetery or the woods.

'So you don't like my outfit?' Jolan asked a second time, no longer feeling inclined to thrust her hand in a skirt pocket while talking with Mr Rimaszombati.

'You own an outrageous skirt that, when you wear it, creates a storm in the Tabán that tickles each and every beard and moustache, even those that are not even fit to be used as oakum . . . That skirt sets everyone's boots a-creaking like whinnying steeds eager to take their master on the road. Why, even the most ancient hats are slapped on at a rakish angle when your little old self decides to wear that skirt,' said Rimaszombati, pronouncing his words as precisely as a meteorologist would his weather report.

'So, which one is that ill wind-producing skirt?' asked Jolan in an impish tone. 'You don't mean the one so tight I can barely walk, the skirt that was so screwed up by the seamstress?'

'I can't speak for others, but as for myself, when I look at a woman I have to see some of her form,' said Mr Rimaszombati with an air of self-importance, as if he had invented this wise saying. 'What else are these two eyes for? I might as well strain and wear them out, as long as I get something for my trouble.'

Possibly Jolan was not the only woman unable to resist when a man explains so earnestly why he prefers to see her in one skirt and not another. Rimaszombati was right after all: one must pick and choose which sights to see in the 'little time' left to live.

Therefore Jolan pulled on the rose-pink skirt she was too embarrassed to wear even when alone in her room.

'Now I see no further objection to our redirecting Galgóczi to the right path he had strayed from,' pronounced the oldest patron of taverns in the Tabán, who hated to see anyone giving up taverns while still in his prime. There would be time enough for that after you were dead.

9

A most important chapter about kissing

Since this was a fast day, perhaps the skirt was not quite appropriate for the spirit of the occasion, because its brevity and tightness tended to evoke days of the flesh, making a man muse about what a feast savages (those cannibals!) would make of Jolan's calves if by some chance she were shipwrecked on some distant island – but the afflicted are not obliged to observe fast days. And Jolan was lovesick, an affliction considered to be the equal of any fatal illness. (Haven't you ever been ready to die for love, if not right away then soon?)

'We still have to rehearse our song, "Bathing in Moonlight", to be sure all goes well,' said Mr Rimaszombati when, as on every other occasion, he examined the pink skirt Jolan was wearing to make sure it had no hidden flaws that only his practised eye could pick out.

'Bathing in Moonlight' was in fact Mr Rimaszombati's favourite tune, the song of his heart that he had, as senior carouser, at one time or another forced upon every single patron of the Green Ace. He had taught Jolan how to perform the song (leaning on

Mr Rimaszombati's shoulder) the way he had once heard it sung one amateur night in the village of Batyi by a young lady whose name nobody remembered any more except for Mr Rimaszombati on certain days. Jolan was very quick to learn the things that form part of a girl's education; seeing Mr Rimaszombati's tears made her eyes moist, for he invariably wept when this song was hummed into his ear.

'And let's make sure to take some wine with us!' the aged bon vivant exclaimed. It was full moon and the almanack had predicted clear and cold weather. The hands of the clock approached midnight, when silence reigns in the Tabán as a rule, regardless of the poor reputation of the district.

The bottle had a bold and jaunty long neck, around which they tied a red, white and green ribbon of the national tricolour after filling it with wine. Jolan carried the bottle hidden under the cape we have spoken of earlier. Exiting the Green Ace, Mr Rimaszombati sniffed at the air: 'I smell an eastern wind, a great rarity in our part of the world where winds mostly come from the north-west or the south.'

Jolan had no qualms about trusting herself to Mr Rimaszombati at the midnight hour, for the courtly gentleman's potential danger to women was limited to the rare days when he 'sensed a feminine aroma', such as he had the last time in 1898, accidentally entering a sewing school where twelve girls were sewing shirts, supervised by a most inviting matron. The 'feminine aroma' saturating that room still haunted Mr Rimaszombati and made him by turns pensive, agitated, musing – a dream that would remain unforgettable until the end of his life. 'For a woman will give off one scent in church, prostrate at a side altar, practically collapsed in supplication and prayer. She will have another smell at a tavern, theatre or ball, when she is ticklish and giggly, overcome by laughter and merriment, for a woman's organism cannot withstand your more powerful stimuli. She has yet another scent at home, immersed in domestic chores, worries and cares, for women at home are preoccupied solely with their own things. Their truly feminine scent can only be encountered in a sewing school, where they confide their wishes, dreams and fantasies to each other while sewing a shirt.'

Such edifying conversation filled the time while Miss Jolan and Mr Rimaszombati roamed the empty streets in the moonlight, streets empty of people, that is. For in the Tabán (as perhaps elsewhere in the world) moonlight wakes the things that are asleep in daytime, or that behave as if they did not belong in the daylight world. Now the roof ridge arches like the back of a tomcat. The moonlit chimney resembles some antique hat worn by a former landlord. The tower of the Serbian church stretches its shadow as if reaching for the spot where treasure was once buried, but no enterprising spirit arrives to dig where the church tower's shadow points at midnight on a certain night of the year. The courtyards may be asleep but moonbeams lend them various colours and shapes here and there where underwear was left to dry on wash lines. Men's ample long johns cast shadows of a different shape to women's slender nightgowns. This is the time when drainpipes jutting from eaves, the baker's shop sign, the grocer's signboard, the reposing wings of the door and the windowpanes can all converse about their lot, because in the daytime they must serve humans. The baby on the midwife's sign keeps only one eye on this nocturnal colloquy for she must be on call even at night. Passing the midwife's house, Rimaszombati was moved to remark: 'One of these days I'll have her give me an enema, for I hear it's supposed to help the digestion.'

But the operation would have to wait for another occasion, for Mr Rimaszombati suddenly remembered something and led Jolan into the shadow of the church tower. No one was there, for any errant soul roaming the Tabán at this hour would choose some moonlit place. They were alone in the dark; Mr Rimaszombati stood protectively by the side of his protégée.

'I'd meant to ask you before: what kind of kisses did you teach Galgóczi?' Rimaszombati now interrogated Jolan.

Jolan did not reply for she did not always answer the barrage of questions her old friend aimed at her; therefore Rimaszombati went on:

'We come across all kinds of kisses in this world before we find the real one, the kiss we never forget until our dying day – no matter what we experience along the way, here and there, the way things go . . . We have to taste many kinds of kisses until we reach the true one and recognize it as such. Could it be you never really gave him an honest to goodness kiss, little girl?'

'Mr Rimaszombati, what do you mean by a real kiss? Everyone kisses to the best of their ability,' answered Jolan, aiming to put an end to the discussion.

'Not so, my child. Kisses begin with a kiss to the hand. For a start, we must know where and how to kiss a woman's hand. There are some who toss off a kiss to the hand as they would some indifferent remark, or as if performing some obligation, as did the citizens of Castile in the days when for lack of the real thing they were obliged to kiss Queen Isabella's gloves or slippers. Real kisses on the hand and foot were already commonplace by then. The hand kiss must be placed where the glove ends and leaves the wrist uncovered; the knowing man positions his kiss over the pulsating artery. Kissing the feet one has to aim at the ankle, and some prefer to kiss behind the knee,' said Rimaszombati. 'Where did Galgóczi like to kiss your leg?'

'Once he bit me on the knee, so I slapped his face.'

'There you go!' exclaimed Rimaszombati, as if he had made

a great discovery. 'Galgóczi bowed down at your feet, which is proper, but instead of kissing your heel or your ankle as another man would, he went straight for the knee. I, for one, can think of a better place on the leg.'

'Galgóczi was drunk,' said Jolan in defence of her young man.

Rimaszombati gave this some thought, staring into space as if trying to imagine from every angle that kiss on the knee perpetrated by Galgóczi. 'You must have placed your foot on a stool, or stepped up on a stone, the way an equestrienne strikes a pose for the photographer, or indeed anyone inclined towards the profession of circus performer. Where did you put your foot when Galgóczi happened to kiss your knee?' persisted the old man.

'I didn't put my foot anywhere. Galgóczi went down on his knees before me and threatened to kill himself.'

'Why can't he think and act like that again!' exclaimed Mr Rimaszombati ardently, as he conducted his protégée away from the church tower's shadow, where the buried treasure lay.

Shortly afterwards they arrived at the shadow cast by the statue that spreads its wings on one of the piazzas in Tabán. This kind of statue is circumambulated by processions of the faithful on a certain day of the year, then forgotten for another twelve months. Rimaszombati stopped in the shadow of this statue and spoke.

'I just remembered why Galgóczi placed that kiss on your knee. In the old days when women still tied their garters into a floppy butterfly bouquet below the knee, the knee itself was considered intimate territory only a lover was entitled to reach. By means of this knee-kiss Galgóczi meant to signify that he was far more intimate with you than those who are satisfied with a kiss on the ankle. Am I right, senorita?' pressed the old gentleman, as gleeful as if he had uncovered some secret.

'Who can tell what's on a man's mind!' sighed Jolan, as one

after another she recalled scenes from the past when she had had no reason to worry about why Galgóczi kissed her in one place and not another.

In the shadow of the statue Rimaszombati grew bolder. God only knows why men are more courageous in some locations. Grasping Jolan by the wrist he looked deep into her eyes in the moonlight.

'We haven't yet spoken about how Galgóczi performed the act of adoration on the mouth and face that some call kissing? Some men, no matter where they are, will start to kiss given the least opportunity. They will kiss behind the fireplace because they believe the inglenook exists for the purpose of stealing a kiss. They will kiss in the wardrobe, closet, cellar, attic or in the pantry just because they believe that a minute without kisses is a minute wasted. And certain mouths were indeed made for kissing. Especially rabbit lips, lamb lips and fawn lips. It is not your broad, thick lips that really know how to deliver a kiss – but lips shaped like the bulb of a lily. Lips like that can cling tight enough to cause in some cases choking, heart attacks and other lethal damage. They can cover every last particle of the mouth like a well-placed seal. They are able to maintain contact for minutes on end, during which true believers claim to be in heaven. Those lips suck at each other, suck until at times they draw blood, which is said to be sweetest in a heated state. It is essential that no air come between the lips, for air stands for the world and the slanderous speech of humans that would forever part those lips from each other. I have heard of cases where lovers kissed so torridly that they became as inseparable as Siamese twins.'

'Hmm!' said Jolan, as if her heart had given a start.

Rimaszombati interpreted this as a sign of success, so he went on faster and faster, as if he were rubbing Aladdin's lamp.

'But most of the time no harm comes to those who kiss only the lips because nature in her infinite wisdom has devised ways to part lips from each other. Kissing makes the lips swell until kisses turn painful, although for some this merely makes it all the more enjoyable. The perils of kissing begin the instant the tongues that lie hidden inside mouths start interfering with the business of the lips; for example when a tongue becomes bored with always receiving only the tastes and juices coming from the direction of the lips and decides to set out from the interior of its lair in order to explore and feel its way around inside the adjoined mouth. They say the tongue has no eye and sets out blindly on its adventures. Blind tongue, my eye! Just ask those who favour tongue kisses if a tongue had ever ventured anywhere it didn't wish to go? No matter how fickle, a tongue feels at home only where it is welcome. It will go out of its way to befriend teeth it has nothing to do with normally, and palpate incisors and molars in another mouth. The tongue gets to know before anyone else how many cavities hide in a mouth that only the dentist had seen until then. It roams through the enchanted garden of the neighbouring mouth and reports if cabbage or cotton candy had been consumed before kissing. I don't mean to boast but I know a tongue that can identify the year of a vintage after meeting the lips of a lady winegrower.'

'Hmm . . .' purred Jolan.

'But the tongue kiss is far more dangerous than it seems at a glance. There are tongues not satisfied with exploring the tastes and mysteries of the mouth, but must venture further down – as far as the throat, for instance. They penetrate, swell into and fill up the throat so that not a drop of air can get by. Women who had been seduced, cheated and abandoned like to kill their men this way . . . The kiss you awake from in the next world,' added Rimaszombati, turning grave, for he had not intended to speak of this category of kissing, only the night had inspired him to utter words that, once pronounced, could not be withdrawn.

Hmm! Lost in her thoughts, Jolan savoured the taste of the above-mentioned kiss. It must be strange to die in the middle of a kiss.

'Jealousy teaches women that kind of kiss. Many a man has met his maker that way. It is called the witch's kiss and many doubt its existence, for those who received it are now silent underground and those who bestowed it would not confess to it even when burned at the stake for witchcraft of other kinds. Why, Queen Elizabeth of England was aware of this type of kiss; she knew far more than her contemporaries gave her credit for. And Empress Catherine the Great knew about it, because sorcerers reveal far more to a sovereign than to a commoner. Catherine de Medici practised it, and possibly Queen Maria of Hungary, to silence her lovers before they had a chance to blab out the secrets of a queen. Before the courtier could spill the beans about the happy hours spent together, about moments of weakness, the loss of innocence and feminine honour, the eternal secrets of womenfolk: here came the witch's kiss and did its job. The Queen stuck her tongue way down into her knight's throat.'

The clock in the tower struck one as if to put a full stop to Rimaszombati's words.

The old man shuddered hearing the stroke of the clock. 'The devil knows which is the better way to go: die of a witch's kiss when death is the last thing on your mind, or in some hospital with saltpetre-seeping walls where your mattress is already being tugged by others who wish to die in the same place?'

Thus spake Mr Rimaszombati as he stepped out of the shadows, before the statue had a chance to tap him on the head because of his godless talk. He was an old man who could only use words to corrupt women, as if intending to leave no soul innocent in the world – a habit of those men who even with their dying words desire to pervert, hoping for more company in hell.

'Let's go, Galgóczi is waiting for us.'

10

A sorcerer passes under the window

Galgóczi, clad in a white sheet, stood on the balcony awaiting his visitors.

The white sheet and the balcony were necessitated by Miss Brunszvik's locking up his clothes, and by her preference for sleeping with the keys under her pillow.

'Oh you enviable, happy wanderers of Life who fly about propelled by health and good cheer, free as the birds and care-free as only those humans are who can escape from worrisome thoughts! While I, in the night of madness, horrors and hal-lucinations, call upon death every fifteen minutes to liberate me from my torments!' exclaimed Galgóczi up on the balcony when in the moonlight he spied his friends who came to rescue him.

'Speak up, let it all out, my unfortunate friend: at this time of the diurnal cycle no one will curse us; it's also true that nobody will say mass for us either, even the monasteries are asleep now,' replied Rimaszombati, briefly appearing in the moonlight before stepping back into shadow, drawing Jolan back there with him, because he did not think it advisable that they should be seen at this hour on White Eagle Place.

'All I can say is that I am atoning for every sin I have ever committed or will ever commit in my life. My sufferings redeem my existence both in this world and the next. I am fully conscious at all times yet I feel myself to be so deranged that waves of insanity keep tossing me back and forth, willy-nilly. Oh, if I could just once more regain my mind as it was before, my former composure, and courage. I've become such a coward! Just like a worm under the stable floorboards. The arms of despicable death reaching for me are my only salvation now.'

Galgóczi went on at length bemoaning his affliction, which can never be understood by those who have not undergone the terrible torment of losing control of their mind and the ability to think rationally. Galgóczi's derangement belonged to a category of insanity that is accompanied by bodily anguish: a madness that hurts!

Not only was his mind unhinged but also his heart, kidneys, liver, stomach: in a word, everything a man calls his own in this life. Even his feet became hated enemies, not to speak of the hands that he kept wringing as if to tear them out by the root. Instead of food he hungered for rusty nails and hooks that would tear up his innards. Galgóczi had altogether become the devil's prey.

'Could wine alone have done this to you?' asked a doubtful Rimaszombati in the shadows, where, holding Jolan's hand, he stood watchful.

Now he shouted out at the top of his voice: 'Hey, Galgóczi! Let me take on most of your sufferings caused by wine. I am an old man and if I go insane so much the better for me, at least I won't be in my right mind to see myself passing to the next world. But what about your other affairs? Who will take responsibility for unhappy love, jealousies, daydreams, Jolan's lovely hair? For those you probably suffer just as much as for the wine that's been forbidden you!'

'I was planning to kill Jolan anyway,' replied the man in the white sheet. (Jolan's hand did not tremble in Rimaszombati's clasp.)

'It's best if Jolan forgets about me and finds herself a better man, worthier than myself. I am sure there are plenty around. I'll never be a whole man again anyway, so let me just go to my well-deserved doom.'

When Jolan heard these words she stepped forward from the shadows. 'Easy for you to say this, you poor maniac, you cannot add any more to your sufferings. You have reached the point where there is nothing more to suffer, your cup is full, not another drop of pain can be added, even if the whole town were to burn down around you. So you think you wouldn't suffer any more even if I left you? But I know my heart would break. Let me continue loving you, I'll wait it out until these crazy bells stop tolling in your brain.'

'Don't sacrifice your beautiful young life to me, what a waste for a flower to ally herself to the worm. I can't say when I will untangle the web I've been stuck in since I lost my mind. I cannot predict how deep the jungle whose thousand perils I must still face in order to regain the sanity I allowed to slip away one unguarded moment. And what will my fugitive mind be like if I ever encounter it again, when I can't even be sure it will ever come back? Go away, girl, leave this mindless madman behind, as Ophelia left Hamlet,' replied the ghost from the balcony and he would have certainly shaken his chains, were there any on hand; as it was he ground his teeth.

'But tell me, Galgóczi, what's the matter with you, so that I can at least pray for your recovery?' the girl cried out, when under cover of darkness Rimaszombati whispered this question in her ear.

'I'm out of my mind!' replied the miserable young man from on high. 'There's no other way to put it, the devil took my brains away. I have contracted an illness that has only one remedy: I must lacerate my heart and worthless being with self-reproach and curses. Only after I exhaust myself with weeping and wailing, tossing and turning, can I catch a few hours of sleep, and I leap out of bed with fresh hatred for myself. I detest myself so much I could smash my brains out against the wall.'

'You've been poisoned, my friend. Somebody must have put poison in your drink, for no one ever went insane from the wine served at the Green Ace!' responded Jolan (once again following Rimaszombati's prompt) and joined her hands as if prepared to swear an oath in support of her statement.

'By now it doesn't matter how; I lost my mind, the way someone loses a cap. By now it's all the same when and where my mind went awry. Perhaps I'll never find out what enchantment dragged me to the window that night, when a sorcerer I had only seen in my worst dreams suddenly appeared in front of my window in the starlight and exhaled his poison into my face and recited his magic spell. Right away I felt lost. My mind was gone. A horrible fear gripped my heart, my teeth were on edge, my heart froze, my throat knotted and everything around me turned evil. Everything turned malevolent, jeering as if I had just then realized how horribly people hated me, for everybody detests the madman.'

As if summoning his last remaining strength, the young man on the balcony pronounced these words with the utmost effort. Rimaszombati and Jolan stood in helpless silence for a while, as if pondering some response that would calm the poor wretch. At last Rimaszombati gathered himself enough to speak up: 'You said someone looked in your window?'

Galgóczi hugged the balustrade as if to summon his strength. The sheet slipped from his emaciated body and he seemed a skeleton in the moonlight.

'The window in my old room opened on to the river, and the sorcerer came from the direction of the river one summer night when the moon hung above the water, almost ready to speak. The sorcerer approached with two women on his arm, the way some gentlemen go promenading when unable to sleep. The older one of the two seemed to have plenty of experience in rummaging through men's pockets. She parted her hair in the middle, like an old-time courtesan whom any man could approach intimately at first sight. This older woman was one who still resents a man who won't immediately embrace her around the waist or touch her somewhere else. She was the one who urged the sorcerer to destroy me, foolish youth, for failing to recall what I owed a woman who spent her best years pleasing my father and his friends.'

'What is the name of this respectable lady?' asked Rimaszombati, as if forgetting he was dealing with a madman.

'Juli was her name, typical for a woman of her sort. The daughter she was parading in the moonlight, called of course Juliska, had just enough wits to know how to hang on to a man; but she'd learn the rest soon enough, I thought. Just then the old woman and her daughter noticed me standing at the window and hated me at once for seeing, observing, and laughing at their nocturnal stroll with the sorcerer – for I loved a chuckle at women's doings, observing how they go about having their way with a man, subjugating him to their whims and moods. Old Juli took the sorcerer by one hand, young Juliska by the other. Well well, I thought, if this does not lead to connubiality soon then nothing will, and I was ready to let the stranger know how much I despised him for being the self-oblivious plaything of such mercenary women. But the stranger, this magician, beat me to the punch. He stepped up to my window, blew into my face and pronounced his magic spell. Nor did the two women remain idle meanwhile. At a gesture from the older one they sprang up, exposing legs sheathed in matching canary-yellow stockings, and pranced up the stairs, up to the attic – in a word, overhead – from where they sprinkled water down upon my head to ensure the success of the spell. Ever since then . . .'

The clock struck two in the church steeple, and in the still of the night one could clearly hear the earlier actors around the tower yielding their places to the new performers of the night. Shadows changed shape as their terms of duty expired. The shadow of the tower shifted from where it had sprawled before. It was followed by the transformations of the yellow-stained underwear hung out to dry in various courtyards. The newborn on the midwife's sign started to screech, whereupon the door flew open as if by clockwork and the midwife stepped out, her little chapeau slapped on askew, a mantilla around her neck, and with the baby now inside her mysterious bag she began her rounds from house to house – where would she gain admission? The wretched young man retired from the balcony, his sheet trailing in his wake like a cloud.

II

A brief report on a cure attempted by a medicine man

By now everyone was tired of listening to Galgóczi night after night just to help him find a way out of his severe malady. 'Incurable' was the verdict passed by the nocturnal folk Jolan sent over at closing time from the Green Ace to White Eagle Place. Galgóczi, given permission to appear on the balcony, repeatedly apologized to his listeners and recounted the tale of his enchantment, the same old song. He burst out in tears when Jolan sent him a medicine man, although in days past he loved to hang on to the tail of this wizard's cloak, roaming through far-off districts in search of undiscovered taverns, for this itinerant scholar's main occupation was visiting each and every one of the capital's 3,240 restaurants, wine cellars and taverns in order to write down in a pocket journal his observations about the specialties of each.

'We have already been to 240 taverns,' said the wizard, from below the balcony. 'That leaves only 3,000 more! Don't you feel like continuing? I know a wine cellar near the old Obuda cemetery where not even the crow flies.'

'I made a promise never to enter a tavern again, and may I break a leg if I ever set foot in one!' whispered Galgóczi.

'So you made a promise to the old lady?' the wizard inquired *sotto voce*. (Although he was getting on in years – some claimed he had been sighted in the Tabán a hundred years earlier – he also liked to make women appear older, once they were past their first communion, no longer schoolgirls, and going to church for reasons of their own.) 'If you made a promise to a woman, I have a way of absolving you. I will simply carry you on my back across the threshold of the tavern – just as I used to give you piggyback rides in the past every time Golden Rooster Street proved too steep for you. Come on, jump down, and I'll catch you.'

This wizard – whose origins, home and family have remained a mystery in the Tabán over the last hundred years, who was forever on the move, in dream and in waking life, rain or shine, but mostly in nasty weather when he could not stand still – this wizard would surely have helped Galgóczi escape, had it been solely up to him. True, he would have taken him away for ever, for he thought 'something was rotten in the Tabán' ever since that philanthropic 'skirt' Miss Brunszvik had set up camp in the neighbourhood.

But not even this former drinking buddy, the wizard himself, could liberate our young man from his enchanted state, still beset by the shivers, crushed by illness, spouting words familiar to no one, as if some stranger had crawled inside Galgóczi's skin.

'The devil is inside him. He must have swallowed the devil in an unguarded cup, the way Kerschanz the barman swallowed the corkscrew. He will never crack open another bottle,' opined the wizard at the Green Ace where Rimaszombati sat mournfully at a table by candlelight like some old outlaw and Jolan crouched sniffling in a dank corner, counting the years she still had left to live. 'I'll be a straw widow for two more years, then I can die in peace,' she said to console herself. Rimaszombati merely emitted an ill-smelling groan, something he had never dared in this restaurant, and shifted his weight from one elbow to the other. And so the wizard soon vanished without a word of goodbye, for he had many a tavern left to haunt because of the curse that lay upon him.

'Another day, another hope gone!' said Rimaszombati, who was now refusing all food and drink, as the all-seeing door of the Green Ace closed behind the wizard. 'I can understand why some men get tired of living when they become unable to resist their fate.'

Jolan kept sniffling: 'How could Uncle Rimaszombati have grown tired of living? You'll always find other pals to play pranks on!'

'But never again the youth, love and wine that your friendship meant to me when my moods served as the viola playing the melody that brought you two together, I'll never again see the likes of old acquaintance like that!' moaned Rimaszombati. 'Oh, won't you please put your little foot over here, on my heart.'

That meant he desired the tavern-keeper's daughter to fill up the wine glass, the one that bore the initials R and J flanking a heart, etched into it at the last Tabán fair. 'What good is drinking by yourself, Uncle?' asked Jolan.

12

The girl with the rainy-day face announces a change in the weather

Galgóczi, learning to walk again, liked to stroll in the churchyard, near the spot where the flood of 1838 had washed away the dead and their coffins, leaving behind empty grave pits as mementoes for careless men to stumble into. Some of the local men, especially in their seasons of intemperance, had slept for a spell in just about every one of these unoccupied graves; only a stranger would send up a scream stumbling into some abandoned hole, and keep screaming until some night watchman came to his aid with a sacristan in tow, who handled ladders and wax candles in the neighbourhood. At one time or another Galgóczi had fallen into one of these pits, but he never called for help except when someone else fell on top of him and started to heave up wines consumed at unfamiliar taverns. Otherwise he would wait until dawn.

But this time Galgóczi avoided falling into a hole, although nearing the church he had such a bad attack of vertigo that he felt like plunging into the earth head-first, in mid-stride, before he put his foot down. In fact the spell cast on him still prevented Galgóczi from taking sure steps, without halting and groping uncertainly in mid-stride, hesitant foot trembling in the air as if he did not know where to put it. The spell also kept him hearing voices behind his back, and all around him, voices of people he of course could not see.

Jolan would only show her rainy face peeking around a corner, like moonlight hiding behind the clouds on Hallowe'en. As yet she had refrained from speaking to Galgóczi, while he staggered about, but some of the dead, who had survived even the flood, spoke to him all the more. The red marble memorial plaque of a burgher named Rottenbiller, set into the wall of the church, was addressed by the crazed Galgóczi in the following manner:

'Mr Mayor, your Honour, if it be true that repentant souls receive forgiveness from their fellow humans while still in this world, then I choose to remain among the penitent. Although I am too poor to make amends for all the wrong I have done, and cannot take back all the lies I have based my whole life upon, I do promise to stop lying and to live a wholesome and righteous life from now on. I will not stray from the path of decency, which will be all the easier since I shall never again take a drink of wine.'

What did Rottenbiller reply from the wall of the church? No one knew, not even those busybodies who lurked in the wake of Galgóczi's footsteps as if here were a dying man about to bury his treasure in some hole.

Miss Brunszvik appeared in the graveyard when she thought it was time for the convalescent to return indoors and stop conversing with autumn leaves, clouds and the dead. Miss Brunszvik, goodness personified, took Galgóczi by the hand and led him back to the house on White Eagle Place, where, like lessons in a schoolroom, Temperance slogans covered all the walls. After all, Galgóczi has been saved . . .

But Jolan refused to let herself be forgotten. Words of encouragement heard at the Green Ace, as well as her own intuition led her to take certain steps in Galgóczi's direction. One night, lying in her bed after all was quiet at the Green Ace, she broke into heartrending sobs. Had Galgóczi died, she could not have wailed any louder; but staying alive as he did, without coming back to her, Jolan's sobs were more plaintive than any sort of female weeping could be. She learned to cry non-stop, at length, setting up a keening that proved unbearable even for those apothecaries of feminine tears, priests and undertakers. Jolan managed to introduce into her sobs all the howling pain of love-tormented womankind ever since the world began. Her sobs were enough to split ears, to crack bones and brains and infuriated even the mildest of men who heard them. Her keening continued uninterrupted, like some wild beast bellowing after her mate, like a mad dog howling at the moon, like some relentless magic incantation that leaves not a moment's peace to the hearer. Jolan had stubbornly made up her mind to succeed through her sobs, even if it broke her.

After she had mastered the art of crying, she went out one midnight and stood under the balcony where she had last seen Galgóczi shrouded in a white sheet, and launched into weeping, like some spirit that had stumbled there from the beyond, her voice allowing Galgóczi no respite, lest he believe, as he had already begun to believe, that during this illness of many months' duration he has expiated all his sins on earth. 'No, not all debts have been settled!' signified this female weeping night after night, without saying it in so many words. Malicious souls, who like to amuse themselves at other people's expense, encouraged Jolan to persist, as they crossed White Eagle Place at night, and hurried away. Mr Rimaszombati, who could have done something to smooth things over, was of the opinion that it was more or less all the same (for him) whether Jolan laughed or cried; he had done his best to instruct her about kissing, but she would not listen to good advice. When a woman takes it in her head to follow her own counsel the results are rarely salutary. After all, love is always the private affair of the one who's in love. The one who drew the Joker from the deck! thought Rimaszombati, as did so many other men, when women nearly break their hearts in pain.

13

The last part of the history of the wine jug, wherein justice and order are restored to the world

Oh young women, you whose saffron and ivory legs step so carefree in the Tabán and elsewhere, prancing through life as you do over the cobblestones, whether sent from heaven as meteors or surfacing from earth's depths to linger here awhile: Oh young women, each of you may encounter some *malheur*, when in your hottest love affair you find yourselves having to compete against some powerful opponent, whereas you had envisioned your love running a smooth course, regular as the moon. Such an opponent, one to upset all your expectations, is wine, wine that has engendered so many thoughts in this world, good and bad alike. Indeed, who could tell if people would be ultimately happier getting drunk only on love and not also on wine? But wine can be an even greater enemy of love when it runs out, vanishes, never again lending its ecstasy to love, which had arisen precisely because of wine. Alcohol may be love's accomplice, but when accomplices fall afoul of each other, foul play must follow, one accessory to the crime murdering the other.

This is what happened in the case of Galgóczi and Jolan. Galgóczi, when sobered up, free of the wine in whose ecstasy he had loved Jolan, as fate would have it, also sobered up from his infatuation, simply because wine no longer transported him to the point where Jolan always seemed the loveliest, most exquisite, most desirable girl in the whole world.

'Just one more meeting, and I can die in peace,' Jolan said, in letters and in messages sent in frenzied desperation, since on the sixth of November Galgóczi was sighted in the Tabán promenading in a new green suit like some schoolboy who has passed his exams with flying colours. The same day Jolan draped a small mourning veil over her chapeau even though she was not quite certain if it suited her outfit. But she dressed in black now, for women will don black whenever given a chance. Jolan wept tears as she darned her black stocking, as if she were already trudging through the rain, on her 'journey to the beyond', as all sentimental women since time immemorial call their road to the final assignation. To go out on a date is no small thing even in everyday life; but a last rendezvous: it's better perhaps not to set out because surely every doorpost, little dog, and wizened, grimacing ancient hag will insist on getting in your way.

Mr Rimaszombati accompanied Jolan at a distance, to be on hand in case there was trouble in the old church where so many had already rendezvoused before. He witnessed how Jolan, at some distance from St Andreas, who was lugging a weighty beam of the crucifix, as well as from St Jacob, who was leafing through a great big tome, had dropped to the flagstone of a side altar, her knees apart, her waist bent, as if no longer kneeling but altogether collapsed, like some little ditty that could fly only this far, to die here and leave the rest to the saints who will see justice done in her stead. Forsaken fiancées kneel like that, sunk into themselves, in seemingly eternal abandonment at the side altar while at the main altar proceeds the wedding that should have been, as promised, her occasion to say 'yes' in front of the priest, sacristan and wedding party. Not even the hawk-nosed, cocky yet teary-eyed best man in attendance, wearing his old jacket thrown over a shoulder, remembers to bother with the abandoned betrothed. (Mr Rimaszombati, as he later explained, was present on the premises just in case he was needed as witness to a clandestine marriage.) There lay Jolan by the side altar as, the stone saints of the old church will readily attest, deceived fiancées had always done.

Galgóczi arrived somewhat tardily to this 'final' meeting, as if after all he would rather be elsewhere. But, as we may see in his case, only wine-drinking men can sit back and calmly linger as long as they like at some establishment while someone expects them for a 'final' meeting somewhere. Whereas the man whom wine did not empower to be cruel will still set out, although he knows in advance that no good can come of this meeting. Thus wineless, cowardly Galgóczi, all his former strength gone, walked into the church and stopped under the organ to wait until Jolan had said all her prayers. Jolan now rose and noiselessly stepped to Galgóczi's side in the silent church that was empty before evensong.

'I only wanted to say goodbye, that's why I asked you to come . . .' she faltered behind clasped hands and cast a timid sidelong glance at Galgóczi's haggard face that, it was said at the Green Ace, was not unlike that of a hanged man cut down from the gallows. (As indeed Countess Brunszvik had cut Galgóczi's rope.)

Galgóczi trembled and remained silent, as men are wont to be at times like this.

'I thank you for coming when everyone said you wouldn't. What business could you have with a girl you've abandoned?' Jolan continued and again looked at Galgóczi, who still had not spoken, although appearing to be extremely moved.

'I will not inquire what you intend to do; all I ask is that you stay away from here for ever, because your presence is unbearably painful for me,' Jolan now whispered, for even in the midst of the greatest torment women are capable of saying things that apparently make sense. But not men, who, if they open their mouths in certain critical situations, are sure to utter the most asinine things.

Galgóczi, too, opened his mouth and said the following: 'I, too, have decided to leave this place and am only waiting for my itinerant friend to appear. He probably knows of inns where the woman of the house is confined with a newborn whose nappies are drying all over the attic. Or at least the innkeeper's wife is pregnant, so that I cannot fall in love as fatally as I fell for you!'

In her dolour Jolan was not really listening to Galgóczi's words, and without weighing what he said, continued her own heart-rending tune: 'I never want to see you again in my life, or hear your name, not even see you in a dream . . . Will you do that for me, Galgóczi, and disappear?'

Poor Jolan. In her world she could not have known the fact that words of that sort affect only bibulous men, men who befriend wine, make friends through wine, feel and think through wine – for wine injects its own sensibilities and vulnerabilities into their hearts. Poor Jolan indeed. She could not have known that forsaking wine most men forsake love as well, and can arm themselves against momentary weakness, something the drinking man is incapable of. And Galgóczi had fortitude now . . .

'I have already vowed to address only women who are in a blessed state of pregnancy, for I deem them safe.'

'I wish you success in whatever you resolve, for I hope you know I will always wish you only the best, even when I cannot see you,' repeated Jolan, opening one last time for Galgóczi the door leading to love, happiness, the beautiful life and the sweetest emotions, for him to enter, as if nothing had ever happened. One could almost hear the little door opening, and Jolan's dearest, devoted voice: Come in, come on in, I am the one who loves you the truest of all. Without me you are as good as dead, you poor unfortunate, even if you keep on living, because I will surely die. Come, come let us love each other, my angel. I am good and I am pure and I love only you . . .

This is what Jolan's unsaid words were conveying, and Galgóczi had to feel it, for if he did not, then nothing mattered anyway.

Love and conscience struggled so hard inside Galgóczi that he nearly collapsed in a heap, for never before could he see as clearly the crossroads of his life as now, when he stood stone-cold sober in the church.

'Not even the devil loves me, and Jolan, most probably you don't love me either, although you happen to be the one I suffered the worst for, it nearly drove me mad.'

Now Jolan turned to stand face to face with Galgóczi, possibly to say something else to conclude the novel of her life. But the words stuck in her throat, not a sound came out. She just stood, feet rooted to the ground, her eyes staring at Galgóczi as if beholding a miracle.

'What is it?' asked Galgóczi.

Of course he had not yet seen the change that came over him in the church, for otherwise he would not have asked.

As we have said, Galgóczi stood under the choir, but one part of him stood inside the nave of the church. About one half of his body could be said to be in the church, and on this half his hair, moustache and beard turned white as a dove during the conversation, as if struck by white lightning that burned his hair white in an instant, unbeknownst to him. This miracle had bisected him exactly down the middle and thus marked him for life.

Jolan, no matter how kind-hearted she was, had to back away in horror from the young man whose moustache was auburn red on one side and silvery white on the other. Rimaszombati, who, as we know, was lurking at the entrance, backed away with equal horror from the young man.

And so Galgóczi, placing one shaky foot before another, afraid at each step that the world would slip away vertiginously from under his feet, at last reached White Eagle Place, where he met the wizard, to whom he confided his resolution about lady tavern-keepers.

The wizard looked hard into Galgóczi's eyes. 'Not possible,' he said. 'I don't want them to give birth to monsters wherever I go with you.'

He said no more, but Galgóczi, on looking at a mirror, understood anyway what he meant. Now at last he was right. Not even the devil loved him. He had given up wine. But he had also abandoned love. He stayed alive, but it was no better than if he had shared the fate of Bitchkey and Botchkay.

(1930)

One Glass of Borovichka and Its Consequences

'Eat lots of carrots, that'll put lead in your pencil,' said the strapping woman who was Kalkuttai's lady love.

And so Kalkuttai unfurled the linen napkin, for he resigned himself to the fact that you must obey women in certain matters. He tucked the napkin into his collar all the way around, and tied a knot in the back, the way he had seen old clergymen do. It was a sizeable napkin, large enough to wrap a whole family's picnic lunch for a summer outing; one corner had, embroidered in red, the name Janet and a five-pointed coronet. It was not Jeanette, no, not *Zhanette*, it was plain old Janet, a family name. So let's call the lady who owned the napkin by her last name, because some women are sensitive about just anybody calling them by their first name or nickname. Especially since Kalkuttai's lady had been given 'Mantzie' for a first name, a name that nauseated her, a name she firmly believed to be unsuitable for a lady as sober and settled as herself. You can only be a Mantzie for as long as you're wearing training brassières.

Our man donned the napkin and used its end to wipe his plate with absent-minded gestures.

'How many times have I told you,' said his lady, leaning forward over the small dining table (for she had had a few years at teacher-training college behind her), 'to save this habit of yours for the caféteria at the Püspökladány train station. There you can polish your plate all you want, just like those itinerant pedlars and horse-dealers who reek of moustache wax. But now you happen to be seated at a family table and there is no cat or dog in my house to dirty your plate.'

Kalkuttai cheerfully undid one vest button. 'Take it easy, young lady, I know you keep the cleanest kitchen in the land. I've never seen chipped enamel on your pots, for you are well aware that could lead to appendicitis, which often proves fatal. And I know for a fact that you use sandstone powder only for whitening your floorboards, and not for cleaning wooden kitchen utensils. See, I am fully aware of all your good points. You can't fool me, not with my knowledge of people.'

Janet eyed attentively the crisped curls on the back of her man's head, a fashion introduced in Hungary by Austrian officers back when King Franz Josef was still a young man. She scrutinized his flared shirt cuffs, the opening of which showed a filigree gold chain bracelet that was a favourite souvenir among old-fashioned ladies' men.

'How come you're in such a good mood, did you stop at that tavern on the way?' she asked suddenly.

'Now, now, little lady, you know very well I haven't been back to that place ever since I socked that red-haired scoundrel Zebrai in the jaw for spreading rumours about you and me.'

She heard him out calmly, with the impassive face of one determined not to swallow lies of any kind. 'I never expected any man, not even my husband, to fight on my account, I hate fighting. I mentioned the beer hall only because I've warned you more than once that beer before noon, your so-called "elevenses", was invented for ne'er-do-wells who can't afford a real lunch or haven't got a place where it's worthwhile to arrive with a hearty appetite. Believe me, it's mostly unhappy loners without a woman who hang around taverns before lunchtime. I make exception for the provincial who's been riding the train all night, jolted, tossing and turning, sighing in his sleep: a man like that has earned his "elevenses".'

'Thanks for the advice,' Kalkuttai replied, 'but ever since I found a long hair left by the cook in my portion of sour lungs, I have given up mid-morning meals.'

Meanwhile the soup arrived, brought by a spick-and-span, barefoot serving girl. Kalkuttai's eyes lingered on her sturdy ankles. 'Goodness, it must hurt when this gal pulls on her boots every Sunday!' he exclaimed.

The lady of the house took her time ladling out his soup with great care before she responded to her man's comment, for she did not want him to think her jealous on account of the serving girl.

'Ever since I was first married, the maid is only allowed to enter my room barefoot. In winter she can leave her slippers outside the door. As for boots, you wear whatever suits you best. I can understand why some men still insist on wearing boots with elastic sides. They are so much easier to get into than laced or buttoned boots,' she pronounced, while counting out six semolina dumplings into the golden broth steaming in the man's soup bowl. 'The soup's piping hot, like every dish that leaves my kitchen. You might as well help yourself to a shot of aperitif from the cupboard. No, not the slivovitz – plum brandy's only good first thing in the morning. This *borovichka*, from Gabriel's still in the Uplands will help fortify your stomach. Here, have a few slices of St John's radish with it, they're in season now. It would have been nice if you'd brought your own radishes from the market. For some reason, don't ask me why, it takes a man to pick out radishes.'

Kalkuttai did as he was told. He stepped up to the venerable antique cupboard that had bunches of grapes and goblets etched into its glass doors; surely many a bygone gent's eyes had rested on this same view before opening the cupboard door to get acquainted with the items found therein.

Yes indeed, Gabriel, the *borovichka* distiller in Szepesbela, truly possessed the knack of squeezing the real scent of juniper into his brandy. Kalkuttai downed the aperitif with a flash of memory of the Popradfelka train station of his youth where he always stopped to purchase sprigs of edelweiss to fasten in his hatband. Simultaneously, a schoolboy mood coursed through his veins, as if a long-rusty chain had shifted the winch of his soul's draw-well, sluggish at first, then more and more sprightly, as if turned by a young girl's hands . . .

'Mama, this *borovichka* merits further attention,' Kalkuttai said, still in his former tone, but something must have stirred inside him, for now he noticed that it was in fact quite dark in the dining room because the cockerel-patterned lace curtains on the window swallowed much of the light; surely the soup would have a different fragrance served outdoors, say, in some verdant garden where distant, white-bosomed blue mountains send their cool breath blowing towards the town.

Janet had no reason as yet to suspect her man's thoughts, since basically she doubted that a man, at the dinner table, was capable of minding anything else but his belly. Therefore she chatted on, as she always did at noon when Kalkuttai showed up for lunch: 'I know that some doctors, such as the scientific-minded Sebastian Kneipp, consider saffron toxic for the liver and the cause of all kinds of facial blemishes, but I simply can't imagine a real soup without saffron. It gives a touch of colour even though its value as flavouring is close to zero. It makes a good-looking soup that's kind of like a woman with a pretty façade but nothing much inside. It's the greens that provide inner content for a soup, especially ruddy peppers just torn from the stem, ripening kales, potatoes with some girth, and then soup bones, with bits of fat and chunks of meat. But a penny for your thoughts, Kalkuttai . . .'

To all appearances Kalkuttai seemed to be spooning his soup in the same manner as he had once observed a certain provincial guest at an old hostelry in Pest delving into his soup, goggle-eyed like some huge fish, ignoring the bored village dames who sat down at the next table probably hoping for a fling in the capital, for something not possible back home in the sticks. That's right, Kalkuttai now slurped and chomped his dumplings with the same gusto that his anonymous paragon had exhibited, as if expecting these sounds of mastication to generate an even heartier appetite. He even indulged in a performance that never failed to please the ladies, lifting his soup bowl and tipping the last drops into his spoon like some country pharmacist vacationing in Budapest.

But as a matter of fact his mind wandered far from here, back to his youth when one dawn in early summer he arrived at the Kassa train station and devoured two portions of the local smoked ham, with a julienne of mild horseradish in long thin strips. (He was no fan of the wickedly mordant, Phtrugy variety of horseradish.) Ah, would he ever in his life eat ham and horse-radish like that again, seeing as how he's got himself involved with this woman whom sooner or later he would have to marry? Those landscapes of his youth were so beautiful; the gentlemen wore cummerbunds of white or blue polka-dot silk around the waist, the ladies had their white gowns trimmed with blue braid, and their faces were the colour of vanilla from all the ice cream, their hands smooth, white and firm as pianists', who always take very good care of their hands.

The lady across the table watched Kalkuttai with seemingly impassive eyes, although these same eyes were capable of beautiful dark flames that would smoulder after peaceful digestion has taken its course, like marsh fires over fertile bottom lands.

She took away Kalkuttai's empty plate. 'Of course you didn't even notice the soup was yesterday's, because a consommé is best on the second day. It must have a chance to settle down, and come into its own, just like a man who in the course of a lifetime had got over-excited about all sorts of phonies and fakes. The real flavour of a consommé arrives only after it's past the first boil. The same way, a man becomes truly lovable only after he's tried a thing or two in life, been around a while, had his ups and downs, tasted both bitter and sweet . . .'

Hmm, thought Kalkuttai, this woman's trying to make me older at any cost, even though I'm not even up for section chief at my office.

'Moreover, you had better give up the boiled beef, although I know it's your favourite. After all, life is not all filet mignons, one gets tired of even the finest cuts of beef – although in the old days women used to enrich the consommé with small pieces of pork. That's why some old portraits show men with pig's snouts and the head of an ox. So, my good sir, what do you say to some sort of migrating bird – say a duck, or a goose? . . .'

Done with the sweet talk, Janet rose to personally supervise the plating up in the kitchen. Ladies always meant this gesture as a great honour, and loved to don the white apron that, upon returning to the dining room, they would undo with a distracted air.

Kalkuttai did not mind being left alone at the table with his droll thoughts that were impossible to share with this solemn and dignified lady.

He was forty years old and took care of his bunions, which was why he could still strut like a cock of the walk whenever his customary even temper flared up into high spirits. But in fact his comfort came first and foremost, a quality he had inherited from his grandfather, along with a predilection for certain kinds of cheese. When his official business called for travel he liked to pre-plan the venue and menu for every lunch. He envisioned entire protocols well ahead of time, down to the amounts of wine he would consume, how many glasses before resorting to the sodium bicarbonate; also, where he would find the picture – or illustration cut out of a newspaper, showing the execution of the Emperor Maximilian by a Mexican firing squad, or else a plate from some decades-old fashion magazine – usually pinned on the walls of WCs in provincial inns, an image to contemplate with teary, blinking eyes for the duration of a proper bodily function that follows digestion. He knew the places where the tavern-keeper gave discounts to travelling government officials, and he made sure to inventory his socks and handkerchiefs in any hostelry where the chambermaid wore too much make-up. His job at the tax bureau required sitting around a lot, so he looked forward to official outings, a chance to drink his fill of beer at the train station without having to worry about his cantankerous supervisor and his busybody colleagues. On the road, he could indulge in feeling superior to a certain extent, mildly ribbing fellow travellers, especially itinerant salesmen of sundries and dry goods, for he had inherited from his grandfather, along with a love of cheese, a tendency to chaff and banter. But he never carried it far enough to be ejected from a tavern; he preferred to leave, complaining indignantly. No, seeing this unremarkable person you would not have suspected he had a clandestine passion for womanizing – another trait inherited from grandpa who, on his deathbed at age ninety-two, married his housekeeper, a woman with cracked heels.

Janet now re-entered the room with the giant strides of a major-domo leading an entire procession whereas she had only that certain servant girl in tow whose two hands now held a great serving tray made of burl wood.

'I see a bird! A fine-looking fowl!' rejoiced Kalkuttai, even though secretly he had been reminiscing about a bean soup brimming with tender bits of smoke-cured ribs and an especially toothsome kind of sausage, along with noodles, so that regardless of whether it was needed or not, you could stir in a few drops of wine vinegar. This vision also included the dark-haired lady of the tavern hovering in the background, undecided as yet about which guest to favour with her after-dinner conversation.

Janet sat down at her place and received the platters from the maid, positioning them with great care in the middle of the table within reach of Kalkuttai. An oval serving platter presented roast goose with an abundance of gravy. The drumsticks pointed upwards, as if about to run off into some green meadow; the thigh meat, sliced into a stack, still swelled as mightily as in the days when the goose took its first tentative flight over a pond.

Janet held forth like some schoolmarm. 'I didn't dare to roast it very long for fear of drying out the meat. Only certain kinds of beef can take that much roasting. This tender goose is for nibbling and "sucking on". Each little bone can be taken into the mouth one by one, some you can chew without hurting your insides. My first husband had the habit of picking up even large marrow bones to gnaw the scraps off, because usually those are the most delicious titbits. You don't need to save anything for the dog since we don't have one. But what are you thinking of, Kalkuttai, choosing that breast piece when there's all that nice thigh meat? Will I live to see you forget to dunk your bread in the gravy?'

No, Kalkuttai did not forget to dunk, although in the meantime his thoughts had secretly wandered back to a certain cashier lady named Gavotte whom he had once seen at a café in Kormend. He knew not why she came to mind, for this cash till queen, courted by lieutenants of the local infantry regiment, paid no attention whatsoever to a transient government official. She somehow managed to look right through him, her eyes aimed in the direction of the market square, where a kaftaned orthodox Jew happened to be bargaining for a shipment of onions. What was so remarkable about him that made Gavotte absorbed enough to withdraw her hairpin from her chignon, only to reinsert it in another place? Kalkuttai recalled the capacious purse the Jew paid from, scornfully pulling banknotes from various compartments, like one who is all too aware of the wretched value of money – he refrained from licking his fingers to count the banknotes, the way Gentiles do, thereby acquiring all kinds of mouth ailments. Anyway, this Gavotte . . . forever remained a dream for the tax official Kalkuttai.

None the less he diligently kept dipping his bread into the gravy, after meticulously paring the crust from each slice. As he carefully affixed the piece of bread on his fork and rolled it around in the drippings, his face acquired the solemn expression of a chemist synthesizing an important compound in the laboratory. The gravity of his face relaxed only when the piece of bread, darkened by all the drippings it had soaked up, was ready to be transferred with an arc-like movement of the fork into his mouth. Alas, a few drops were wasted; they fell on the napkin. Kalkuttai repeatedly shot indignant looks at the napkin suspended from his neck and shook his head in disapproval, as if blaming someone for the waste.

Before attacking the goose proper he used his fork to plant pieces of bread crust at various strategic locations in the platter of goose drippings, the way a fisherman casts the baited hook. Having disposed of these coming attractions, he pulled back the flaring shirt cuffs on both wrists, and with thumb and forefingers picked up certain pre-selected morsels of meat.

'Don't mind my fingers, little lady!' he said in a conciliatory tone before taking the first bite of tender young goose breast.

'That's how I prefer it, too,' responded Janet from the other side of the table, likewise picking up a piece, the smallest and boniest, as befits the hostess.

Even though Kalkuttai smacked his lips, clicked his tongue, licked his teeth and the corners of his mouth and his moustache while eating the meat that was dripping with goose fat, Janet kept up a stream of talk, as if to conceal some inner anxiety:

'Please make yourself at home. If your seat is uncomfortable, try another chair. Feel free to lift a leg every once in a while, for good circulation is paramount, and gas and bloating causes serious damage in a man who bottles up natural impulses. The pit of the stomach must stay unencumbered during a meal. Alas, we womenfolk have too many strings and bands in our skirts and underthings to do what is required for proper digestion. But you men have it easier – all you need to do is loosen the belt, let it out a notch, undo one button, and your circulation gets a tremendous boost.'

It would have been truly enjoyable to listen to Janet go on, if Kalkuttai's shoes had not started to hurt him. His corns occasionally flared up, sometimes even right after a trimming, and this gave Kalkuttai a doleful expression.

The omniscient Janet noticed this at once. 'Go ahead, slip your shoes off under the table. My husband used to do the same, with his comfortable elastic-sided boots. After lunch he always rose from table and walked to the sofa in his socks. I like a man who acts naturally.'

Kalkuttai was too ashamed to confess that he could not untie his shoelaces until bedtime, because that morning his shoelaces had broken and only with a great deal of trouble was he able to make them usable again. He chose to suffer in silence, and the home-fried potatoes paid the price. He failed to praise them sufficiently.

Janet complained: 'Give me a man who, as soon as he comes home, gets down to shirtsleeves and slippers. With that kind of man you never have to worry that at your first word, your first little comment, he will grab his hat and run off to some smoky gambling casino or worse, to some stinky tavern. My kind of man settles in for a stay at home, because he knows that a woman needs some "looking after". Take those home fries for instance. At this time of the year not everyone would dare to make them. They say it's best to save potatoes for the winter when fires burn throughout the long evenings. Then a husband will rush home even from the next county if he catches scent of the young potatoes his wife is frying up.'

'True, home fries are an excellent family meal,' replied Kalkuttai, 'but they still need those winter evenings, just as crayfish is best in June and July, when you soak your feet in a basin of cool water, next to which you place a wicker basket full of small crayfish that you can eat a hundred of, if you have nothing better to do.'

Janet wrinkled her forehead, and was not appeased even when Kalkuttai dipped a few potatoes in the drippings of goose fat. She had expected greater acclaim for her potatoes. She said nothing, and, to break the uncomfortable silence, Kalkuttai ventured a remark: 'Come to think of it, maybe I'll have some of that cucumber salad,' as if he had just noticed, whereas he had been eyeing this favourite delicacy for some time.

Then, after preparing further bits of bread for dipping, he went on in a storytelling vein: 'Once I had an acquaintance, a man of course, who was a wizard at concocting all sorts of salads. He wasn't a cook; he was a land surveyor and assessor by profession. I had run into him during official field trips at a number of inns, at Vac among other places. Now Vac is known for its penitentiary, but you must also know that women from there go to Budapest for their rendezvous, just as women from here like to meet their beaux at Vac. Well, there's an old hostelry called the Kuria in Vac, and it is quite a reliable place. That's where the surveyor liked to mix his salad dressings. He travelled with a case full of various mustards and sauces in little bottles, because in the provinces you can't always find authentic Dutch or English mustard. True, there are Hungarian mustards, especially home-made varieties, that will stand comparison with any foreign brand, but this surveyor was a fanatic when it came to his recipes. He used four different mustards for his lettuce salad.'

'And what about his cucumber salad?' asked Janet with a trace of mockery, reminiscent of a schoolteacher interrogating a student she had caught in a lie.

Kalkuttai was determined to go on, but first he stirred up the cucumber salad in its capacious serving plate, using his fork to herd back into the thick of the salad those bits of black pepper, paprika and slivers of onion that had fled to the edge of the dish.

'He used no mustard in his cucumber salad, but he had the presence of mind, whenever he had a rendezvous at the Vac hostelry with some woman from Budapest, to blow thirty-one kreutzers on a telegram, requesting advance attention to a properly prepared cucumber salad. This way he never had to contend with a cucumber salad that was bitter or not marinated, for the cucumbers had a whole night to imbibe all those devotional articles, the spices and flavours necessary for producing a decent salad. You can always find the right wine vinegar in a place that sells unadulterated slivovitz – usually in the neighbourhood of an orthodox synagogue.'

Janet started to smile now, which did not suit her character as a grave and serious woman. Her smile was a meld of a certain amount of disappointment, a bit of sorrow, but also resolve. 'Well, I confess this cucumber salad has been marinating only since this morning, maybe that's why it fails to meet Mr Kalkuttai's approval,' she said in a restrained tone of voice. 'In any case one can certainly learn from that surveyor because any man who takes his own case of mustards and condiments to the inn at Vac cannot be a total loss. Tell me, Kalkuttai, have you ever done any surveying, by any chance?'

Kalkuttai, still in a playful mood, answered in a rather jocose manner: 'I would have liked to, had I not chosen government service.'

. . . After this, the lady of the house had little more to say, other than wishing him good health after the meal. She cleared the table, coming and going, disappearing for a while only to return and find Kalkuttai staring at the ceiling, nursing post-prandial daydreams. We may very well guess the nature of these after-lunch thoughts, and so did Janet, and therefore it is understandable that she took her revenge upon her lover in the following manner.

After a while Kalkuttai retired to the small chamber without a window or any other egress, to stare at yellowing fashion plates and an illustration depicting the execution of the Emperor Maximilian pinned to the wall. Immersed in his reveries he did not notice that Janet had silently locked the door from the outside, sent the servant girl away, and gone out to visit a girlfriend whom she had not seen in a long while.

(1926)

The Ejected Patron

In the manner of storytellers of old, I respectfully warn my readers before they jump to any conclusions about the title of this piece. No, we are not talking about some infamous pub-crawler, some notorious drunkard who vomited torrents of lies and jests reeking of garlic, and whose shamelessly provocative behaviour made him unwelcome to those tavern-keepers and their patrons who, in the former Hungary that stretched from the Carpathian mountains to the sea, had at least once a day occupied every available tavern seat (that is, the guests did); had filled every single glass (that is, the tavern-keepers did), glasses that were as much in evidence as the painted ones, topped by an abundant head of white froth signifying since time immemorial a freshly tapped keg, calculated to put thoughts into the head of every thirsty man passing by these weathered tin signs that protrude into side streets. Why, on some occasions (holidays or fair days) they even filled up the glasses that had apparently been enjoying a much-deserved rest in some melancholy niche or on a cobweb-laden shelf that the ageing tavern-keeper rarely uses, thereby avoiding unsavoury quarrels with patrons because of certain items (chipped glassware or vessels containing funerary ashes) on the same shelf alongside glasses that happen to be perfectly good, but possess an iridescent rainbow tinge . . . (Yes, it can be disheartening to see rainbow colours, vibrant as a blast of organ music, on the side of an old drinking glass! As if some drunken devil had lifted the rainbow from the sky to beautify the glasses he drank from during his wicked benders, just as certain experienced females often daub the hues of innocent maidenly charms on their cheeks.)

Well, the hero of our story had been thrown out even from those taverns where the Slovak pedlar need not bother trying to sell new glassware, taverns where the bricked-in windows' ledges hold only the wassail cups of guests who had long ago migrated to the cemetery. So why on earth did they eject our man from taverns when he never paced the uneven floor of the taproom with mayhem in mind, nor peeked into the kitchen with intent to filch a roast rib or anything else stealable? Nor did his raincoat reek of stale stuffed cabbage, an aroma that would set even the most ancient barflies sniffing at the air, with nostrils that had never probed anything but musty, antique wine casks at the request of the superannuated tavern-keeper who wanted to know if a barrel was still redeemable and worth sending to the cooper for a makeover – such as a physician might attempt for an old man on his last legs. No, the raincoat in question had no odour whatever as he swung it off his shoulder, no excuse for the few lingering old veterans to recall the cholera epidemic of 1868 when you couldn't step out of the house because of corpses littering the street.

So let us see now, why was our hero tossed from every tavern he entered? True enough his name was Draggle, a name likely to remind most wine drinkers of grapes and vintages drenched by rain and rendered undrinkable. However, in those days it was not customary to give your real name as you introduced yourself upon entering, not even if you were addressing his lordship, the almighty tavern-keeper himself. Most guests traipsed in, crossing the threshold as lightheartedly as a bird alighting on a branch, without elaborate greetings. Some did enter the tavern, spouting all sorts of jocose salutations, having had this habit for as long as thirty years without ever noticing they were the only ones laughing at their own clownish greatings. Most guests entering a tavern mumbled something into their beard – you couldn't tell if it was good evening, good day or goddamn – but then it's no news that people don't frequent taverns simply to exchange hellos.

Now Draggle, with whom we are concerned here, always chimed out his greetings loud and clear and appropriate to the time of day, like a schoolboy with an ear out for the school bell. For instance, he would never be caught saying 'Bon appetit' when it was past lunchtime! Respect for your fellow man means assuming they have eaten their lunch at the proper time. Whoever has failed to do so is an object of pity to be heard out with sympathetic nods as he relates the unexpected event that prevented him from tying on the napkin at the sound of the noontime church bells. Draggle liked to hear a man who was late for lunch blame the long wait at the tax office, wiping clean his plate almost apologetically on account of the lateness. Truth to tell, Draggle had never in his life entered a tax office, and hearing such complaints made him feel vindicated.

The aftertaste of his lunch still lingering, Draggle liked to drop in at those Josefstadt taverns frequented mostly by patrons who on the first or the fifteenth of the month paid in advance for their meals, or else purchased one of those little booklets containing various meal tickets the size of postage stamps. In certain establishments such as the 'Matty' (indicating the restaurant bearing the name of King Matthias), these patrons received smaller portions, but not so at the Plum Tree, where the widowed Mrs Teneri gave her stamp-carrying customers larger than average portions. This good woman clearly intended to keep all her patrons for the duration of their lives, her rough treatment having sent Mr Teneri to his grave far sooner than her guests would have believed possible. Therefore she now lavished all her pent-up affections upon her guests, bachelors, widowers or divorced men with more than their share of troubles who had quietly resigned themselves to lunching at taverns for the rest of their lives. Some of this landlady's affection overflowed in the direction of Mr Draggle, even though the sagacious lady was well aware that sooner or later she would have to eject Mr D. from her eatery.

'Today's main course must have included tomato sauce,' was Draggle's innocuous opening statement as he sat down at a table where he had spied an acquaintance. 'Don't ask me how I know, when, as usual, I had lunch at home, prepared by my housekeeper. It's just that tomato sauce is the kind of food that stains your suit even if you pass in front of the restaurant serving it. There's simply no escape once they open the jar it was locked into last summer, like some genie. The very colour of that sauce entices, especially when served liberally, as in this place. Why, some men are such fools for tomato sauce that they almost plunge right in when dipping that forkful of meat. Some people claim this phenomenon has a scientific explanation, but as a layman all I can say is that this sauce is one of the least expensive to prepare, especially if the customer does not insist on extra sugar in it. This sauce, although inexpensive, accomplishes all that you could expect from a sauce: it gives a reddish hue to those portions of the meat that the patron would otherwise cut off and discard, parts that remain on the beef only through the neglect of the butcher or the cook. For even if you welcome, around the edge of your steak, a thin rind of lard that casts a dreamy glow like the moon's halo, you might still look askance at suspicious snippets of skin and titbits that belong in the gullets of those gluttonous dogs that hang around near a slaughterhouse, and reconsider dunking your forkful of meat in the tomato sauce along with these soft, tripe-like scraps that are liable to be tainted – and perhaps trim off these pendants which actually give meat its food value, and make butcher boys and their dogs grow so big.'

From behind the tomato-stained napkin, the acquaintance countered: 'As for me, I can't think of real beef without these loose, untrimmed, skin-and-bone titbits.'

'I am not talking about bony parts, because at restaurants where the beef is served with the bone, you can be sure you're getting a prime cut. It is next to the bone that one can best tell if the meat is spoiled – no matter how many sauce-boats or bowls of tomato sauce are lavished by the management. Not even a mushroom sauce can camouflage the taste if the meat is not fresh, although I grant you that a well-prepared mushroom sauce is perhaps the only one that can vie with the lively effects of tomato sauce, which stays youthful even in wintertime. True, mushrooms always have a taste of maturity, the savour of a man or woman past his or her first youth. Mushrooms just happen to be born old, for they have a chance to mull things over before they emerge from the soil, whether it's in the cellar, greenhouse or the woods. Yes, mushrooms are little old men even as the forester's laughing daughters stumble upon them after a rainy night. Fresh mushrooms! Think of all that subterranean deliberation preceding the decision to meet humankind! In any case there is a basic difference between tomato and mushroom sauces, in as much as the former, that is the tomato sauce, always needs a bit of meat, bread or rice to be enjoyed, whereas a mushroom sauce is sufficient unto itself, you can sop up the remaining spoonfuls while contemplating the plate that's getting cleaned, seeing your past, as it were, in an ever clearer light. When the last spoonful of an abundant portion of mushroom sauce is gone, you may still have a crust of bread in hand to wipe the plate with, if you wish a reprise of certain flavours.'

'But your philosophy of life shouldn't have anything to do with the savour of food. The best appetites belong precisely to those who never worry about life or food.' The tomato-stained napkin had barely had a chance to finish his say (clearly he had further observations to make) when Mr Draggle pointed to the small ticket the waiter at the next table was putting away into his grandiose accordion-pleated leather wallet.

'Let's see that ticket, Lajos!' cried Mr Draggle in the voice of a gendarme collaring a counterfeiter. 'Lo and behold, here you have a meal ticket, obviously the product of some wretched little printer's shop in the basement of an alley reeking of rats and newsprint. And this printed ticket, ever since the widow Mrs Teneri has blessed it with her restaurant stamp, has been emanating a clearly perceptible scent of tomato sauce. This ticket is well aware that its owner tore it from the book for the sake of ordering tomato sauce. The same way, a funeral wreath signals from far off whether it has seen service on the sarcophagus of an old man or a youth. Take a whiff of the bouquet of the tomato sauce and right away you'll smell the top shelf of the pantry where the jars of tomato sauce stand at attention, arrayed in rank and file.'

'My dear man,' replied the besieged guest, still trying to take cover behind his napkin, 'I've heard that everything on earth, every object, human, vegetable, animal or mineral, has its own unique unmistakable smell, but I simply cannot fathom why this piffling little scrap of paper should smell of tomato sauce.'

Here Draggle turned towards the glass of wine he preferred as his après-lunch mouthwash (for which he would invent so many different names that he never failed to confound and amaze the bartender, dubbing it, by turns, a whiff, a lark, a long step, a cat's pounce, a watchbox, a puffball), and having pushed away the glass with a certain finality that implied a settling of accounts with his opponent, in a gesture of ravenous vehemence undid the last three buttons of his vest and, turning away from the table, delicately cleared his throat, as customary in such small restaurants, acting to all intents and purposes as if about to order a second lunch – although according to certain malicious tongues you could never be certain that Draggle had in fact had his first.

He launched into his tirade with a mighty invocation: 'Let me, at this very instant, meet again the small portion of braised beef I had enjoyed before noon in the course of my official rounds at my friend Hintenreiter's on Wreath Street. Although this kind of braised beef is only available when the restaurant owners' social circle happens to gather at Hintenreiter's for their Thursday brunch, as announced in the *Restaurateurs Weekly*. Naturally it is not only attended by restaurant owners from all parts of town, who arrive after their trips to market (having sent the horse and carriage and the cook home with loaded shopping baskets, usually topped by cauliflower, sorrel, shallots and fresh asparagus for home consumption), but also by those good friends who care enough about their stomachs to check the paper every week for the current venue of the brunch. And since my official post leaves me free to get away from slaving at the desk (this was all that Mr Draggle would ever reveal about his official post), I just pick up my walking stick with a light heart and proceed on my merry way to these intimate gatherings that are always marked in my pocket diary. Of course I usually run into some of my restaurateur friends with beet-red faces shaved for the occasion, who pound me heartily on the back to inquire, "Well, well, my friend, how did you like last week's brunch at Geza Neuzidler's?" No disrespect is meant by this familiarity; their curiosity about my opinion implies just the opposite. And in fact I sang the praises of Geza's brunch, and I'll praise it again now, because nowhere else do they favour the guest with the kind of dumplings he serves with sour lungs.

'I also lauded the brunch held two weeks ago at Schwab's, for I could still recall those smallish but most toothsome, bite-size but still substantial stuffed cabbages, which, although served as an appetizer, were prepared from cabbages that were the first of the season at the open air market on the Danube quay. Baron Podmaniczky may wear his pantaloons ironed to a razor-sharp edge, but I doubt that he ever tasted a stuffed cabbage like we had at Schwab's. Why, somehow you managed to convince yourself that it wasn't so much the stuffing that made the difference but the flavours of the cabbages themselves, cabbages that had seen only a small shredder, or were sliced with a knife, and went into the pot with runt, stump, knots and veins intact. These heart-roots of cabbage in their first youth are capable of vying with the taste of first love. They let you savour the aroma of springtime fluids, you can tell that these knots and veins actually filter their juices from the fresh rains that hover over the garden, choosing, like savvy little housewives, those most favourable for raising cabbages.

'Yes, those little cabbages at Geza's brunch were superbly raised to envelop the stuffing lightly packed within their leaves, awaiting not so much the knife and fork as the spoon, which is far more suitable for doing a thorough job. Of course Geza did not forget to stir in a few chunks of ham, of the reddish, home-smoked variety, whose attraction lies precisely in its small size, making it easier to smoke. A ham like that comes with bones that are delicate and diminutive, and its so-called "whistle bone" can be nibbled at both ends, even by an old man. I repeat, even though we happened to be at our friend Hintenreiter's on Wreath Street I did not shrink from uttering loud words of praise for Geza Neuzidler's bravely innovative stuffed cabbage brunch (after doing justice to it, much to Geza's delight, most of us groaned "That does it for today's lunch", but as consolation someone chimed in: "It's always like this at the restaurateurs' brunch"), oh yes, I had the courage to speak the truth – while cursing the brewery that sent extra kegs for the occasion, for we old-timers know full well the kind of scheming that goes on behind these "extra" kegs, even if they do come from the same special batch that was formerly brewed for old man Dreher and the Emperor Franz Josef himself.

'Since restaurant owners like to think the brewery leeches off them, my words were received with approval, for no matter how far their connections go back, when the brewery is mentioned restaurateurs don't need to resort to absinthe mixed with Chinese drops to whet their appetite for angry complaints and loud oaths. So it was in vain the bartender hauled in the keg to tap it in front of us with the copper tube. The guests shivered at first as they eyed the golden brew in the glass that had a collar like an officer of the guards, but truth to tell the first glasses went down in one gulp – after all, it was a pleasure to drink the same beer that was once brewed for Franz Josef. However, that Old Gentleman does not drink any more, that is, not more than one fat glassful, somewhat less than a stein.

'Therefore we soon switched to wine, for a tavern-keeper is ultimately judged by the wine he serves. Certain dishes can succeed or fail, as a fricassee of turkey necks may vary according to the cook's mood, but when it comes to wine, there's no room for mistakes when connoisseurs sit at the table, some of whom will chew the wine not only with their molars but their incisors as well, before letting it trickle down the gullet. Not to mention those ultimate cognoscenti whose tongues start to whirl like a reel as the inside of the mouth turns into a sieve when they sample an unknown vintage. An acquaintance of mine in Buda, where there is reason to beware of adulterated wine, has been known to snort a noseful before making a purchase. This wine here, for instance, would never pass my friend's muster,' said Mr Draggle and he made as if he were about to snort up through his nose the *rufke*, as he sometimes liked to call his wine.

But instead of raising the glass to his lips, he resumed lecturing his table companion, who now turned the napkin tied around his neck inside out so that it showed traces of the sorrel sauce served yesterday or the day before.

Draggle was stunned. 'They served sorrel sauce here?' he exclaimed, as if he had learned something extraordinary. 'Real sorrel sauce, without my knowing about it, although I stop here just about every day, whenever my official duties allow? Tell me, did you actually have some of that sorrel sauce? And I don't mean wild sorrel, that makes cows' bellies swell, but fine, authentic, cultivated garden sorrel, that women await so eagerly in their little vegetable gardens at the coming of spring? Hats off to sorrel sauce that is prepared the right way – it stands for youthful zest in life, in food, in mood, in appetites. One woman alone knew the secret of preparing a righteous sorrel sauce, and that was Teneri's first wife, whom he followed to the grave, in order to escape his second wife.'

'Look, I have no interest whatsoever in your complicated family histories,' said his table companion, aware that the landlady had started to stare at them with eyes that could charm a snake. And the restaurant patron remains a coward even when he has a book of meal tickets in his pocket.

But Draggle would not be silenced. 'Each dish, and each person, has a different taste at different times of life. Take me, for instance: only now am I beginning to appreciate sorrel sauce made with sour cream, at my time of life, when I have pretty much seen it all, as a result of my official post as well as personal experience. Life and food are best in springtime, when you still believe yours is the first leaf of sorrel in the garden, when you are convinced that you are the only one charged with living life to the fullest. A time when you take no one too seriously, for people come and go, good ones replace the bad – a time when a failed lunch is no tragedy, for there are still so many lunches awaiting you, and you still have plenty of time left to forget all the landladies that had ever played a role in your life. As Draggle is my name, that's how I too used to think once upon a time – it was no big thing if I missed out on a sorrel sauce, because I knew for certain that mountains of sorrel still awaited me. But now I am beginning to feel the pang of each missed meal and each bypassed dish, for I think I'll never be able to make up for it in this life. Oh, who knows if I'll ever eat sorrel sauce again?'

. . . This melancholy thought made Mr Draggle reach with solemn finality for his untouched Bit o'Sorrow (as he liked to call his glass of wine at times), intending to raise the iridescent glass to his lips.

But the waiter behind his back stayed his hand. 'Do you have any money, Mr Draggle? Because you used up your credit long ago.'

Mr Draggle released the wine glass, stood up, and without a word to the waiter, paused only to admonish his table companion: 'I'll drop by again after lunch and we'll continue our chat about the peculiarities of food. The goodness of bread. Or the sweetness of wine.' And he walked out with head held high.

(1927)